HOPE FOR UTTER

Christopher Adrian

In a world marred by adult greed and irresponsibility during the tumultuous period leading up to the Financial Meltdown, the quest for salvation takes an unexpected turn when destiny intrudes, making hope the fragile lifeline upon which one must rely. "Hope for Utter" is a narrative that explores the odyssey of two adolescents – a young boy and girl – as they valiantly grapple with each other's desolation in the aftermath. To prevail, they must confront the bitter irony of redeeming those who played a part in driving them to the brink of despair.

In this emotional tale, it is Naomi, the girl, who possesses the unwavering determination to undertake this daunting task, carrying the burden of the other. "Hope for Utter" unfolds as proof to faith, forgiveness, and the audacious pursuit of the seemingly impossible. It is, at its core, a chronicle of hope – a bright flame even in the darkest of times.

ISBN: 978-1-7370060-1-5

I dedicate this book to all those who contributed to my life, bringing me thus far in life's journey.

Table of Contents

(1) Help

Amid the bustling December afternoon rush, Naomi sits beside her mother on a downtown-bound train. The rocking motion of the train seems to mark a somber countdown towards an inevitable end: the home her father promised for her tenth birthday celebration and the home where her mother had intended to welcome a new baby brother are both fading away into oblivion. With her chin resting on her mother's shoulder and her hands gently gripping her mother's arm, young Naomi gazes into her mother's eyes. A bittersweet smile passes between them as they share their mutual pain. Warm air puffs through the subway car vents, temporarily holding the cold winter air out.

As her eyes begin to close, Naomi utters softly, "Mom, do we really have to leave our home?"

In response, her mother presses a tender kiss onto her forehead.

Naomi's voice trembles with a mixture of frustration and sadness, "What am I supposed to tell my friends?"

Another kiss from her mother, accompanied by a tear, provides the answer. With a gentle touch, Naomi places her hand on her mother's abdomen, her voice a whisper of sorrow, "I'm sorry we lost him, Mom."

Amid this emotional backdrop, Naomi's attention is caught by the movement near the door separating their subway car from the next. Her eyes fixate on a tall man who staggers in; the man has a gray beard and wears a fedora. Amidst her melancholy, Naomi's curiosity is piqued by this newcomer. His appearance triggers a sense of recognition within her, and she observes his worn trench coat, staff in hand, and a bulky leather bag slung over his shoulder. The man leans against a subway pole, and as his gaze sweeps the surroundings, when another passenger offers him a seat. The stranger drops his bag onto the seat and releases a sigh of relief.

The stranger's voice rises above the train's ambient noise.

"Don't reject me now!" he chants, striking his staff against the floor attempting to mimic the train's beat.

"Be generous, my friends, for greed shall destroy you!"

His proclamation prompts nearby passengers to shift away, clearing space for his disruptive performance.

With a boisterous voice, he addresses the passengers, "Ladies and gentlemen, thank you for your warm welcome. Allow me to sing to you about greed."

This intrusion causes varied reactions among passengers – annoyance, pity, and curiosity. However, for Naomi, a sense of hope and curiosity emerges within her sorrow.

As the train speeds on, the man's performance takes an amusing turn. His swaying and the antics of his shabby trench coat provide a comic distraction from Naomi's sadness. The man's gray beard triggers a faint memory, further captivating her attention. He attempts to sing his song, but the train's motion disrupts his balance. Leaning against a railcar pole, he holds his staff with his right hand, allowing his left hand to dangle.

Retrying his tune, he begins, "Once upon a time, father and son, came from far, looking for fare, father and son, happy as can be."

However, his singing is met with disdain from a passenger who retorts, "Shut up, old man! … Moan somewhere else!"

Yet the man continues.

"The father, Morgan, the son, Morgan Junior,

They came each morning, looking to toil,

And work they found, in this big city.

Father and son are happy as can be."

"Yo, shut up!" another voice rises.

The man ceases his song, stops his pounding, and secures his staff beneath his right arm. Then retrieving a flute from his pocket, he proceeds to play a melancholic tune. This melody evokes a mix of strange sorrow and long-lost joy within Naomi. Her attention is drawn to him, and the annoyance of the other passengers fades in the wake of the man's captivating melody.

Naomi reaches out to the old man, crying out, "Hi!"

Her attempts to communicate go unnoticed, lost amid the crowd and noise. Even her mother's cold glance fails to deter her. Naomi makes another, louder attempt, rising from her seat and boldly announces, “Hi!"

Her mother's intervention pushes her back into her seat. The old man, now observing Naomi, tucks the flute into his pocket. He braces against the subway pole, maintaining balance, and turns his attention towards her.

"Hi there!" He greets her with a twinkle in his eye.

Enthralled by the encounter with Naomi, the man resumes his raucous tune, accompanied by a slight jiggle. Though not melodious, it entertains visually. The man begins singing again.

"The father was Morgan, the son Morgan Junior..."

Despite her lingering sadness, Naomi finds herself giggling and clapping along. Others join in, sharing her amusement.

The man with the gray beard bows, takes off his hat, and moves about the subway car with hat and staff in hand. Accidentally, he jabs a passenger with his staff while offering his hat to others. Some teens riding on the train find this jab amusing, but the jabbed passenger sees no humor.

“You gotta be kidding me,” is the glare of the passenger who gets the jab. “I don’t know who allows this.”

A woman acknowledging the comment, “We see this everywhere now … on the subway, on the streets, and it’s getting worse.”

“These people should be arrested, they’re a disgrace to our society,” continues the man who got jabbed.

“And they promote crime too,” responds the women.

Now voices of dissent rise from a few other passengers too, condemning the behavior of homeless people in public places.

As the train announces its arrival at "Bowling Green," and passengers prepare to disembark. The old man also readies himself to leave.

As the train doors open, Naomi's cry rings out, "Wait!"

The old man hesitates briefly, tucking his staff beneath his arm while extending his hat towards her.

She seizes the other end of the hat, pleading, "You must help me, Grandpa Hope!"

In the midst of this tug-of-war, her mother intervenes, exclaiming, "Naomi, let go! He's not Grandpa Hope, nor anyone's grandpa!"

Naomi persists, clutching the hat and her mother, unwavering.

"You must help me, Grandpa Hope!"

Meeting her gaze, the old man's eyes lock onto hers. Confusion gives way to recognition, and shared laughter and joy fill the air.

The train doors close. The man remains inside, standing in disarray next to the little girl. Eventually, he succumbs to exhaustion and settles on the floor beside her. Naomi's mother glares at him, her anger palpable but unspoken. Meanwhile, Naomi's focused attention and the man's mixture of delight and melancholy create a unique atmosphere.

In curiosity, the man inquires, "I never asked your name, little girl."

"Naomi!"

He introduces himself as Morgan Sr., explaining that he's known as Grandpa Hope. Their exchange hints at a connection, a history that gives Naomi hope.

As the train speeds beneath the bedrock of the East River, the man sways in tandem with the train's movement, his staff rolling beneath a seat. Amidst the rattle and sway, Naomi appealing once more.

"Your help, Grandpa Hope!"

Scratching his head, memories haze his thoughts. He recalls a time before Naomi's birth when he, his son, and a new daughter started a business – a cafe and an ice cream store. Naomi's understanding gaze prompts her to inquire about his plan to help her.

Looking into her eyes, he offers a glimmer of a solution, "They call that place the corner of Hope and Main," he exclaims. "That's why they call me Grandpa Hope."

Naomi pleads for assistance, her desperation evident.

"Please tell me if you can help? Otherwise, I don't know what will happen next,"

Not answering Naomi, the man stands up and looks out through the glass window. He only witnesses a gloomy and blurry exterior. The doors of the train crackle; the scornful silver paint on the door reveals a gash - corroded through time.

Fatigue and wretchedness loiter beside him, and within this anguish, sorrow, and hope, the train hollers through a shadowy long pathway.

(2) Hope and Main

Morgan Sr. disembarks from the train, his pace measures inconsistent in contrast to the bustling urgency of other passengers. He moves with an unhurried grace which is surrounded by a quiet stillness of nothingness. Gazing back at the train window, he sees little Naomi. Her farewell wave is delicate and painful as the train gains speed, fading into the distant horizon.

Her words echo in his mind, stirring dormant memories that tremble and come alive, resurrecting better days in fragments of abstraction.

"Can you help me!"

Her question lingers, conjuring sentiments of a time when life was simpler, and kindness was the language that bound them. In her simple gesture, he finds a reminder of the warmth of a family once held close, a warmth powerful enough to outweigh the winter coldness of the world outside.

He ascends the solid concrete steps, stepping out into the frigid embrace of the city. The sky is a pallid expanse, and light snowflakes descend, fading into the air as they fall. With a misty breath, he exhales, his hand nursing frostbitten skin from a lifetime of labor. To his right, a congregation of towering structures and a maze of streets lie in place. On either side of the streets, bare trees reveal gnarled stumps and withered branches, once lively and lush with hues of yellow, orange, and green.

Crossing the street to his right to satisfy his thirst, he makes his way towards a store, but his own reflection on the glass façade arrests him. The image that stares back at him is a stark contrast from the reflection etched in his memory. It's a somber portrayal of a man standing beneath a barren tree, a specter of a bygone era when he was a robust factory worker in the Rust-Belt region adjacent to the

Great Lakes. He was once stronger and younger than the figure captured on the glass, a man who arrived in New York and set forth a new life for his son—a life carved through the silent sacrifice of one's very soul.

Walking beneath the skeletal trees, over fractured sidewalks, and against the chill wind, he seeks refuge from the hollow emptiness that seems to follow him. He turns in various directions, allowing the twists and turns to offer respite from solitude. Above, streetlights isolate the dense sky, pedestrians scurry, and the walkways gradually accumulate a blanket of snow.

Fatigue claims his steps, forcing him to search for a place where he can find refuge and warmth against the relentless cold. He crosses another street, only to realize that his wandering has brought him back to the same store, its glass façade a mirror reflecting his altered self. Hesitating, he chooses not to enter. Instead, he leans against the store's side, his body sliding until he's seated on the sidewalk. With a weary sigh, he extends his legs, yearning for comfort. Snowflakes descend once more, this time melting as they touch his warm body, dissolving into his attire.

A passerby's act of charity, coins dropped at his feet, briefly interrupts the stillness. A man from the store yells at him to leave, a reminder that he's an intrusion in the world of commerce. Struggling, he rises with the assistance of his one functioning hand, finding it difficult to walk. Leaning against the store's wall, he sways and then notices a dumpster at the corner. Surrendering to exhaustion, he lets himself fall between the wall and the dumpster which moves to accommodate him. His leather bag becomes an impromptu headrest, and snowflakes cling to him as he rests, bridging the gap between nature's chill and the embrace of cherished memories.

In his mind's eye, he revisits a bygone winter night, a profound night infused with aspirations, spent sharing a drink with his friend, John. Snow fell that evening, slowly evolving into a blizzard. The scene is a pub nestled at the junction of First Main Street and Narrow Hope Avenue, nestled within a dilapidated storefront. John owned the pub and often compensated Morgan Sr. with drinks for his maintenance work.

"Hey Morgan, have you ever noticed how bustling this place is during the day but desolate at night? … It's not a good sign for my dam business."

"I've observed the same thing …even mentioned it to my son."

"First Main Street is a major road with two lanes on each side, and Narrow Hope Avenue collects at this corner … there's hardly a dam soul around."

"Yes, regardless of the snow."

The two men mull over ways to draw a nighttime crowd to the area, their conversation revealing the contrast between the lively daytime atmosphere and the stillness of the night. They contemplate the handful of surviving stores, the dollar store where Sophia works, and Sally's pizzeria, contrasting against the backdrop of an almost deserted locale.

“Morgan, I even lowered my rent on these stores, but nobody wants to rent my stores, and the few stores that operate here, close shop by six.”

“Except the dollar store where my Sophia works and Sally’s pizzeria. Then what about this pub.”

“You’re right. Sally doesn’t have a life with that man. ... he doesn’t even show himself.”

“He was not like that before, Sally and he had a life, a good one, the loss of their son shattered them … John, people escape their hurt in different ways!”

“Like how you said, how you were after losing your wife.”

“Yes, but I had somebody to live for ... my only son.”

The conversation shifts to Sophia, Ramona, and their respective partners, Malcolm and Morgan Jr. The memories evoke laughter and affection - the bonds of youth and love that thread through their lives. The men reflect on how their children's exuberance illuminated the neighborhood, even as John's own child ventured far from home to pursue her dreams.

"That dollar store guy keeps his store open till late. Does he pay Sophia OK?"

"Yes, but she is planning to stop when the baby comes."

"Can your dam son afford that, does he have a steady job, you haven't thought of that, My Man."

"I might have to work extra until they get settled."

"And how long are you going to do that for them, one year, two years? No, there must be another way."

As they shovel snow together, the conversation turns to the possibility of revitalizing the neighborhood by encouraging their children, Sophia and Morgan Jr., to start a business.

"Hey John, I was thinking, can you let my son and Sophia start a business in one of these stores. I will give you something for it."

"I don't see why not. The center store was once a café and ice cream store, but that didn't go well for the owner. The good thing about the center store is that it faces both streets. If your son and Sophia can energize that dam store back to life, it might liven up this place. What do you say, My Man?"

The idea of reviving a café and ice-cream store takes shape, an endeavor that holds the promise of breathing life back into the community. The conversation pivots to the practicalities of the venture, discussing costs and the need for repairs and redecoration. They envision a future where the storefront transforms into a thriving hub, and John pledges his support, recalling an old Welsh saying that underscores the value of nurturing what's one's own. Their enthusiasm is palpable, and they agree to clear the sidewalks before returning to the pub for more drinks.

Morgan's eyes flutter open; he meets darkness around him; yet a glimmer of light shines from the far end of the alley, a delicate promise of hope upon his weary body.

"Rest at last," he ponders into the silent night.

His leather bag remains a pillow, the once barren ground, now cloaked in a blanket of snow, and frostbites touch upon his numbed limbs. The streetlight, a silent watcher, paints a tableau of snowflakes in diagonal motion, each flake a fleeting comet colliding with the alley's sidewall. The snow's tempo is one of oscillation - a hum of fragility that wanes and waxes, caught in the bright embrace of the lamplight.

Memories weave through like fragments of a long-forgotten dream. He recalls the tempestuous winds of economic Social Darwinism that swept through the small enclave known as Hope and Main - a neighborhood where he played the role of the catalyst, a harbinger, a sweeping changer.

His son, Morgan Jr., emerges in his recollections, a figure of poise and grace, chauffeured through life's corridors, adorned in formal attire that spoke of breeding and achievement. The description unfurls: athletic-fit shirt neatly tucked, obsidian pants cinched with a belt, and shoes polished to an ebony sheen. A clean-cut visage crowned by closely cropped hair, exuding charm and extending greetings like an ambassador of goodwill.

The memory continues, and the past unfolds its vibrance. The nights of Hope and Main, bathed in an electric ambiance fueled by neon splendor and the digital incandescence of an LCD screen.

Yet, even amidst this splendor, a dissonance emerges - the silent cries of those left behind, the voices smothered by progress, and the souls ensnared in a web of opulence. A question lingers like an unspoken confession: Did he, Morgan, harbor genuine concern for these forgotten souls, or was his paternal ambition for his son's ascension the sole lodestar guiding his actions?

The shades of the past, veiled in obscurity, conceal the anguish of the defeated, the anguish of the wounded, the anguish of those imprisoned within a facade of sophistication he had orchestrated. Could they ever escape this web they tangle, or were they destined to traverse alongside him into eternity, like shadows of their own existence?

A light, so radiant and so ethereal, radiates with unparalleled intensity; within this luminance, stands his beloved wife, draped in the purity of a bridal gown- the vision of her youthfulness and splendor.

"Why have you come back, my dear?" he inquires with a sense of awe softening his words.

"Morgan, I have come to take you home," she replies in a comforting voice.

“Home?”

His memory surfaces images of Lex, the son of Sophia, and Naomi, the daughter of Ramona.

"It is time," she announces gently.

Taking her hand in his, he rises from his earthly tether. Her touch is a warm benediction, soothing away the vestiges of the world he leaves behind. As they traverse the alley's expanse, they pass the storefront's glass façade, and there, he sees his reflection once more. This time, the mirror echoes the visage of his youth, an image animated with life and unblemished by the years. Beside him, his wife emanates a with eternal beauty, the essence of her being undimmed by the sands of time.

In this timeless embrace, the rapture of happiness converges with the serenity of the night.

(3) Farewell

The cemetery became a gathering place for mourners, gilded in their finest tuxedos and elegant gowns that fluttered softly in the breeze. At the heart of the scene rests a polished wood-toned casket adorned with delicate roses and fragrant lavender. A sash, gracefully draped over the casket, bore the words, "We Love You Morgan!"

The silent monuments which surround the gathering, interpret a different tale. These monuments, beaten by the weather and human presence, yet being silent and motionless, absorb human follies drifting through the somber landscape and appear as if jeering back at this gathering.

"How did he die," a mourner asks the other.

"Nobody knows, but they found him next to a dumpster - frozen."

"Seriously!"

"They say he had a stroke, then he was recovering at a nursing home, nobody knows how he got to the dumpster."

"Did the dumpster belong to the nursing home?"

"Who knows!"

"These nursing homes, they only want your money. How could they let a patient just walk out without anybody seeing!"

"So, why did he even have to be at a nursing home, surely the family could have afforded a visiting nurse service."

"This shows who they really are."

Another mourner points to her friends, "Look at Sophia, doesn't she look so arrogant, even on a day like this."

"Yes, she thinks she is almighty, we knew each other when she was working at that dollar store for minimum wage, that's when she met this guy."

"Was he rich when they met?"

"No, the guy made money building cheap houses and selling scam mortgages. He got people to invest in his construction business, I think he scammed his investors too."

A man, being irritant over the conversation, asks the group of gossipers, "Did any of you even visit old Morgan in hospital, or even ask him if he was doing all right!"

The group moves to a different location to continue their conversation; then, two other women take that spot in the graveyard.

"Wait, somebody is about to speak. Oh, that's Mr. Williams, Morgan Jr.'s business partner."

"Yes, I know, that's his wife Audre next to him, she is a very nice person. Those two kids are their daughter and son."

"Yes, I know that. I always ask myself how Asher got involved with that whack, Morgan Jr."

"Do you know that Asher knew the old man from back then, they had worked together."

"Stop talking, I can't hear a thing."

"Let's move forward then."

"Many years ago, I got to know a man with profound character, he was a senior factory worker, and I became his foreman. I was a young graduate with few years of experience, hoping to make a name for myself, and I met this man with a lifetime of experience. He was never arrogant, but always willing to help those in need. He was strong but never emphasized his voice. But to speak on behalf of the weak, yes, he did emphasize his voice. Yes, I knew this man well, he was Morgan Sr.

At one point, we traveled on different paths in life, but we met again in New York, and we were business partners. He became my big brother and sometimes even my father. I am sure you remember how hard he worked to rebuild the Hope and Main neighborhood, he was an activist who wanted the best for people. Some even called him Grandpa Hope.

My wife and I were not in the country when we heard this sad news, it broke our hearts to lose a great comrade. Therefore, we hurried back home to be with his family and wish him goodbye.

No human is perfect, but the good quality in him is, he understood that he was not perfect, and was willing to acknowledge it when he was wrong. Therefore, in this last journey of his, I would like to say to him, thank you for being our big brother, thank you for being a patron to the community, and thank you for being selfless. Farewell Morgan, we will always remember you!"

After a gentle round of applause, the casket begins its descent.

The man that was earlier irritated over people's gossip speaks to another group of people, "I too regret not visiting him in hospital, not asking him if he needed help, or reaching out to his family. I am ashamed to be here to only say farewell to a dead body, yet when he was in hospital with his life intact, I went about my own business knowing well that he may not last long."

People gestured in acknowledgement.

The man continues, "I guess if that Morgan Jr was in hospital for … catching a cold … people would queue outside to make a visit … hypocrites!"

Sophia walks up to Asher and Audre, "Asher thank you so much for those beautiful words. Audre, thank you for being with us, it is a great strength to us."

Mourners gather to personally sympathize with Sophia, Morgan Jr., and son. A family to offer condolences is, Antonio, his wife, Veronica, and little daughter, Juliet.

Sophia acknowledges the family, "Thanks for being with us Veronica, without Antonio my husband would have been a wreck."

Then to Juliet, "Hi, my sweetie, you look so cute." Sophia kisses Juliet, then Juliet rubs Sophia's son's head, as he has his head down, not wanting to speak with anybody.

Amidst this emotional exchange, a butterfly unexpectedly breaks the melancholic atmosphere. The butterfly hovers over the graveyard, and Sophia, perplexed by this sight during winter, watches as the delicate creature ventures towards a departing family - Ramona, Malcolm, and their daughter, Naomi.

Naomi sees the butterfly approach and holds her hand out. The butterfly rests on her hand and takes a ride for a few yards, then flies off, fading into the melancholic panorama.

"Mom why are we leaving while the others are still waiting."

"We paid our respects to them, we did our duty, now we are going home."

Malcolm opens the car door for Naomi, "Dads don't we say goodbye to them?"

"Some other time, Baby Girl."

"Mom, come, sit with me."

"I will, My Sweet Baby."

"Are we angry with them?"

"Yes!"

"Then why did we come here today?"

"For the old man, I can't forget the past."

"But you ignored him on the train."

"Because he ignored us when we wanted him the most."

"Moni, shall we speak about this some other time," Malcolm suggests.

"Our daughter has to know the truth, Malcolm."

"Is that why we haven't visited them for a while?" asks Naomi.

"Yes, when they got rich, we were too poor for them … After all we've been through."

"Is that why we are angry with them now?"

"No, I didn't care about that, I am angry with them because they took away the little we had ... when they had plenty."

"So, we'll never see them again?"

"Oh no, I am sure our fates will cross paths again … what we do then matters."

(4) Lost Soul

Years have passed, and now it is a Saturday night in August. The "Star Sisters," graces the stage at the Hope and Main Amphitheater. Inside the theater, euphoria overflows and extends beyond its walls through the giant LCD screen, reaching even the senses of a young boy who sits on the steps of a storefront. The neon ambiance charms the passersby, who are immersed in their own joy, oblivious to the figure in the blue hoodie, who has his head partially covered.

While the boy sits in contemplation, his eyes scan the street; he looks for familiar faces. He checks on his friend Jaylen inside the Café Ice Cream Store and Juliet who is busy at Sally's Pizzeria.

"They're so lively," the boy thinks, as he looks towards the heavens.

He absorbs the glower of the full moon shining over the amphitheater and is unhappy with the dark clouds hovering towards the moon.

"No!" he thinks, as he brings his gaze down.

He feels as if the row of lanterns that stand along the sidewalk gaze at him; they depict a monotonous hue and wink at him, but little insects buzz around those lanterns claiming attention.

Then the tempo of the Star Sisters most popular hit, "… what a beautiful night …," heightens the rapture at the Arena; the screams, the applause, and the cheers, become endless, "… star please don't leave me..." the song continues.

He looks up to the partially covered Moon and hums that tune, trying so desperately to cry out the lyrics. Jaylen and Juliet leave their work behind, and sit on either side of the boy, and sing the song for him.

The song narrates the tale about the Moon falling in love with the North Star; yet, the Moon can't be together with the star, for the Moon is condemned to orbit

Earth for eternity. Therefore, the glimpse of the Star's twinkle makes the Moon rhyme with that silent hymn sung by the Star Sisters.

"Did I sing or was it only them singing," he wonders.

Jaylen and Juliet return to their work, leaving the Moon, the steps, and the lanterns for his company. More clouds shield the Moon, he looks up in annoyance, the clouds sprinkle raindrops on his face as if to mock him. The audience at the Arena cry in delight, it is the final applause for the Star Sisters. The pulse of the Star Sisters captivates the night with their last song, and as the song dies, noisy crowds appear on the empty streets. A haze hovers beneath the Moon amidst the mild drizzle on the storefront.

The storefront becomes busy. Crowds flock into the pub, the ice-cream shop, and the pizzeria. A mom, a dad, a little boy, and a little girl, walk into the ice-cream store; the mom shows the little girl all the available flavor choices, and the little boy tiptoes onto the ice-cream cabinet, looking for his own flavor.

"Fragments from my past," he reminisces.

A couple walks past him and the pizzeria, hand in hand the couple giggles at each other, in a rush, the girl turns back dragging her partner behind her, and the couple hops into the pizzeria through the partially open French door.

"Could I experience happiness!" he wonders.

The French door opens again, and in the glimmer of lights Juliet shimmers out. Her hair floating away from the border of her orange cap and her cheerful eyes affixing straight as she carries a tray and two pizza boxes in her hand.

She passes the boy, "Raining now!" she tells him.

He nods.

"When Dad is not around, Boss Morgan only wants me to carry his food," Juliet chuckles.

"Afraid of somebody poisoning him," the boy thinks.

He watches Juliet drift down the storefront walkway towards the last store. Once again, he is back on the steps: the moon still hiding, the lanterns still gazing, and the insects still buzzing. The sprinkle of rain transforms into a downpour, he moves to the top step and rests his head on the banister. The roof over the storefront walkway blocks the rain for him, yet he needs the spray of raindrops to soothe him. The insects leave the lanterns, yet the clouds stand between the moon and him. He sees Juliet returning to the store and knows that she cannot see his smile - the Moon is still hiding behind the clouds. She pokes his hair and scampers into the pizzeria. The rain hisses onto the asphalt.

He will join Juliet in the same high school soon, she is a junior, but he will go in as a first-year student. Nevertheless, they were in the same classes throughout middle school. Flashbacks of middle school bring joy to him and sometimes ease his pain; he wishes he could go back to those moments: the chatter, the yellow bus, and the basketball court. Juliet was the genius; he was the orator. She was the sister he did not have; he was the brother she did not have. She became the middle school valedictorian while Jaylen became Salutatorian.

A jolt of lightning flashes across the sky, etching a dead branch of glowing ember on a gloomy backdrop. Life is like that lightning bolt, energy, light, thunder, or may strike like vengeance. Another bolt of lightning cracks the sky, he turns his head away to avoid its wrath. He sees the reflection of the streak on the store window, and Juliet watches its final luster melt into the night sky.

Juliet's family owns the pizzeria at the storefront; Juliet helps her family to run the business. Her mom takes orders and manages the pizzeria. Her mom's sister, Sally, is the acrobat, her fingers transform spherical dough into circular pies, her arms paddle pizzas in and out of the silver ovens, then performs a precise cut leaving neither slice larger nor smaller.

"O' Sally, how you try to forget, but how I try to remember."

Sally pulls out pizza rolls from the oven; most go in the display while a customer gets three and four left aside for Jaylen and him.

A man in a tuxedo with reddish glasses and a leather briefcase chained to his wrist, stands at the counter of the pizzeria, trying to make an order.

"Not him again," the boy laments.

Juliet, ignoring the man, signals that the grub is ready, but the boy sits on the top step, with head resting on the banister, and waits for the man in the tuxedo with reddish glasses to leave. But the man lingers at the store waiting to place his order.

Turning his back to avoid the view of that man in the tuxedo with the leather briefcase chained onto the wrist, the boy observes the rain splatter. An array of puddles form on the empty parking lot, the splattering rain initiates ripples on every puddle, and the ripples float across the water, conveying a hypnotic trance on the boy. He envisions puddles becoming larger and connecting to each other forming mini waterways. The waterways convert into one giant river. The river rises, and water flows above the storefront steps. Another wave of water flows from Main Street and crashes into the storefront and finds its way into the ice-cream store.

"Got to save the children!"

He sees the children safe, Mom holding the little girl up, Dad carrying the little boy, water waist high gushing past, but the parents stand resilient and unmoved.

"Juliet!" He remembers.

He runs into the pizzeria and finds it immersed in a mini ocean, and water up to the neck of Juliet.

"I will save you, Juliet!"

"No, you won't," says the man in the tuxedo and reddish glasses, who has a leather briefcase chained to his wrist. "I promised her this."

"No, I will save her," says the boy.

"You can try, but you will fail."

"I will not fail."

The man moves Infront, attempting to obstruct the boy from saving Juliet. The boy pushes the man away making the reddish glasses fall into the water. The boy sees his own reflection in the man's eyes, and steps back; then remembering Juliet, the boy dives into the water.

She sinks deeper and he tries to pull her up; he just can't, she is caught by the current. He holds on to her as they both sink into the water. Down, down they go! He closes his eyes.

(5) Block Party

Steel drums and banjos take turns toning nearby buildings, barbecue smoke reminds the neighboring populaces of their fun afternoon, and showing off their glitzy outfits, children dance on the stage. Flags and décor are in animation acknowledging the breeze, and a large banner illustrates, "Thank You Our Hero!"

Yet, inside her apartment, the apparent hero is going through another meltdown.

"Naomi, stop!" yells Ramona. There is a crash and the sound of shattering glass.

"Moni, what's happening," Malcom rushes into Naomi's room to witness a shattered mirror, glass on the floor, and Naomi crying.

"Who else, it's your daughter," explains Ramona.

"I hate my life!" says Naomi.

Malcom embraces Naomi saying, "I love you Baby-Girl, relax … breathe in … now exhale … relax …"

Malcom holds onto Naomi as Ramona stands in distress, glaring at father and daughter. Malcom releases his embrace, and Naomi switches embraces with her mother. Malcom notices Ramona's hesitation to return the embrace, but eventually gives in.

"Therapy is not helping her, Malcom; this is not working. I don't want to take this anymore."

"Moni, you take Baby-Girl downstairs, people are waiting for her. I will clean this up."

"Take her down this way? Malcom, I don't want her to get this attention."

"It's all fun, Moni. People want to thank her. I agree with you though, I didn't expect it to be this big."

Malcom sees Naomi walking into the bathroom, then he hears the slamming of the bathroom door and the clicking sound of the bathroom door lock.

Ramona beats her forehead against the wall, "God give me strength," she utters. "You know what, Malcom, you go down … it's you who encouraged this behind my back."

"Moni, we haven't had a party for Baby-Girl since her ninth birthday, she's going to high school next month. I thought of making up to her this way."

"I don't know how she will do high school with a broken hand and this temper."

"Moni, you know the hand is recovering. About the temper …"

There is a tap at the door, and Ramona answers, it is Sally.

"Hi Moni … it's not a good time, right?"

"If I wait for a good time, I'll be waiting forever … come inside, Sally."

"Where is our hero; I brought this for her."

"In the bathroom going through another meltdown. And the therapy is not helping … Oh Sally, I don't know what to do, I just can't go on."

"Let me speak to her," says Sally, and softly taps at the bathroom door.

"What?" is the reply from the bathroom.

"Mami, it's me, Sally. I brought you something nice."

In a few minutes, they hear the lock click open, and Malcom is thankful that he does not have to force open a door lock, which he does often."

Then they wait anxiously for the door to open, which finally happens.

"Hi," exclaims Sally, smiling with open arms. "Look how pretty!"

Naomi ignores everybody, pulls out a dining table chair with her foot, and sits cradling a cast hand.

"I brought something you like," says Sally to Naomi, "I left a large tray at the party for the others to enjoy, but this is for you."

Malcom carrying the debris out of Naomi's room, "Sally, don't go bankrupt, we love your pizzeria too much for that to happen."

"Oh no, Malcom, when I heard how our hero saved that child, and when everybody is thankful for her, I have to do my duty too."

"Thank you, Sally!"

"Moni, give us a smile," Sally looking at Naomi, "a smile like her smile."

Naomi looks at her mother, and Ramona walks up to the window, smiling.

"I can't remember the last time we had a block party here," adds Ramona, looking out of the window and mimicking the drumbeat with her fingers on the windowpane.

"See, isn't it worth it, Moni!" Malcom comments.

"Baby-Girl, come, look at those children dancing."

Naomi walks to the window and looks out, Sally follows. Naomi leaning over Ramona, peeks through the window, and Ramona fixies Naomi's hair.

"When I was small, Mama used to take me home to spend our summer break, her family used to party like this," says Ramona.

"I used to party like this too," adds Sally, "but that was a long time ago."

Malcom understands what Sally is referring to, she may be still in pain over her lost son. If her son was living, he would be an adult by now, "How time flies," Malcom thinks. "Why do good people have to suffer!"

"Come Mami, let's go down and enjoy your party," says Sally.

Ramona, Sally, and Naomi descend the stairs and step outside into the warm and bustling atmosphere. The steel drums still echo, the band plays on, and children continue to dance. Naomi finds shade under a canopy, her mom sits beside her, and Sally heads to another canopy to speak to a boy in a blue hoodie.

People approach Naomi to greet her, and children eagerly scribble messages on her cast. She notices Sally serving food to the boy in the blue hoodie, and Naomi's and the boy's eyes meet. Naomi sees the emptiness in his gaze and the coldness in his demeanor as he clutches his food and eats quickly.

"Wow! nice party, right!" says Mom.

Two boys and a girl from the neighborhood walk up to Naomi and offer her their high fives, and one boy tries to sit next to Naomi.

"That seat is taken," says Mom in a bland voice, the boy walks away to join his friends.

Naomi looks for the boy with that blank expression and sees him at a distance, following Grandma Olivia.

Sally joins them, "Mami, can I bring you something?"

"I was about to get something," says Mom, "if you can just stay with her for me, please!"

Naomi observes the joyful crowd; she realizes how a small gathering could foster a sense of community among neighbors and friends. She sees other teenagers like herself, carefree and happy. The sunlight shifts, and Sally offers to move, but Naomi declines, finding comfort in the warmth of the sun.

"Mami, you're a hero, you saved a child, and I am sorry he hurt your hand."

"No Sally, I hurt my hand, myself."

"What… how?"

"When I saw him grabbing that child and walking down the steps, and the child's grandma screaming, my anger came back to me."

"Weren't there anybody else around?"

"Two people were just watching, they were frightened to do anything about it, so I charged at him, and he fell down the stairs. Then I picked the child and ran into the apartment."

"Did he try to follow you?"

"I saw him trying but he couldn't get up the stairs, I think he hurt his foot. Then he drove off and was later arrested."

"Gosh, you went through a terrible experience here. So how did you hurt your hand?"

"In the process ... I don't know exactly how it happened."

"You have to be careful, Mami."

"Sally, I want to ask you something."

"Go ahead!"

"Are you still angry for how you lost your son a long time ago?"

Sally taking a deep breath, "When you lose something dear to you that way, you become angry … and you become sad. Although the sadness never goes away, and it may stick with you forever … you must overcome the anger."

"Why?"

"Because anger prevents you from being you, it puts you in this unending vicious cycle."

"How did you overcome your anger?"

"You have to overcome hate. I did, and it made me feel better, but my husband could not do that."

"But why can't you hate those who hurt you?"

"You have a choice of hating and being like them ... or moving on and being who you are."

"But then, aren't we setting them free?"

"No, you're setting yourself free!"

"Then, how do I overcome hate?"

"I don't know, each one has to find their own way, but one way is to do something bigger than yourself. Then turn back and you will see how far you've progressed."

"How do I do something bigger than myself?"

"It could be an ideal, it could be an action, but it should be something that channels out your anger."

"Where can I find what you're talking about?"

"Keep looking, and when you find it, you will know what to do."

(6) My Name is Utter

It is the first day of high school, and the hallways of Admirable Academics High School buzzes with excitement - a cacophony of eager voices and a palpable sense of anxiety. Students hurriedly make their way through the corridors, eager to embark on this new chapter of their academic journey.

Outside the principal's office, two students, a girl, and a boy, sit with Miss Grace, the school social worker. The girl wears a bright pink cast that extends from her fingers up to her elbow. The word "Brave" is boldly engraved on the cast, surrounded by various comments and artwork rendered in black and blue. The boy sees how she wears it with pride, and as students pass by, they can't help but offer compliments or gaze at her in admiration. All eyes were on the brave girl, her cast, and her sling.

In contrast, he who sits beside her goes largely unnoticed, overshadowed by the girl's courage and her eye-catching cast. Yet he doesn't mind because he's happy to be back in school once again.

"There's my brave girl," comments the principal who enters the office, then stepping back out and pointing towards him, asks Miss Grace, "How is he doing."

"That's what I am here to talk about," explains Miss Grace. "In fact, about both of them."

The principal waves Miss Grace into the office.

The girl with the cast speaks to him. "I think I've seen you in my neighborhood."

"Me too, Naomi … it was nice seeing you again … after that day at the block party," he thinks.

Hoping that Naomi won't speak to him, he sits motionless, fixating on the opposite side of the waiting area, observing the secretary's typing pace.

Naomi repeats, "Hi, my name is Naomi, what's yours, I think I know you; don't you live on block 4B?"

While trying to recollect his memories from his early childhood, he hears Naomi repeat her question.

"What's your name, don't you live on block 4B. Do you know Grandma Olivia? I live on the next block."

The name, Grandma Olivia, grabs his attention and delight for a moment since that's his grandmother. Then the emotional incentive ends, because Naomi would hate him, knowing who he really is. Once again, he fixates at the secretary's typing - fingers beating on keys so swiftly and her lips flickering as if speaking to herself.

"What's your Name," Naomi asks again.

"Shh," snaps the secretary. "This is the principal's office."

The room becomes silent where the only sounds are the pitter-patter of the secretary's keyboard and the whispers between Miss Grace and the principal.

Naomi gets up, peeks into the principal's office.

Observing the secretary looking at her, "I am just checking out this school."

"Sit!" demands the secretary. "Now!"

"OK!" responds Naomi, then to him, "If you don't want to talk, it's fine."

He mentally responds, "I would love to speak to you, but I can't; even if I could, speaking to you is not possible."

Naomi sits next to him and pulls out her tablet to do her reading. He pulls out a book off his backpack and begins writing; Naomi flips a page on her tablet and keeps reading.

The secretary types on her computer, and every few minutes she looks towards them and notes their tranquility. She seems to be pleased.

Miss Grace's and the principal whisper; the secretary, tries hard to decipher the whisper by cracking on her keyboard as softly as possible.

Miss Grace and the Principal continue their conversation.

"He has been cleared to attend school by his doctors, but we got to monitor him from our end. He has become nonverbal, and he has gone through facial reconstruction due to the accident. To make matters worse, he has been separated from his parents. His grandmother is his guardian now."

"Yes, I was reading his report, Miss Grace."

"Also, he wants to have his face covered under that hood."

"We can allow that under special circumstances."

"I thought so."

"Also, did you read the newspaper article about Naomi?"

"I did! The neighborhood organized a celebration for Naomi for saving that little girl."

"So, Naomi got attacked while trying to save a little girl from being kidnapped."

"Yes, that guy had been preying on the weak, he had also beaten and robbed an old woman."

"This child puts herself in danger!"

"Thanks to Naomi they arrested this guy, and their neighborhood is much safer now.

"What a child!"

But we need to teach her to be safe, to take care of herself and not put herself into danger."

"I trust that you could guide her on that, Miss Grace."

"I will."

The secretary feels sorry for the teens, and regrets snapping at Naomi; then walking to a filing cabinet, she peeks at Naomi's tablet, wanting to smile at her.

"Now that's sad," says Naomi.

"What's sad, sweety," asks the secretary.

"No, I am just commenting on the book that I just read, it has a sad ending."

"What's this book you ended?"

"A Tale of Two Cities. It is a story that connects with the French Revolution. At the end, this innocent man and woman get condemned to die along with the others, but they are happy because they have done something great in their lives."

"Wow, so sad!"

The bell rings, indicating the transition of classes, a rush emerges within the silent hallways, and dies. Naomi gets up from her seat, with her tablet in hand, once again peeks into the principal's office.

The secretary smiling, "The meeting is still on, are you getting bored?"
The boy notices the secretary's change in mood, "This is an interesting start," he thinks.

Naomi walks back towards him, "You write so fast, but I didn't see your name written on the cover."

"You never give up, do you," exclaims the secretary.

Naomi bending towards him with her hand hanging in front of him, "So you don't want to say your name to me. Why is that now? I think you don't like your name, or you don't have a name… right!"

Naomi is right, he does not like his name. He does not know how to answer, he keeps writing.

The secretary speaks to Naomi, "Sweety, why are you bothering him?"

"No Miss, I get the feeling that I know him from somewhere, I just want to know his name. That's all."

"He doesn't want to speak to you, so let him be."

The secretary continues typing.

"You look a unique person to me, boy; maybe, I'll call you Mr. Unique … no, that sounds cheap!"

How could he tell her that he's smiling at her humor, but she can't read his smile!

"Who knows? You may think that talking is tortuous," Naomi continues. "Maybe Double T would be a good name for you ... but I think there is somebody with that name."

"Yes, talking is tortuous, but Double T is a cool name," he thinks.

Naomi's humor creates a pleasant feeling within him, and he notices that his hoodie has fallen back.

"You're just gazing that way. Oh, trying to be exclusive right?"

"Yes, but not the way you interpret," he ponders.

Wait a minute! I think I got a name for you."

Naomi thinks for a moment.

"If you don't have a name, I will give you one. Utter boy, that's what I'll call you. Do you like it, Utter Boy?"

Naomi waiting for a response, and finding no response, "U stands for Unique, the double T's stands for Thinking that Talking and Tortuous. Then 'E' stands for Exclusive."

"That's 'T' repeated three times, that's fine, I will take two." he thinks with an inner smile.

Naomi thinks further, "Utter Boy sounds awkward, maybe Utter would do, yes that's good."

The secretary in a hilarious mood, "Sweety, what does the 'R' stand for?"

"I can't come up with something for that, I'll go with what I have for now."

"Sweety, you crack me up!"

Naomi looks around, "Now how do I make this official? … got it!"

From a nearby drinking fountain, Naomi collects drops of water in her palm, then pours it on his head saying, "I give you the name – Utter!"

Water drips from his hair and along his face. He uses his fingers to gather the pouring water and sprinkles it back at Naomi.

Naomi ducks to avoid the sprinkles. "Ha, you missed!"

Miss Grace rushes out of the principal's office crying, "What's happening here?"

The principal follows Miss Grace.

"Sweety, I expected you to be calm while I was inside the principal's office. But I feel let down now."

"I am sorry Miss Grace, I didn't mean to, but since he was feeling so down and not talking, I thought of livening him up ... I had to!"

"He's feeling down because he can't talk ... He can't talk, sweetheart, he can't talk!" blurts the secretary.

With that comment, the four girls glower at each other, each trying to speak, but it seems that they can't convert thoughts into words; the principal crosses her hands and looks at the secretary, the secretary drops her head and continues typing.

Naomi, walking towards him, "I am sorry, I didn't know! I am so, so … so sorry!"

He brushes off the stagnant water from his hair, takes a pen off his bag, and brings the pen close to Naomi's cast.

"Go ahead, you can write something, but it's coming off today… Sadly!"

He imprints on the cast, "When your wing is restored, may you ascend like an eagle! Thank you for my new name, it is better than the one I have - Utter!"

"See! He likes his new name; he just began using it."

Once again, entertained by this juvenile mischief, the secretary tells the principal who still has her hands crossed, "They're so cute!"

The principal invites the two students and Miss Grace into her office and begins her conversation with the two students.

"I know what both of you have gone through. Tragic! However, I admire the fact that you're bold enough to face your future and report to school on the first day. For that reason, I am proud of you! But just learn to control yourselves, self-control is a virtue."

The principal pauses, waiting for the students to reflect on her statement. The students stand in front of her, waiting for her to continue the conversation.

Thus, she continues. "Now, Miss Grace wants me to assign a staff member to take care of you during your school day, but I don't think that's necessary. What do you think?"

The students shake their heads.

Naomi adds, "Miss I could take care of myself, and I will take care of him if you want me to. He lives close to where I live, just the next block."

The secretary adds to the conversation, "She is so cute, bless her heart!"

"Good!" continues the principal, "I see how well you're taking care of each other, and please do that without any disruption."

"One more thing," the principal adds, "since you must use public transport to get home, and taking Miss Grace's advice, starting today and for the next two days, a staff member will be accompanying both of you home. Just until both of you become familiar with your travel routine."

"But Miss, I can go home on my own."

"No arguments there, if this person I send with you tells me everything is fine, then from next week onwards, you can travel alone."

"Thank you, Miss."

"Any questions?"

Everybody is silent until Naomi breaks the silence, "One question Miss, what's your name?"

"I am Mrs. Shepherd."

(7) Voice

It is Monday, the first day of the second week of the new school year, the teens are back in school, Jaylen and Juliet are in the junior's classes while Utter is in the freshman's class with Naomi.

"Hey, Utter, why do you run off as soon as you approach your building, is it to get away from that guy who's been following us home?"

He shrugs his shoulders.

"Guess what… Miss Grace said that we could travel on our own today. So... if you can't find me after school, meet me at the exit."

He nods.

"One more thing, I see Juliet's dad driving you to school in the mornings, if you miss them, my dad and I can bring you in the morning too."

Shuddering his head hastily, "No!" he thinks.

"Oh, don't worry, Dads won't mind. He's a nice person."

"And a huge contrast to mine," Utter thinks.

"The writing piece today is describing how you and your family spent your summer break," yaps Miss Pet, the ELA teacher.

Although the new school year began the previous week, because there were only three school days that week, because Mrs. Pet thought that it was unfair to begin school during the middle of a week, and because she was not in a mood to teach, students in Mrs. Pet's third period ELA class, not wasting precious education time, had used that time to get to know each other better.

Cursive writing in white chalk against a trite blackboard, illustrates a common topic which Utter, Naomi, and most other students in that class have much narrated while in elementary classes. Utter knows that the assignment insults high school intellect, yet he, along with other students begin forming their initial sentences. In the midst of this literary slur, Naomi gazes upon their instructor, where Naomi holds in the unspoken contemplation about this insult to education.

"Now stop looking at me and do the writing, if you do not have anything to write, write about yourself, or at least describe a friend's experience," the teacher echoes.

Another teacher peeks into the class, and the two begin whispering about how they spent their summer breaks.

"I was in Florida, we got a timeshare," boasts Mrs. Pet.

"Great, were the beaches crowded?"

Miss Pet turns as she speaks, making sure her students are busy. "A little bit, you should join us next time."

"So much for education," Naomi murmurs to Utter.

He nods in response to Naomi.

"She's throwing baby work at us, and we are in high school," Naomi continues.

He nods again.

Overhearing the conversation between the alleged educators and its substantive content, Utter feels a compelling urge to offer counsel to Miss Pet, conveyed through his written words.

"Since my hand does not want to write, you can add what I did during summer … into your writing piece ... if you don't mind."

He passes a note to Naomi -You got it Naomi! Quick, tell me what you did or can I write about your party.

Naomi whispers, "No, wait ..."

"Got to go, I just remembered my work." The other teacher walks away hastily, ending the conversation with Miss Pet.

Seconds later, "Don't work too hard," screams Miss. Pet, slanting herself and hanging her head towards the outside of the classroom entrance.

Soon, his writing is complete, and he raises his head. He observes Naomi adding Depth to the illustration of the human heart, which she began doing at the science class this morning. The arteries sprout out of a slant heart, all deviating out of the page and entering the third dimension, to match with realism.

"Da Vinci wouldn't have done this better, but I would have liked color," he thinks.

He notices Mis. Pet glancing at students' work; occasionally squinting her eyes, then pushing her glasses up her nose bridge, sometimes bringing the glasses to the tip of her nose, and randomly grumping, "I miss Florida."

Miss Pet abruptly stops next to Utter, "You wrote something there, too bad you can't read, "she shrugs her shoulders, her palms facing skyward, then setting her glasses.

She peeks at Naomi's book, "Naomi, where is your work" she asks, swaying her head left to right. "Use that pencil to write, not doodle."

The teacher mumbles, "Some can't read, some can't write, I don't know how they got to high school."

The pencil in Naomi's hand shatters in two against Naomi's fingers, then she attempts to further shatter the pencil; to prevent it, he rests his hand over Naomi's hand, looks into her eyes. He senses the pulse in her hand as she lets go of the shattered pencil. The pencil stumps roll off the table. Naomi gradually pulls her hand away from him, and he picks up the two pencil stumps and leaves it back on her table.

Naomi rises, "Miss, he is done writing, and I'll read for him."

Naomi's voice resonates through the classroom, transferring students' attention from writing to listening.

"Naomi, do your own writing," yaps the teacher.

Naomi picks his writing book, flips it, and brushes past students, moving to the front of the class.

Miss Pet screams, "Naomi, back to your seat," but Naomi reads his writing.

"How a student enjoys a summer break," then bending towards him and flickering her eyelids, "Utter, where's your title, don't you even date your work."

"Forgot that, didn't I," he thinks.

The teacher yells again, "Naomi, back to your seat."

Naomi holds the book in embrace, and in a soft, polite, voice, states, "Miss, I did not write for a reason, and he did not read for a reason. But, since I can read, and he can write, that makes Utter and me a team. So, may I please read. … Please!"

"His name is not utter," says Miss Pet.

Naomi ignores.

"His name is not utter," repeats Miss Pet.

"Yes, it is! He wanted a name change, so that's his new name now. It is Utter, with an uppercase 'U'."

"Whatever!"

Naomi clears her throat, "How a student enjoys a summer break varies on the student's life circumstances; also, how a student enjoys a break, may not necessarily be how that student wishes to enjoy that break. A person should not make a general assumption that all parents and guardians of children also have that same long break. What about parents who live paycheck to paycheck; will they raise enough money to take their children on a splendid vacation? What about children living in shelters; they depend on budget allocations and donors for a vacation. What about those who go on summer camps, don't they enjoy their summer break? How students spend their vacation should not be a judgmental discussion for a teacher, for each student's experience is different.

For example, my friend Jaylen and his family spent two weeks in Australia and two weeks in Kenya, during their summer break. Photographs of moments they enjoyed, beautify their social media pages. Their Safari in Kenya exposed how close they were to nature. Images of the lion, the elephant, and the zebra, roaming along the banks of the Mara and the Talek rivers were captivating. His vacation was about travel and adventure.

Meanwhile, my friend Juliet's experience was different. Their family wants to buy their first home; therefore, the family worked hard this summer. Their summer goal was to keep their family business afloat and add money towards the down payment. Juliet's vacation was working eight hours a day, five days a week, and resting two days to re-energize. Juliet also enrolled for six college credits, credits that may benefit her when she enters college. Her vacation was about progress.

"Where did you write about me Utter," Naomi looks at him, looks at the students, then back at him. "Add my paragraph," she says and continues reading.

My friend Naomi, "Oh, there it is, sorry Utter," she grins. "This is about me."

My friend Naomi spent her summer helping little children in a day camp. Most children at the camp did not have a place to be, while their parents were busy at work; thus, the camp was an immense service to those children. The children at the camp looked up to Naomi as their big sister, while she saw those children as if they were their siblings. Sadly, she could not end the camp due to an accident that occurred to her while she was trying to save a child from getting kidnapped. The children at the camp created a giant collage praising her, and she was happy that she brought joy to children during her summer break. Her vacation was about compassion.

Random claps become a roar of claps, and become silent to her powering voice, "I am not done yet!"

Mine was a total contrast to their vacations; "This is about him now."

I spent this vacation trying desperately to hold on to all my vacations from a different life: a different life that seemed normal, a different life that seemed forgiving, and a different life I wanted to return to. This summer I wondered if my past moments were a dream, or if my present is the dream; when will I wake up, or will I ever wake up. I wished a giant flood would wash away my present and recreate that past, but my wish did come only in a dream, and sadly in that dream, drowns a person that I care for so much.

"What was your vacation about, Utter? Whom did you dream of?"

Naomi hands the book back to him. Students applauding, she bows, and bows again.

"Naomi, bye," the teacher yells.

"Wait Miss, not yet."

Naomi moves through the middle aisle, twisting left to right giving high-fives.

Shaking her head, Miss Pet moans, "I miss Florida."

The bell rings, the children rush out of the class, as Naomi and he follow. They walk briskly down the corridor towards the next class, Naomi walking in front of him, as he follows shielding his appearance with his hoodie.

A foot appears Infront of him, he trips and hits the ground.

"Why did you do that?" yells Naomi, at a group of boys who are congregating in the hallway.

"Your puppy should look where he's going," says one of the boys.

Others laugh.

"He is not a puppy, and one of you tripped him. The one who did it should be apologizing … now!"

The boys laugh.

Naomi, making a fist, takes rapid steps towards the boys. Utter hurries back on his feet and not wanting any confrontation, pulls Naomi's hand, but she shrugs it off. The power of the shrug throbs up to his shoulder, but worthy of preventing a confrontation.

Standing Infront of the boys, “I saw one of you do it, so apologize now.”

“Or what,” asks one of them.

“You will answer to me then,” says a voice from behind.

It is Jaylen.

“Who’s he to you, aren’t you one of us … and why are you so annoyed when he deserved what he got?”

“You’re bothering my brother,” says Jaylen.

“That loser,” says a boy from the group, “He’s nothing like you.”

“He is still my brother!”

“Oh, we’re sorry,” cries out another boy. “But you’ll find us one day, and we won’t be there for you.”

The group of boys disperse.

“Thanks, Jaylen.”

“Anytime.”

“Good luck for tomorrow’s game Jaylen, add to the touchdowns.”

“I will.”

(8) Walk

Planning to wait for their next bus, Naomi and Utter get off at the intersection of Hope and Main.

"Utter we got seven minutes for the next bus, let's get ice cream."

Utter shakes his head refusing Naomi's request.

"I will buy for you, I got money."

Utter still refuses by shaking his head abruptly.

"Is ice cream bad for you, are you on a type of diet, or are you just wanting to be difficult?"

Utter turns his face at Naomi. Naomi, not giving up, pulls him by his hand towards the ice cream store.

"Don't resist Utter, you will hurt my other hand too."

Utter not resisting Naomi, follows her into the ice cream store.

"Nice and cool here! Wow, look at that line. Utter, watch for the bus, I will order."

Utter keeps watch, but looks around the store, and becomes fixated at the mural on the sidewall. On one side of the mural are framed photographs of varying rectangular dimensions, hung in a decorative pattern.

"Hey Utter, the man on that Mural, is somebody I knew when I was little."

Utter becomes attentive, with his eyes wide open.

"His name is Morgan, I called him Grandpa Hope. His son's name is also Morgan. Grandpa Hope was a good man, he did so much for the people around here. That's why I asked him for help."

Utter listens thoughtfully.

"The things that his son had done, had made Grandpa Hope incredibly sad. So, Grandpa Hope died and couldn't help me, and all was lost for me ... forever."

Naomi sees Utter's eyes take a reddish shine.

A woman standing behind them and holding onto a walker, says, "You got that right my child, that man in the mural was a good man. God bless his soul!"

"Did you know him too?" asks Naomi.

"Very well, my child, very well! … You know, I met him a few days before he died."

Naomi adds, "I too, met him just before he died. I asked him for help, but I didn't know that he couldn't help me. They say that he had lost the will to live."

Naomi notices tears running down Utter's face, "Oh I am sorry! I didn't know sad stories make you cry that much."

Utter wipes his tears.

"Let me think of a different story to tell you."

Utter seems uneasy, and now he looks out for the bus.

"The line is moving fast; it is our turn next. Utter I am getting us option three on the menu, is that good?"

Accepting Naomi's choice, Utter pulls out his money, but Naomi pays for them both.

"When I was little, I used to come here with Mom, and Mom never waited online. If Mom's friend Sophia was around, Sophia would just bring the ice cream to us. When it was cold outside, we used to get hot pumpkin spiced lattes … Sophia was nice."

Utter dashes out of the ice cream store.

"Hey, where are you running off to, is the bus here, hold it for me, Utter!"

The woman who is with Naomi shouts, "Hold the bus for me too, please."

Naomi walks out with two ice creams in each hand, she does not see a bus, but she sees Utter sitting at the bus stop, resting his face on his hands. She walks up to him, and the woman with the walker trying to keep up.

"Did we miss the bus?" asks the woman.

Utter shakes his head and Naomi hands him his ice cream. The woman sits next to Utter, "Hope this ice cream won't melt before I get to my grandchildren."

"When I was little, my mom used to push me on the stroller down this road, there were no buses running on this road back then," Naomi says.

"Good infant-memory my girl, I remember that time," says the woman.

"I remember a lot; this area was not this way before. It was all rundowns."

"Yes, my children, this neighborhood went through drastic changes that were implemented through the hard work of Morgan Sr., we called him Old Morgan although he was not that old, but we saw how his brown beard and hair had turned grey so suddenly ... so sad."

"Yes, my mom speaks about that change. I remember seeing it too. I called him Grandpa Hope."

The woman continues the conversation with Naomi, "Morgan, I am talking about Old Morgan ... he petitioned the city asking for a bus stop at this intersection and a new bus route to be in operation along Narrow Hope Avenue. He also requested the support of people living down Narrow Hope Avenue. People did not care, some people had already made plans of leaving this economically deprived locality, while some other people thought it was comfortable living like that."

"Yes, I know," acknowledges Naomi. "You know Utter, we got this bus running, I made this happen. My mom and I, and other moms and other babies, stood for days protesting."

Utter is in deep thought or enjoying his ice cream.

To gather his attention, Naomi, standing on the bus stop bench, the vacant seat next to Utter, and yells out, "Don't make my mom freeze when pushing me down Hope Avenue," then jumping off the bench she yells out "Don't make my mom get a heat stroke pushing me down Hope Avenue."

The old woman tells Utter, "That was the saying on the banner, we carried it all the way to the mayor."

Then the woman asks Naomi, "Were you there too, my girl."

"I was a baby in a stroller, I told you, remember?"

"You have a good infant memory."

Naomi explains, "Actually, I am relating to the photographs posted next to the mural, the black stroller with the red handle and two yellow ducks hanging, is my stroller. My mom told me the whole story of what we did."

"Yes, it was that man Morgan who planned it, the father not the son. The father did good things in this area."

"See Utter, I told you that he was a good man."

"I don't know if you two children remember," the old woman pointing towards the Amphitheater, "that was a park over there, they built a theater after he was gone. There was nobody to protest for the children."

"I remember playing in that park, we felt sad when they blocked it out to build the Amphitheater."

"That man cleaned that park by himself, sometimes he got help from John, the previous owner. They say Old Morgan used to be a skilled machine worker. We saw him fixing the park equipment, painting, and cleaning out the weeds."

"Did you ever go to that park Utter?"

Utter shakes his head.

"They say, it was good business for his son and daughter in law," explains the woman, "soon, children began playing in the park, more people gathered at this intersection, and there were more people visiting that cafe ice cream business. That place got crowded."

"Utter, do you want to walk home, I think the bus is late."

Utter nods.

"Let's get two more ice creams for the road," suggests Naomi.

Utter begins walking fast down the street.

"Hold on Utter! I was only kidding."

"Let me walk with you, I don't know what's happening with the bus today," the Woman says. "Do you live far, my child?"

"At the end of this street, I am used to walking this distance."

"That's far, I just live two stops away. My grandchildren would be waiting for me ... Old Morgan needs to come back to get everything organized around here."

"Did you know him well?"

"The woman continues, "I knew Old Morgan because he was a friend of my late husband's. It was my husband that introduced Old Morgan to the former storefront owner, John."

"I see."

"The storefront didn't belong to the Morgan family at first, and a year after they started this cafe ice cream business, John wanted to move to California to live with his daughter's family. John was selling off the storefront, and the Morgan family managed to get a bank loan to buy the storefront."

"That was smart."

"But … people were surprised that John sold the storefront so cheap. My late husband was too."

"How did that happen?" inquires Naomi.

"There are so many stories, I don't know what's true or what's false. Anyway, I survived after my husband died of a heart attack when he found out that Old Morgan's son, Morgan Jr., had scammed us."

"What? ... Morgan Jr., scammed my parents too!"

"Did he? Many fell for that Morgan Jr.'s bait. He had a partner, now what was that evil man's name, I can't remember. Although, I will never forget his face or the way he looked."

"What did he do?"

"He scammed my poor husband by getting together with Morgan Jr. Yes, that's what they did."

"How did they do it?"

"They looked so nice at first, always in a tuxedo and ever so polite. I don't know why that other man had to have that briefcase chained to his hand or wear those reddish glasses."

"Oh!"

"You are too young to understand these stories my daughter," The woman pauses, "I got to turn here."

Looking towards a house off a side street from Hope Avenue, "I live in that house with my daughter's family, I help them to pay their rent when I can. My daughter and her family were to move to my house, but that's the house we lost because of Morgan Jr.'s scam."

"We lost our house too; my mom says that she will never forgive them."

The woman stops walking, Naomi and Utter stop with her too. Naomi shows interest in listening to the woman's conversation.

"I forgave him, my child. I said that to Old Morgan."

"You met him after that?"

"Yes, when we were having trouble, we were looking for him, then we heard that he was at a certain nursing home. My daughter, not being that forgiving, met him at his nursing home."

"Oh!"

"Yes, but my daughter didn't tell me what they discussed."

"Did he feel sorry?"

"I don't know, but he came for my husband's wake. I was hurting too. I told him everything his son and that man with the briefcase had done to us. I also told Old Morgan that it is because of him that I trusted Morgan Jr. and that other man."

"Did he say anything?"

"No, but he was sorry, he knelt near my husband's coffin and prayed until it was closing time at the funeral home."

"Did his son visit you too?"

"No, the father had come alone, because when we were going back from the funeral home, we saw him walking down the street with his head down. Then I noticed that he was limping, and his hand was dangling. He was walking alone in the cold with no jacket on."

"I think he felt sorry for what had happened."

"You are right my child; I think so too. I asked my daughter to stop so that we could ask him if he needed any help."

"Did you stop to ask?"

"Yes, but he shook his head."

"Then?"

"I had my husband's trench coat and fedora in the car, I wanted to give it away to somebody, so I gave it to Old Morgan."

"Oh!!"

"I am happy that I forgave them, because a few days after that, I got to know that he died too."

A honking sound gets the attention of the teens. The front window of a pickup truck rolls down. It is Juliet!

"Hi," says Juliet, "need a ride?" Then pointing to Utter, "We're going to your grandmas," smiling she adds, "We're taking her dinner and there is plenty for anybody else who can eat well."

Utter promptly gets into the back seat of the truck, dragging Naomi with him. Naomi follows Utter due to being tired of walking.

"Hi Naomi, I am Juliet, and this is my dad."

"Yes, I know you. But how did you know my name?"

"Who doesn't know you in school Naomi! And you're in his class, right?"

"Yes! We were walking home because the bus is late."

"We know, people complain about that bus. But it's good for our business ... and his." "Juliet's dad says laughing wildly.

"Dad don't act crazy, and this isn't time," Juliet reprimands her father in a stern voice.

"What did your dad say," Naomi asks, "I am confused."

"I will update you in school tomorrow, that's if we meet," replies Juliet. "But feel free to drop into our pizzeria at the Hope and Main Plaza, I am there on the weekends. That's next to where you bought that ice cream, it's called Sally's Pizzeria."

"I know that place, we go there often, Sally is our friend ... our dear friend."

"Oh!"

(9) Housewarming

The clock's hands point resolutely at 9:00 AM, heralding the arrival of a Sunday morning in the crisp embrace of October. Utter wakes from his slumber, greeted by the comforting aroma of tea brewed by his loving grandmother. Seated on the edge of his bed, he clasps the warm cup in his hands, the nurturing gesture reminiscent of the tender care of his grandmother for as long as he could remember.

His gaze wandered to a portrait adorning the wall opposite him, an image fraught with both familiarity and mystery. On the left side of the frame, the countenance of his mother smiles back at him, her eyes seeming to follow him no matter where he stood. In contrast, the right portion of the portrait lay torn and incomplete, leaving behind the haunting impression that someone had deliberately excised a figure from the tableau.

Utter's reverie was interrupted by the soft voice of his grandmother, a soothing presence that he had momentarily forgotten was beside him.

She speaks with a quiet promising tone, "You will see her soon, sugarcane. I won't let my children suffer for his crimes."

With those words, she retreats from the room, leaving Utter to prepare himself for the day ahead.

A short while later, her voice drifted in from the other room, "After church, we are going to Juliet's for their housewarming … Naomi's joining us."

Utter contemplates wearing a hoodie, a shield against the prying eyes of the congregation and the guests at Juliet's gathering.

Yet, a piece of advice from Naomi echoed in his mind, "If you have a weakness, expose it as if it defines you."

With his newfound sense, he discards the hoodie and instead selects a dress shirt, fastening each button before a long mirror. As he scrutinizes his reflection, he marvels at the profound transformation from the moment he had emerged from a harrowing coma to the present. In those initial months of recovery, he had been incapable of rousing himself from bed at this early hour, often waking at noon and rising from bed by 2:00 PM. The outside world had seemed an ominous place, and it was his grandmother who had guided him on daily strolls around the block, coaxing him back into the realm of the living. Nightmares of Juliet's drowning sometimes torment his restless nights.

His fingers trace the contours of his face, a touch that the mirror reflects but his own skin could not fully perceive. His memory of a smile remains elusive. Unfelt by him, two teardrops trace silent paths down his cheeks.

Doctors had cautioned that the road to recovery would be arduous, possibly stretching over a year. Yet, the unwavering faith of his grandmother, the unwavering support of Juliet and Jaylen, and the tenacious spark of hope within him were serving as catalysts for his healing. Meeting Naomi gives him confidence to face the unforgiving world.

With his shirt neatly tucked in, Utter steps out of his room, ready to face the day which lay ahead, his journey from the depths of despair toward the light of possibility.

Following their church service, Grandma Olivia arranges for a cab to whisk Utter and Naomi away to Juliet's home. As the cab rolls to a halt, Naomi emerges first, stepping onto a cobblestone pathway that meanders amidst an elegantly landscaped front yard. The sight of the light brownstone façade and the gracefully arched second-floor windows evoked memories of her childhood home, a place her parents had reluctantly surrendered to foreclosure. The past seemed to blur momentarily, causing her to blink away the wistful haze that clouded her vision. When her eyes flutter open, she finds Utter gazing at her, his expression of silence to his understanding of her unspoken pain. Though the pain endures, the seething anger that had once accompanied it had gradually subsided in recent weeks. With a soft smile, she acknowledges his empathy while waiting for Grandma Olivia.

With smiles lighting their faces, Grandma and Naomi crisscross the cobblestone path, leading them toward the entrance of Juliet's home. Nestled along the left periphery of the front lawn stood a freshly painted wagon wheel, its vibrant hues of periwinkle, sunflower yellow, and lime green offering a striking contrast to the serene surroundings. Juliet's parents warmly greet their guests at the threshold, a flurry of gifts, embraces, and kisses exchange against the backdrop of cozy interior hues painted in shades of warm orange and rich red.

Juliet takes Naomi on a tour around the new house; and tours not being his favorite, Utter picks a tall glass of Sally's favorite punch, and occupies a comfortable seat in a corner. He only hopes to observe the day's events.

"You will need this too," says Sally, offering him a spoon. "If you need anything, let me know."

He nods.

More friends and family gather; men's laughter and woman's cheer are overlain by teens dancing to Thalia's music. Naomi ends her tour around the house and joins the other teens dancing.

"Come 'on Utter," she yells at him.

He shakes his head.

A little girl chases after a little boy who wears a cap with silver lining; the little boy drops his hat, as he runs up the stairs, and the hat lands by the feet of the little girl. The little girl wearing that hat, joins Naomi in the dance area. The little boy tries to grab his hat back, but being unsuccessful, runs crying to Juliet with his complaint.

In a secluded corner, Sally's husband strums a guitar, to the music playing on the audio system.

"Sally's husband is a great music teacher," Utter reminisces. "Wish I could remember what he taught me."

On the sofa, Grandma, Juliet's mom, and Sally are whispering to each other.

"My husband had to invite him, I hope he doesn't show up though," says Veronica."

"I will have to leave then…...hate to do it to these children, …. they're having a good time," replies Grandma.

To solve the dispute over the hat, Juliet and Naomi escort that little couple to the canopy outside. The little boy is still wailing, asking for his property, but the little girl, not wanting to give up her trophy, holds onto the hat. The four begin a mini round table discussion leaving the hat on the table. The teens, using their charm, offer an alternate solution to the little couple's dilemma. Soon the little couple walks inside to help each other with snacks and drinks; and the two teens seated on either side of the table, having the hat in the middle, start their own discussions. Peeking at the little couple and seeing them enjoy snacks and drinks, and being pleased with their own problem-solving skills, the teens slap each other's hands.

"Ouch," yelps Naomi.

"Sorry," squeaks Juliet.

"Is your hand getting better?" asks Juliet curiously.

"Progressing! But hurts more when I am in Miss Pet's class, but Utter writes for me, he writes at printer speed."

"You mean Lex."

"He doesn't want to be called that name!"

"Yes, I know, we don't call him that when he is around, but to me … he's still Lex."

"If you didn't explain to me who he was, I would have never guessed." reminds Naomi.

"Did you ask him why he wanted to keep it all a secret?"

"Yes, I did. Then he passed me a long note explaining why he didn't want me to know who he was and saying that he was sorry! … I was annoyed, I crumpled the note and threw it back at him."

"What did he say in that note?"

"He was afraid that if I found out who he was, I may hate him. He also mentioned that he knows what his dad did to us, and how our family hates his family."

"How did you feel when you knew who he was?"

"I felt … nothing. By then, I had already decided to give him a hand ... to do something bigger than myself."

"What did your parents say about him?"

"Mom said that the family is trouble, it's better to keep distance."

"Oh!"

"Then, I asked Mom, if the actions of one person in a family makes the whole family bad."

"Wow, what did she say?"

"… Nothing much ... actually, a lot."

"Oh!"

"During that summer block party, Utter suddenly appeared in our neighborhood. I couldn't make out who he was due to his facial reconstruction, but there was some resemblance."

"That block party, they celebrated for you?"

"Yes, I felt bad that day, my parents ignored Grandma Olivia when she tried to speak to them. But Utter was seated in a corner, all alone. Then, when I met him in school, I wanted to find out if he was all right."

Juliet explains, "Yes, Lex lived in their mansion, he came to his grandma's after everything went wrong for him. Jaylen's family, my family, and Lex's family are close to each other. We used to hang out at their house or travel together, quite a lot."

"I wanted to know his name, and when I asked, he didn't want to tell me his name. He gave me an annoyed look. I didn't know that he couldn't talk, so I gave him the fun name - Utter. He liked it. So, that's what I call him now."

Juliet acknowledging, "That's what everybody in school calls him."

"Except Miss Pet, she is annoyed about that name. Too bad ...."

Juliet explains, "The doctors said that he would never wake up, they wanted to pull the plug on him. Grandma Olivia said that they could do it over her dead body … I wanted to say that to the doctors too."

"Oh my ... is that so! That's why he calls this his second life."

"Nineteen months is a long time to sleep though, but he is awake now, that's the good thing."

"What happened to him?"

"What happened to him is another story, we all know bits and pieces. He can't remember anything. But we know that the incident sent his mom to prison and gave him a coma. And now, he hates his dad, and misses his mom."

"Was he suffering when he woke up?

"Yes! He used to give everybody, this blank stare, then try to say something, but he couldn't say anything."

"Did he recognize you?"

"It took him weeks, then one day, on a little whiteboard he wrote my name. Then on another day they were showing him a portrait of his mother and father, he ripped the photograph in two, threw away the father's part, embraced the mother's part and there were tears rolling down his face."

"Something terrible has happened to him!"

"Yes, his grandma says that he wrote - I am not Lex Morgan, never was one, never will be one."

"Did he visit his mom?"

"Yes, Grandma Olivia took him one day to see his mom, all they did was cry. When they came back, he did not eat or drink for days; he spent most of his time sleeping. Finally, Jaylen and I somehow managed to get him to eat and drink."

"Interesting! Did they find out why he can't speak?"

"The doctors say that there is no physical damage, they think it could be something psychological due to the trauma."

"Did he say why he hates his father so much?"

"He didn't, the psychologist and the investigators asked him to draw or write whatever he remembers. He didn't, he just pushed the paper away."

"Why were the investigators there, Juliet?"

"Because it was a fatal accident. And, besides his mother, he was the only person alive out of the three passengers. But he could not remember anything when he woke up."

"Three passengers?"

"Yes, there was a third person, a man who came out of the trunk of their car."

"What?"

"Yes, a guy called Segarra just popped out of their car trunk."

"This is so strange." Naomi anxiously asks, "Then how did his mom end up in prison, Juliet?"

"My father said that it was through circumstantial evidence."

"Then, his mom may have been linked to how that guy went into the trunk. They may have found evidence to incriminate her."

"Something like that. But she is such a nice person, she couldn't have done it."

"Did you know her well?"

"Yes! ... Yes, she was like a mother to Jaylen and me, she took care of us."

"Took care of you?"

"There was a time when Mr. Asher and my dad were so involved in Morgan's business ... because things were getting difficult ... then Sally and Mom did all the work at the pizzeria because business was slow. Due to those reasons, someone had to take care of us, and Lex's mom did it."

"Then, there was a difficult time."

"Yes, even Jaylen's mom began her practice once again."

"The three of you would have been like family."

"People in middle school thought that Lex and I were brother and sister."

"Oh!"

"We have to find out the truth about what happened," Naomi murmurs.

"Who knows, sometimes the truth may be staring at us … but we can't accept it," Juliet murmurs.

They go back into the house, everybody is having fun, Jaylen and Utter are sitting next to each other in their own worlds: occupied on their smartphones. Grabbing food and drink, Naomi walks out with Juliet, to be under the canopy, to have more conversation.

She tells Juliet about the incident that damaged her hand, and how a little accident like that would not stop her from doing what she wants.

"Besides, I will be better soon, then I will show all those teachers how to write. Also, Utter will show them how to speak."

"Ha!"

The little girl and boy who were previously having a dispute, are now playing with a toy car. The little boy gives the little girl the toy car, and she rolls it along the paving.

"I wish life was simple as that," Juliet comments.

(10) Fragment

Would you like to go home Sugarcane?" asks Grandma. "You look so bored, that's why I am asking."

He shrugs his shoulders; he does not mind either way since he has not been in a mood to socialize with anybody. Even if he did, how could he say anything? Jaylen and he were on a texting marathon for a while, Juliet and Naomi joined it too, but they have their normal lives to live; he appreciates the goodwill of his friends, but he expects them to enjoy their lives and not deprive themselves of their freedom by trying to nurture him.

Grandma continues, "Jaylen is on the dance floor with the girls, why won't you join them too, if you are feeling bored."

He once again shrugs his shoulders, and Grandma walks away.

The music has been pulsating relentlessly since their arrival. Naomi and Juliet extend him an invitation to dance, and although he wants to join them on the dance floor, he opts to defer to another time. Today marks his inaugural foray into social gatherings since awakening from his coma, and a subtle undercurrent of social anxiety lingers, an emotion he was determined to conquer. Nonetheless, today's atmosphere proves significantly more inviting than that fateful day when Juliet and Jaylen had taken him to the "Star Sisters" performance at the Amphitheater.

"Can I bring you something else to eat, or at least another drink," asks Sally.

Sally has been so generous to him in serving all the food and drink she has prepared; she is a great cook, but a belly has its limits, thus, he shakes his head gesturing, "no."

But he wants to use the bathroom, he does not know the sign language to ask her.

He looks around for a bathroom, and Sally observing him as if she can read his mind, "That's occupied, but there's one upstairs."

He walks upstairs, and sees a closed room door with the sign, "No Permission - No Entry." A clear indication that it's Juliet's bedroom. Next to that room he finds the bathroom.

Walking out of the bathroom he finds those two little kids whizzing past him; they were running out of Juliet's room leaving her room door wide open.

"Wonder if they got permission," he thinks.

Inside her room, not far from the door, he sees her Forensic Science textbook lying on the ground, with a few pages coming out.

"No! The kids have ripped her textbook."

Observing for a moment, "I don't need permission for this."

He picks up the book and puts it back on her bookshelf.

A piece of paper falls out of the textbook. Noticing his name written on the paper, he scrutinizes the paper. He sees a graphic organizer with a dart drawn in the center and arrows drawn to his name, to his mother's, and to his father's. Another arrow points to the name, Valentine. Mom's name is crossed out with the word innocent written above and a teardrop drawn on the side of her name; there are question marks next to the other three names.

"Detective Juliet is working on a case," he reasons.

He Inserts the paper into the textbook, closes Juliet's room door, and hurries down.

"Getting ready to go home?" asks Grandma.

He nods his head.

That night, Utter is on his bed, thinking of the graphic organizer Juliet had inside her textbook. He understands that Juliet has been thinking about his mom's case and she is evaluating her newfound knowledge and skills. He is happy that Juliet understands too, that Mom is innocent. He guesses that the question marks are for suspects and wonders how that kid Valentine who was in his eighth-grade class, connects in Detective Juliet's investigation.

The question mark next to his name surprises him, "Hey, that's not cool!"

The phone rings and Grandma replies to the caller, "I will come down."

Stepping out of bed and looking outside through the slightly ajar third-floor window, he observes the rear shutter of a black sedan rolling down. He can't identify the passengers inside but can identify that car with the glistening silver shell and triple-band LED headlamps affixed on either side of the shell. Grandma approaches the car.

"The other suspect." He says in his mind, leaning his head against the wall.

He hears Grandma say, "You got nerve showing up at this time."

"I came to see my son; I hear that he was at Antonio's party this afternoon."

"Yes, he was, but thanks to you, he can't even enjoy something like that. He was seated by himself, watching others enjoy themselves."

"Can I see him, I missed him at the party," the voice in the car asks.

"The court order says you can't see him, and he doesn't want to see you either."

"I don't care about any court order, did he say that, or is it just your opinion. Besides, he can't talk or remember much."

"It is his wish and mine too. Also, it is time you started respecting the law."

"How many times am I to tell you that I didn't break any law."

"What you have done to people I know, is quite enough. It's funny how people like you are out enjoying, and innocent people are suffering without any help."

"I just want to take him on a ride in my new car, just to say hello. Is that asking too much?"

"Did you ever ask your wife if she needed help. Did you even just visit her to say hello. Is that asking too much? … Take responsibility for your actions, bring her home, and then he'll see you."

Utter eases the room's window shut - the world outside silenced by the embrace of his earmuffs. As he settles into his bed, his gaze falls upon the cherished picture of his mother, a guardian presence that watches over him, both in life and in memory. The events of that fateful day are on his mind; If only he could recall the circumstances that led to the accident, if only he could traverse the currents of time, would the trajectory of his life have been different?

Nonetheless, he is happy for Juliet and her family as they embarked on this new chapter in their lives - with a new home. Fond reminiscences flood his thoughts—the days when Juliet graced his home with her presence, his mother's warm smile as she baked muffins for them, and the shared joy of watching movies in the home theater. Sometimes, Jaylen would join their gatherings, and the trio would engage in spirited basketball matches on their backyard half-court. On special occasions and holidays, both Jaylen's and Juliet's families were among the cherished guests, celebrating well into the night, dancing until they were utterly exhausted. During more extended breaks, they found reprieve and relaxation at the idyllic Morgan Holiday Villa in Port Aransas.

One indelible memory etched in his mind was a time just before the accident, the July evening at the Port Aransas Villa when their families had convened to commemorate three graduations: Juliet's, Jaylen's, and his own. He had stood on the balcony, overlooking the sunset, with Juliet by his side. Down on the beach, Jaylen's parents reveled in the thrill of dashing into the incoming waves that encircled their jubilance and collided into the shore. The spectacle, while joyous for others, stirred an underlying anxiety within him.

Juliet's mom and his own mother strolled along the sandy shores, their Turkish towels billowing in the breeze. These maternal figures clung to their towels like sails resisting the wind, but how could he have resisted his own burgeoning desperation? The remainder of the gathering were in the pool, passing a beach ball among themselves, their excited shouts echoing in the warm evening air, though to him, those exclamations were harsh screams.

Juliet marveled at the serene beauty of the reddish-magenta sky's reflection upon the foaming ocean, but all he perceived was an unsettling crimson hue, a contrast to every other shade. The ocean's gentle whispers seemed to pacify every heart, except his own.

Food had lost its flavor, nights were devoid of comfort, and his friends seemed distant and alienated, save for the ever-present concern of Juliet. That evening, as the setting sun cast a radiant glow upon Juliet, he had found the courage to confide in her about his deepest fear. Juliet had offered consoling words, although their content now eluded his memory. In response, he too had conveyed something of significance, though the precise words remained a fragment of the past.

Yet, he vividly recalled the paradoxical sensation of the setting sun's warmth and the chill of the sea breeze intertwining within him. The mysterious man, clad in a tuxedo and sporting reddish glasses, with a leather briefcase securely tethered to his wrist, lingered persistently in his recollections.

"What must I do to rid myself of you, Segarra?" Utter's voice echoes the question that has become a haunting refrain in his mind.

(11) Family Time

On Friday evening, Naomi and Malcom walk down Hope Avenue: they do this often for relaxation, then they take the subway to the City, meet Naomi's mom after work, and have a family dinner in the City.

Naomi, still fascinated with Juliet's new home, remembers the home she had to leave.

"Dads, when are we moving to a better house, I am tired of living in our apartment. Besides, after my accident, I don't want to live in that building."

Malcom, walking with his hands inside his pockets, "Baby-Girl, I am working on it, but what you experienced was a random incident. It's been taken care of."

"Another excuse!"

"Hey, one of your teachers called me while I was at work."

"Which one?"

"Miss Pet, she tells me that you don't write in class, that you talk back at her, and she is worried about your first marking period grades. Besides, my girl, you can't tell others to always write for you."

"Yes Dads, about that, Utter is writing my notes for me, I don't see what's wrong about that. Now, he doesn't speak, I speak for him; so … I don't write, he writes for me…Is that wrong."

"Baby-Girl, Lex…"

She interrupts, "Dads do not use that name on him, he's called Utter now."

"But he has a real health issue, you are cured, and as of this week, you have been doing your own writing in all your classes except Miss Pet's class. Don't you see the problem."

"All right Dads, as of this week Miss Pet is teaching us social studies too. The school excessed the real Social Studies teacher, Mr. Anderson, who is now walking around the school as a substitute teacher, and Miss Pet, who has an attitude, wants to throw work at us."

"How is that connected to your writing in class?"

"Well… the truth is, I want to give Utter a purpose, a focal point, and I thought making him write is the best way to do it."

"Have you become his therapist now."

"Dads, all Miss Pet does is complain. On the second day of school, she yelled at Utter for not speaking out, now she yells at kids for speaking up."

"Baby-Girl, choose your battles in life! Fight for something that you really want. When you begin criticizing every little thing, you lose focus on your greater goal."

"Good advice for Miss Pet, I am sure she graduated with a degree in grumbles rather than a degree in teaching."

"That was funny! I know Baby-Girl, if you have any problem with schoolwork, just come to me, I will help you; but Miss Pet is the one that gives you a grade that goes onto your transcript, grades which colleges see. Now you, wanting to be an attorney, you need to write."

"Dads, attorneys hire secretaries. Anyway, Miss Pet is not there to teach, she wants to just kill time. She gives a lame writing assignment for ELA, and all we do for social studies is random disconnected work that has no meaning."

"I know Baby-Girl, we need to navigate the system here, be patient, and give others a chance to do their job too."

"That's the problem Dads, we follow tradition. We need new thinking, we need progress. For example, Miss Pet is so concerned about us writing in cursive script."

"That's how we were supposed to write back then."

"You don't get the point Dads; she looks down on us because many of us don't write in cursive script."

"Did she tell you that?"

"No, she implies that with her awkward comments."

"Like what?"

"She says a lot, like, your generation can't read or write because all you can think of is about your smartphones."

"Smartphones are a distraction to our thinking, especially while studying," explains Dads.

"I told her that technology evolves, and if she wants to use a feather-pen to write in script, we have no problem with that, but if she wants to teach us, she should update her content knowledge."

"That was rude, what did she say then?"

"She sent me to the principal, complaining that I was not letting her teach."

"What did the principal do?"

"She listened to my story, spoke to Miss Pet over the phone, then asked me if I would like to present something to the school for Social Studies Day. I said yes! Then she asked me if my hand hurts while typing on the computer. I said no. Then she gave me 'How the Other Half Lives,' and asked me to do an activity for Social Studies Day, analyzing if that analogy is relevant to current times."

"That's big! Then what happened?"

"I helped the secretary sort out some papers, and when the bell rang, I left for my next class."

"Did the principal say anything when you left?"

"No, but I said to her that this whole thing may have not happened if Mr. Anderson taught us social studies instead of Miss Pet."

A moment later she continues, "you know Dads, I will get him back to class. I will organize."

"Now, don't start a situation where I will be sitting Infront of your principal trying to explain why you did something you were not supposed to do. And, you don't know whose side I may take."

"Of course, I know whose side you may take. Your daughter's!"

Later that evening, Malcom and Naomi are at the restaurant waiting for Ramona to join them. Malcom, sitting by the window, watches vehicles go by. Ramona enters in her light blue work clothes and in exhaustion.

"Parked four blocks down, were you waiting long?"

"A little bit, shall we order Moni, you must be hungry."

As the family progresses through dinner, Naomi thinks it's time to get an answer to her unanswered question.

"When are we moving to a better house? I asked Dads, and that conversation went somewhere else."

"As soon as I finish my BSN, which is any moment now, I will have time to focus on a new house, we need a down payment and have to show good income," says Mom.

"Both of you … work hard. Dads is a chief security officer. Mom, you work in a hospital, and we still live in a small apartment, in an apartment building where I got hurt."

Hearing no response from either parent, Naomi continues.

"How come Dads, the last time we bought a house, you had that old job you hated and didn't even earn enough money," Naomi questions. "Mom, you too didn't have a good job because I remember each time I asked you for something, you said that you didn't make enough money so that you can buy everything that I ask for."

"Those were different times, sweet, due to those errors, now they have strict rules," Mom explains. "Now, we need to have good credit ratings too."

"All those rules now. When you didn't have money, they gave you a big loan to buy a big house. Now, when you have income, they have so many rules. Am I missing something here?"

"Baby-Girl, we got caught to a crooked mortgage lending system that not only brought us down but the whole country down."

Naomi in an agitate mood, "Now we're still here after all these years."

"Thanks to Morgan, we got a house, and thanks to that same Morgan we lost that house, now we have to run in circles," says Mom. "Run in circles!"

"Dads, and you Mom, I know you blame Utter's father for losing our house, and I hate that man too. He took away our house, which was so special to me. He put my grandma under stress, and we lost her quickly. And worst of all, due to the stress he put on you Mom, and I never got to even see my baby brother. Nobody knows how I felt when I lost everything … I was hurt more."

"Sweety, were you keeping this inside you all these years?"

"Yes, it was hard to let go ... I had become somebody else."

Ramona moves her chair closer to Naomi. "You didn't discuss this during therapy?"

"Would it have helped; would it have put the clock back?"

"But you should have spoken out on how you really felt!" Ramona says.

"Also, how could you have heard me … you were venting out so loud, I didn't want to add to the problem."

"Oh, my poor Baby Girl!"

"But now, how could we move on Mom?"

"See what I mean Malcom, look what they have done to our daughter ... and I forgot to tell you, Sophia … yes, Sophia Tosco … she has sent a message to me ... through Olivia."

"What did she want?" asks Dads.

"I don't know, she wants to speak to me after all these years. It's funny how people remember you only when they're down, or when they need something from you. When they are all doing well, or when they are all done using you, you are like trash to them … I thought she could just wait there."

"Forgiveness is a virtue Moni. When Olivia asked me the other day if she could take Baby-Girl to Antonio's housewarming, I didn't mind. Besides, the Morgan kid and Baby-Girl have turned out to be good friends."

"Dads, he is Utter!"

"Sorry!" Dads continues, "It's that clown who messed us up, not Sophia."

"Don't go on about her with me, she acted all innocent when things went wrong. She was in command when she thought things were going well." Mom chants. "Then remember how stuck-up she was …When they had nobody, we were there for them … I did a lot for her."

"We have to move on, Moni."

"It is easy for you to say Malcolm, remember how sad it made Mama, we had to bury her while we were going through foreclosure, she died of sadness …. Remember how Mama called Sophia … remember how Mama was with the breathing tube when she spoke? … Remember what Sophia did – nothing!"

"Moni, Olivia was with your Mama when Mama was so sick … she was in hospital with Mama."

"Right! ... Yes! I don't have a problem with Olivia or the son. Olivia was there during Mama's last days, for that, I will always be grateful. She treated me like a daughter, I think of her often, even though I pretended to dislike her to get even with Sophia."

"Mom! You didn't let me speak to Grandma Olivia because you were pretending and trying to get even with Utter's mom?"

Mom wipes a tear off her eye and continues, “I was wrong, but she was the closest person to vent my anger. I was so hurt after all what happened to me.”

“When I came back here, and because we had lost Grand-Mama too, I wanted to speak to Grandma Olivia, but you didn’t let me.”

“I am sorry for that ... It’s the other two I will never forgive for what they did to us, see how karma works now. Where has that got her now! That Morgan still thinks that he’s so big …ok let’s wait.”

“Then Mom, do you think Utter’s mom could have done that? … what she’s accused of … you were once friends, weren't you; so, tell me, is she capable of doing that.”

“The Sophia I knew a long time ago, was a good person. That’s why I was her friend, but that all changed with that Morgan’s new business.”

“It’s all right Mom, I understand. Like you, I was hurt too … all these years. But I learned to move past that, I think I have made myself free.”

“Malcom, I need to get home fast, I am so tired I need to take a warm shower and sleep.”

“Mom, you can make yourself free too.”

(12) Case Load

Monday morning, before the school bell rings, Naomi is at the principal's office. She expects the door to be open as usual, but finding it closed and hearing the principal's voice inside the office, she knocks.

"Just a minute," says the principal. "Who is it?"

"It is me," replies Naomi.

The door opens and Naomi greets Mrs. Shepard, "Good morning, Miss!"

"Good morning, Naomi! Give me a minute."

Miss Shepherd is ending a meeting with two individuals; Naomi recognizes one person to be an assistant principal of the school but does not recognize the other person. The assistant principal and the other person keep speaking with each other, she overhears them discussing the lack of funding for the school.

"Naomi ... did you have trouble with Miss Pet again?"

"No Miss I did not, I wanted to hand in my draft proposal and write-up for Social Studies Day."

"Great, I will go through this when I am free. Anything else?"

"Yes, what's the meaning of our school's name, Admirable Academics High School."

"Admirable means something to admire about, something great, and Academics is the content that's taught."

"Something great is taught?" exclaims Naomi.

"Yes, the content of what you learn, the content that's taught, how it is taught."

"How is it taught?" repeats Naomi.

"Yes, you need good teachers to transfer knowledge to students."

"So, Miss, you agree then, that we need good teachers who have mastered their content and also who can transfer that content to students."

There is a moment of no conversation, raising her eyebrows the principal looks at the other two who were at the meeting, then turning towards Naomi, "Sweety, why are you really here?"

"Miss why did you pull out Mr. Anderson from our social studies class?" pleads Naomi. "He was a good teacher!"

"It is complicated to explain, it is about budgets. To put it in a simpler way, this school does not have money to pay for an outside teacher to come in and teach when a teacher gets absent," explains the principal.

"Miss a substitute teacher hardly teaches because students don't allow them to teach. If their regular teacher is absent, most students don't want to work."

"That's why we have Mr. Anderson covering those classes," further explains the principal.

"Miss, just one more thing please. just to let you know, the teachers who can teach just move from class-to-class babysitting students, while teachers who are talented in babysitting, are desperately trying to teach. What's happening doesn't go well with the name, Admirable Academics."

"I see what you mean, who is your guidance counselor, I will give you a note requesting for a program change."

"No miss, I don't need a program change, besides it won't bring Mr. Anderson back to his regular class schedule. Put Miss Pet to babysit. Mr. Anderson is a good teacher - we learn from him."

"I understand what you are trying to say. For now, you go back to class and show me that you can do your studies without causing misunderstandings with any teacher," advice the principal.

"Thank you, Miss! Please reconsider Mr. Anderson, he is a good teacher."

As Naomi leaves the principal's office and during her walk through the long corridor, Naomi meets Miss Grace.

"Hi Naomi, how is your hand now?"

"Good, progressing well. Thanks for your support, Miss!"

"Aw! Thank you, Naomi, I saw you coming out of the principal's office, is everything all right?"

"Yes, I was working on my cases, Miss."

"Cases?" Miss Grace asks. "What cases?"

"I am working on two pro-bono cases, one short-term and one-long term. I met the principal about my short-term case. The long-term case is another story."

"I am so confused now," says Miss Grace. "Please come to my office when you're … we will talk more about this."

Mrs. Shepherd finds time before the school bell rings to review Naomi's writing.

Naomi Martínez

Social Studies

<u>Would Jacob Riis Capture Something Different Today?</u>

In the latter eighteen hundred, we were on a journey to becoming a world industrial power; manufacturing, finance, and energy were some of the leading industries helping in this prosperity. With these advancements, rose new infrastructure, and these new infrastructures defined the American Landscape. The Brooklyn Bridge, the Statue of Liberty, and the Fuller Building were new iconic landmarks specific to New York City, which related to America's new story. Yet, hidden from the world were a group of people who lived in misery, in slums, and tenements. As the rich lived in their mansions while dining with the finest cuisine; as the middle-class rat-raced to scrape for a better living; overlooked by both these classes lived a group of poor, with crumbs to feast on, rags to dandy with, and shacks to rest in. Jacob Riis, through his remarkable work of photojournalism, captured the lives of these poor multitudes: the people he defined as the other half. One of his famous photographs, "the Lodgers in a Bayard Street Tenement," portrays a group of people sharing a little room, owning only a little space where they could lie down. The extent of such photographs by Riis is unknown, and we recollect the conditions of that period by the few that were published. Much of Riis' work was criticized by those who were not willing to accept reality; however, society understood the need for change, and some progress was made. However, was sufficient progress made to eradicate that situation?

The world progresses after the days of Riis; today, in this twenty-first century, we have become the superpower of the globe. We control the financial destiny of the world, we control the information highway, and soon we will conquer deep space - such is the economic and industrial progress, a century after "How the Other Half Lives." Amidst all these changes that have taken place over the bygone century, society could still ask how the "Other Half" lives. Has the "Other Half" progressed with similar stride, or do the "Other Half" still loiter, mingled within this prosperity. A recent broadcast on television displayed the dismal conditions of public housing in my neighborhood: Rat infested environments, cracked walls, lack of adequate plumbing were some of the conditions. The growing amount of homeless people we see along the streets in major cities, or a healthcare system that deprives certain people in some States to the extent of making them choose between day-to-day living or living healthy, are evidence that the "Other Half" still exists.

If Riis lived today, would he pick a different genre for his photojournalism, or would his lenses still capture the same images once captured a century ago. Would he see a better world filled with prosperity or a frazzled world torn apart by an immense wealth gap? If Riis lived today, would the title for another photograph be "the Lodgers of a Homeless Shelter:" people resting for the night in overcrowded, unsafe, and degrading circumstances! If Riis lived today, will the title of another photograph be, "Wasted Tears:" a little girl crying to get into her home where she and her family who fell victim to a mortgage scam are driven out by Marshals …

The school bell rings, and Mrs. Shepherd puts away Naomi's writing and walks out of her office to manage the day's proceedings.

"Naomi, where are you going with this!"

(13) HEART

Two years in high school has made Jaylen mature, stronger, and an emerging high school football star. This is his first season as the Quarterback player and has scored forty touchdown passes; his goal is to achieve over fifty touchdown passes by the end of the season.

"Your mother and I are so proud of you, my son," says Asher as they drive home after one of Jaylen's practice sessions. "Do you think you will cross that fifty, I think you will."

Jaylen imagines that fiftieth touchdown pass and the roar of the crowd, he imagines Juliet saying, "I knew you could do it!" He imagines the Thanksgiving Eve game where his team may face their toughest opponent, he imagines the media coverage and how colleges may compete to recruit him.

"I am trying Dad. Yes, I think I will."

"Good! Now, I got to say something, your mother and I will do everything for you, but there is something you have to do for yourself."

"What's that, Dad?"

"You see, right now you are on your way to becoming a star, but that comes slow. Making a name for yourself is a slow and hard process."

"Ok! ... I know! ... I know!"

"But Son, everything that you build can be washed away with one bad move. How that bad decision may come is unknown, and you must be strong to overcome any adversity. Do you get what I am saying?"

"What do you mean, Dad?"

"What I mean is always do the right thing, don't get too involved in something that may destroy your career, your name, and everything you have built so far."

"Yes Dad! Can we stop by the pizzeria and get food?"

"Also, is your coach talking to you about your diet?"

"Yes, yes, a lot."

"Getting back to what I was saying, for example, look at that Morgan guy, if you take his money away, he has nothing. Now, I know he has promised your school money to build a new science lab, but you should have values in life."

"Yes, I spoke to Mr. Morgan about funding our school after what I saw and heard on Social Studies Day."

"I forgot to ask, how did that go. Mom said you participated in organizing the event."

"Yes, me and a few others. Everybody was speaking about Naomi's presentation; it was a powerful theme. I saw another side of life which I have never experienced."

"Trust me, Son, I have seen many sides to life, but sometimes we ignore just to make believe that they don't exist. I am happy that you're opening your eyes."

"It is disappointing that we're heard only when we become loud, who is there to speak for the weak anymore?"

"I know, Jay, if we don't lend a hand to people on time, they may sell their souls. Like what Morgan did."

"I think he can redeem his soul back, but he has to try," says Jaylen.

"Good luck with that."

"Morgan wants me to be at the ice cream store on days when I am free, for promotion. He thinks that I am a little popular, so there will be more sales when I am around. ... He needs a chance to redeem his soul, dad."

"Is that the only reason you come to the ice cream store?"

"What does Dad mean ... Yes, I like Juliet being there, next door!" Jaylen reasons to himself with a smile.

"Don't get caught to his angle, he's after something. I am putting your sister through med school; I will take care of your education and your little brother's. I want the three of you to grow my business too. Just don't let him use you or influence you, I don't like his methods of doing business. You're better than that."

"I know Dad, I am also there for my friend Lex, he just woke up, he needs us."

Dad says, "Bless that kid, I am sure his grandfather is watching over him and has arranged an angel to take care of that kid."

"I think he has ... but I don't think Angels come from above, they're created from within."

"I am so proud of my children. My daughter will graduate from med school, you are turning out to be a star, and my little boy is exactly following the two of you. What I am trying to say is something that my mother taught me."

"Dad, change your lane."

"My son, Asher," she used to say. "Follow HEART!"

"What's HEART, you mean you got to have a heart, right?"

"It is H. E. A. R. T. son. So, H stands for humility, E stands for effort, A stands for adaptability, R stands for responsibility, and T stands for Teamwork."

"OK!"

"What I am trying to say is, in life, you may face tough situations, then think of the code H. E. A. R. T."

"Do you follow that code or whatever that's, Dad?"

"Hey son, I am not perfect, I have made my share of mistakes, but yes I try to follow HEART."

"Dad, you got to change your lane; we need to turn."

"Nearly forgot that."

Asher drives the car to the left lane as they arrive at the intersection of Hope and Main. The arrow turns green, and he makes the left turn planning to take another left into the parking lot of Hope and Main Plaza. As he parks the car, he sees Antonio at the pizzeria.

Getting off the car, "Ah, there's my boy Antonio, got to have a word with him!"

"Antonio!"

"Will! What's up, what's up!" Antonio greets Asher, with a fist bump.

"I am sorry man, I couldn't show up at your housewarming party, got held up with work."

"That's no problem, we can hang -out sometime. Anyway, Jaylen and Audre were there, they had fun. They were there when Boss Morgan came too."

"Yes, I heard that he came, he has bought a new Mercedes, right."

"Yes, he said 'I paid all cash!'" says Antonio with a side smile.

"Just like him to say that. I miss the old man; I don't know how long this guy's pompous would last. Anyway, how are your wife and little girl?"

"Good … good … at home enjoying the new house. Now they have no time to be with me here. Anyway, my daughter is too involved with school now."

"That's nice Antonio, I am so happy for you. We should hang-out sometime, not done it for a while now, with all the things that went around."

"Dad, we got to take this food for Mom," interrupts Jaylen as he wonders if their conversation will ever end.

"Jay! You're in a hurry to leave today!"

As Jaylen and Asher Walk to the car, "Call me Antonio, our families will hangout sometime."

Back in the car, Jaylen thinks of a way to avoid Dad's conversation, which is dubbed as preaching, by the family. But talking about Dad's past seems interesting.

"So, My Son, where were we now?"

"Hey, Dad, Antonio and you are good friends, right?"

"Antonio and I first met during the construction boom period, when the Morgan family began investing in real estate development."

"How did you get to know the Morgan family, Dad?"

"Because I have an engineering degree, I was made a foreman in the factory that Morgan Sr. worked. Son, I followed my code that I was talking about, HEART. I got commendations and promotions on the job. But, you know, few people hated me for being a young person holding a senior position, and for certain others it was ...you know what I mean!"

"Was it that bad there?"

"A few people treated me badly, but thanks to old Morgan, life became much easier for me at the factory. People respected old Morgan there, he had been there for a while, and his father before that. People say that his grandfather was one of the founders of the company. Then when I left that factory to begin my own construction tool manufacturing business, old Morgan helped me in the initial startup operations."

"Mom said that he stayed in your garage, right?"

"Yes, we had a small house, and when he came out of prison both, Senior and Junior, had no place to go. We converted our garage into a room for them to live."

"How did he get sent to prison."

"The factory that we were working, began outsourcing, and they were getting rid of employees, so Morgan organized a strike."

"They sent him to jail for organizing a strike?"

"No, they cut everybody's health benefits, and old Morgan's wife was due for surgery and treatment."

"Damn!"

"Yes, then he had an argument with one of the directors which led to a fight that hospitalized that director."

"Why didn't you stop him, dad?"

"I had moved out by then. But those who stayed back had worked for that company for years, they had given their lives to the company, and Morgan felt their pain."

"How unfortunate … sad."

"So, he went to prison, his wife died while he was inside, and his son was devastated."

"That's why you helped them?"

"Yes, then his house went into foreclosure, and they got thrown out by marshals, so I brought them to our house."

"Did he stay there for long?"

"Not for long, he was too depressed to stay, Morgan Jr. was going all crazy, one night, they just drove off."

"How did you meet up with him again?"

"Many years later, I was doing well on my own ... and he had made it in New York, he was doing well too. He asked me if I could be an investor in Morgan Jr.'s real estate operations."

"Dad, then you were OK working with Morgan Jr."

"First it was the father doing all the work, then when the father became a social activist, the son came more into the picture ... I got to work with that Morgan Jr., later ... much later."

"I see, Dad!"

"Here's the lesson my son ...."

"Dad, why didn't you advise Morgan Jr.?"

"Things were happening fast, there was a lot of money involved, there was no time to think, only time to act."

"People say he sold scam mortgages, to push the houses he built. Is it true?"

"It looked all legal on paper, nobody questioned anybody back then."

"Why didn't you question him, Dad?"

"See son, Antonio and I were involved in everything other than the mortgages, he and that scammer did the mortgages ... we found out about the scams later ... when everything was slowing down."

"You mean you and Antonio, who was so close to them, didn't know anything until the end?"

Asher is silent.

"You knew about it … right?"

Asher is silent.

"I see dad, you and Antonio knew about what he was doing, … nobody did anything after finding out the truth!"

"We suspected it … but my son, I am human … I am not proud of what I did, but in life, when you benefit from something, and when it seems legal, you don't question the ethics."

"Wow!"

"As I was saying son, here's the lesson ...."

"Dad, we're home.

"I didn't break the law like him, I had to protect what I had built so far. I had put all my money to his business."

"Mom must be hungry, got to take this food to her," Jaylen says as he gets out of the car and slams the car door.

(14) Investment

Morgan Jr. reclines on the rooftop porch of his lavish mansion, his mind drifting back to a time when the bay's breathtaking views were a source of comfort during moments shared with Sophia and their son. Now, that once captivating bay is a dreary, monotonous expanse. In the distance, a tugboat tows an aging ship, a sight that triggers memories of their modest beginnings – the days when they ran only the ice cream store, when a new bus route opened on Narrow Hope Avenue, when their son was a toddler, and when they sought new business ventures.

Their fortunes took a turn during the housing boom, when government restrictions on real estate investments and financing eased. The opportunity presented itself when John, diagnosed with cancer, needed to sell their storefront urgently.

Morgan recalls boasting, "I spotted a great deal and seized it!"

But there's a shadowy secret lurking beneath the surface. Will Sophia ever discover the questionable means by which he persuaded John to part with the storefront at such a low price, as his disappointed father did. Antonio knew the truth, but he knew how to handle Antonio.

He remembers how Sophia and he went beyond the purchase. Due to the storefront being old and rundown, they decided to demolish the storefront and rebuild a state-of-the-art shopping complex in its place.

He remembers the time Sophia and he had just invested in the cafe and ice cream store, how they lived in that old basement studio down Narrow Hope Avenue. One night in their basement apartment, Sophia was preparing food, and he was at the side table running through paperwork. His son was asleep on the bed nearby. This was their home, their little castle, their warm basement studio. Their most valuable possessions were, the center table where they sat for meals and planning, the king-size bed they all slept most often keeping their son in the middle being afraid he may fall off the bed, the dresser with three shelves, and the refrigerator.

"Are you sure these numbers are right honey?" He remembers asking Sophia.

"Yes, father and I went through the numbers twice this afternoon … before we left the store," said Sophia.

"Good, now we can get financing so that we put that rot down and build a mini shopping area like in Manhattan … What do you say, honey?"

"Father wants to build the two sides first, he wants to keep the ice cream store and the other two stores operating, then work on the center part after moving the stores to one side," Sophia explained to him.

"Sounds good to me."

He remembers taking an old grudge against Sophia's former employer who said to Sophia, "You're too good for him."

Then how he told Sophia, "I also told your former boss, the dollar store guy that I am not extending his lease … Let him go somewhere else."

Surprisingly Sophia agreed with him. "That's okay with me, he made me work so much ... He used to tell me that I can't get a job anywhere else because I didn't graduate from high school."

He remembers saying, "Honey, I like when you and I are on the same page. The old will go and the new will rise."

"That's great," said Sophia "it will change the face of this neighborhood."

"This neighborhood will still look ugly with all that rundown, old looking, and abandoned houses, gawking along this street."

"Morgan, unless we buy them, put them down like what we plan to do to our store, then build new houses."

"Good idea honey, we still have a small problem."

He remembers the idea Sophia ingrained in his mind, that idea that became an obsession, and he envisioned the neighborhood transforming into modernization through him. But he wanted money, and he wondered where he could find such financing. He revealed his idea to Sophia and Father; Sophia was eager with the plan, but his father was skeptical.

"Dad, I need you to believe in me," he remembers saying to his father.

A few weeks later Sophia broke the news to him, "See Morgan, father was mentioning this guy, now what was his name ... I think he said, Williams Asher."

"Asher Williams! What about him? I know the guy; he has a construction tool manufacturing business."

"Father said that he is willing to invest."

And now Asher wants to get into this real estate market too? That's great!"

"Let me talk to father tomorrow, I think your plan may just work."

He remembers how after Asher decided to invest, how other investors became motivated too. He felt that his vision was becoming tangible.

He remembers how his fortune changed when he met Segarra, during the housing boom. He was at a construction site watching Antonio instruct the workforce, when a man in tuxedo and reddish glasses approached him.

"Mr. Morgan, right."

"Yes!"

"You have a lot of houses coming up, do you have anybody to sell these houses."

"Why? Are you a real estate agent?"

"No! Anybody can be a real estate agent these days, but people need money to buy what you're building."

"What are you trying to say?"

"I am somebody who puts money in the hands of people."

"I am a mortgage broker; I know every loophole that puts money in people's hands. I am here to give you a business plan if you are interested only."

"There are so many mortgage companies these days, why do I need your help?"

"Supposing you had a mortgage company that automatically qualified people to buy one of your houses, supposing people got a good deal only through you, and suppose people came knocking at your door to buy a house, how would you like it?"

"That will be really good."

"Supposing I can make that happen, would you like to work with me?"

"How much do you want for your services?"

"You don't have to pay me anything now, I only want a place to set up shop and somebody to be the boss. I will do all the work and you only pay me one percent for everything you sell."

"Let me think about it?" He remembers saying, but he had already made up his mind to test Segarra. One percent for anything that sells was a super bargain.

Morgan dims his living room lighting. He notices a voice message from his family doctor.

"What does he want?"

"Hi Mr. Morgan, this is Dr. Phillips, I need to speak to you about something important, also I am sending you for a biopsy. Please call me."

He sees his wedding portrait with Sophia, the photograph that father took with that old camera, the photograph which was framed at that corner store which was later put down by him.

Back then, the real-estate business was flourishing, he, Sophia, and their investors were busy accruing old houses, vacant lots, and abandoned properties; then building brand new single houses or blocks of townhouses. As fast as they built new houses, they also needed to sell those newly built houses to make a profit.

That's when he used Segarra.

At a meeting, He said to his investors, "The faster they construct, and the faster they sell, the faster the investor's wealth accumulates. That's us I am talking about. Now, the government has relaxed lending policies for the people, the government wants to help the people to buy their own home. So, we need a plan to help these people fast."

"How do you plan to do it, Morgan?" Asher Williams asked at that meeting.

"Asher, you will see when my plan works. You will be happy that you invested with me. Trust me!"

He analyzed the relaxed mortgage lending regulations banks followed during that period, and he also observed the business potential for mortgage lending. The real estate investment and construction companies were under his and Sophia's name, therefore, as Segarra advised, he incorporated a mortgage lending corporation under Morgan Sr. and hired Segarra as an employee.

Along with Segarra, he visited other mortgage lending companies and studied the products those companies had to offer. Finally, he and Segarra produced a mortgage product or a lending plan that looked better than his competition: a plan so attractive at face value, but a plan with a major longtime setback for the innocent borrower.

Segarra began traveling around with his briefcase cuffed to his hand, people thought that it was funny. Segarra did not care.

"I don't want to lose valuable information, this way I will never lose them," Segarra used to say.

People also wondered why Segarra wore his reddish glasses.

As months went by, there were new constructions emerging through his investors. The new storefront and the first group of houses were almost ready. As commuters passed the Hope and Main intersection, they observed the giant LED that portrayed a motion video of a happy family moving into a new home, and a storyline that illustrated how his lending company helped that family to own a house with zero investment.

A storyline he made, played on the LED. "If you have a few thousands, move into your own home."

Another storyline he made was, "No down payment - No out-of-pocket closing cost." The promotions were so successful that the first housing development sold off before completion, and people were booking showings for the next housing developments.

During that time, he understood that the greatest motivation to the human being is money, money even in the form of a loan. He understood that people would overlook divergences if a path to money is open, and he wanted to exploit that greatest weakness in people. With Segarra's help, he did.

At the end of that year, he threw a grand celebration for the investors and friends at this mansion in Staten Island, the mansion he bought from his first earnings as a businessperson.

He thinks of how people even lose their souls in the process of accumulating wealth, he knows he has, and he wonders if it was worth it.

"Let me call the doctor in the morning," Morgan says as he retires for the night.

(15) Visit

"HI, my sweet Naomi, come inside," says Grandma Olivia after answering the doorbell. "Let me call my Sugarcane, he is in his room."

"No," says Naomi. "I came to see you, Grandma Olivia."

"Me?" questions Grandma. "How nice of you, my angel!"

Utter comes out of his room rubbing his eyes and greets Naomi with a high-five.

"Sleeping at this time, Utter?"

"He needs his afternoon nap, could be also the medication," explains Grandma. "And you wanted to talk to me, My Dear?"

"Yes, do you have old photographs of Utter's mom, I mean your Sugarcane's mom and my mom, when they were friends."

"Of course, I do! But why do you want it now?"

"It's for my case, Grandma Olivia."

"What case, my dear?"

"I am doing research about my family and Utter's family." Naomi corrects, "I mean your sugarcane's family."

"That sounds interesting!"

"I have never asked you this, and I don't know why I always call you Grandma Olivia, is that all right?"

"My sweetheart, your grandmother was my best friend. Your mother and I go way back, I knew you when you were a baby, I took care of you when you were a baby, you lived in this next apartment before your family moved out, your mom is a daughter to me, and you have always called me Grandma Olivia."

"Yes, that's why when I think of you, or speak of you, I just remember you as Grandma Olivia," Naomi pauses, "I remember one day, when I was in grade five, we had just left our nice house and moved into this apartment, I saw you."

"I have seen you many times."

"Yes, me too. But that day, I tried to wave at you, but Mom took my hand and walked away from you. Later, I asked her why, and she seemed very annoyed. I never asked her again because I didn't want to annoy her, that's until a few days ago."

"What happened a few days ago?"

"Never mind, were they good friends, Grandma Olivia?"

"Yes, they were best friends, like two sisters, I could not separate them, nobody could."

"Please can you bring the photographs and tell me and Utter all the stories."

"First let me get cookies, and would you like to have a panini?"

"And do you still have that hot chocolate that you gave us the other day Grandma Olivia?"

"You got it!"

The children enjoy the food and drink that grandma serves them, and they enjoy even more the stories she tells them. Pages of old albums turn one after the other, fascinating Naomi.

"This picture is his baptism," Grandma says pointing to Utter. "Look, that's your mom and dad."

"Wow, they were so slim back then, Utter's mom and my mom are very pretty here."

"Yes, but they still are and will always be. It was a small get-together, me, your grandma, your mom and dad, and Grandpa Hope."

Tears come to Grandma's eyes as she continues, "He was a good man, Grandpa I mean, he did a lot, he was a diligent worker."

"I remember him, Mom used to push me in the stroller to get ice cream. If we met him, he did funny things to make me laugh, he used to play a beautiful tune on his flute."

"Yes, the flute was his favorite."

"Sometimes I don't know if I went to get ice cream or went just to listen to the flute … maybe both."

"Both, I think."

"When we go to Utter's house or when they visit us, Grandpa used to give me nice gifts."

"Yes, that's who he was, he never comes here without bringing something for me. God bless his soul!"

"Then one day, when I was much bigger, I think before we moved back here ... I met him while riding the subway with Mom, he did not want to talk much. I never saw him after that because he died. I wanted to know his story. I wanted to know what happened to him."

"Yes, that's when he became the bad person in society. My child, one error can destroy everything you took a lifetime to build."

"How did it happen Grandma Olivia, how did it happen?"

"I don't know the whole situation, that's the time when your mother swore that she will never speak to Sugarcane's mother again. In fact, she cursed her, she cursed everybody in Sugarcane's family. They had a horrible exchange of words."

"That's terrible, Grandma Olivia, terrible!"

"Naomi honey, I think we are stressing sugarcane here with all these stories, we will talk another time." Grandma squeezes Utter's hands while speaking, and Utter sits serenely.

"Naomi, you could take the album if you want, but bring it back to me," says Grandma Olivia as she pushes the album towards Naomi.

"No, I will leave it here so that I could hear your stories."

"Oh boy!" Grandma Olivia carries the album away saying, "Let me know when you want to leave, we will walk you home. It's getting dark outside."

"I am not afraid anymore. My dad said I could restart my taekwondo classes as soon as the doctor says I am all right. You can join me, Utter; it makes you strong."

"Of course, I know you are not afraid, but we will still walk you home."

(16) Meltdown

Naomi's conversations about Ramona and Sophia's friendship troubles Olivia. One night, Olivia has a dream, a vivid and intermingled dream of actual events that transpired years ago. She sees herself on the head seat at the Morgan family dining table, and in front of her, on the other head seat, she sees Morgan Sr. On her right side, sits Sophia and Morgan Jr., and on her left, over the empty seats is the view of a green expanse stretching towards the bay.

Olivia questions Morgan Jr., "Just tell me what happened with Ramona's mortgage."

"I got them a beautiful house that did not cost a penny to them, gave them a mortgage they could afford, and they lived there for three years. Did you hear them complain at any point before? … Weren't they singing my praises, Olivia?"

"Yes, but now their mortgage has suddenly doubled, and Malcolm is on a reduced pay at work."

"Tell Malcolm to find another job that pays him better, and besides they knew that their mortgage was going up after three years."

"Did you tell them that before? … Morgan, did you tell them that when you arranged the loan?"

"I did thousands of mortgages, I hired people to work for me, do you think I had time to go over every little fine print on the contract?"

Olivia continues with Morgan Jr., "They were not everybody, they were people we knew. Sophia and Ramona grew up together!"

"Good! Then she should have read it for them, they're her friends. If you cared so much for them, you should have read it for them too, why didn't you do it?"

"Morgan!" yells Morgan Sr. "Have respect!"

Olivia attempts to talk, but she stammers. She walks away crying and Sophia follows her.

Sophia takes her to the pantry, and as her daughter and she sit beside each other, they hear the father and son argue with each other.

"They trusted me to get them a house, I did it for them, now what are they complaining about? Just asked them to sell that thing if they can't manage it."

Morgan Sr. clarifies, "Yes, Son, you got them what they wanted, but at what cost. You cost them their livelihoods. They can't sell off the property because the market has crashed."

"Dad, don't go there with me talking about livelihoods, they knew what they were getting into."

"They trusted me more," continues Morgan Sr. "Because of that they never questioned you … I failed them here!"

"Were you their attorney, didn't they have an attorney to advise them. Dad … couldn't their attorney have said something … Now when things go wrong, I am to blame."

"You introduced an attorney that worked for you, not for their interest."

"So, their relevance is greater to you than mine, is it?"

Morgan Sr. with hands on his face, "Son, what have you done!"

"You know what I have done Dad, I built a business enterprise out of nothing, do you remember the rotten life we lived when we first came to New York. Can you say that now? That's what I have done. Look at that neighborhood, I changed it. You should be proud of me as a father, not blame me … By the way, I was not the only person doing this, people around the country were doing this. Olivia and you are acting as if I was doing something illegal."

"Son, just because everybody does something, it does not have to be the right thing. Life gave you better skills, you could have used them wisely. I came to New York to give you a better life, to forget our past, and rebuild what we lost. Not to live off other people's misery."

"Dad, you are still going on as if it was my fault. There is a global financial meltdown and that's the cause, not me."

"You should have been more careful."

"What were you doing Dad, were you careful? You were here most of the time looking out of the window with a bottle next to you. Or you were puffing a cigar on the balcony. Sophia was taking care of Lex or was shopping. I had to do everything."

Morgan Sr. walks into the pantry and holds Olivia's hand. "I am sorry Olivia, that was rude, please forgive us."

Olivia acknowledges through her facial expressions.

Olivia wakes up, she knows it was a dream, but she also knows that her dream was a replay of factual conversations that occurred in the past.

It is too early in the morning to be awake, but she can't fall asleep again. The dim lighting guides her past her circular dining table and onto her armchair by the window. She sees the articles which she collected for Naomi, lying on the side table. Naomi wanted articles about the Financial Meltdown, and these were articles that she accumulated during Sophia's trial.

Olivia switches on the side lamp and begins glancing through the articles, thinking that reading may make her feel sleepy.

… In an era marked by a startling lack of oversight, financial institutions extended loans to individuals through lending firms, which peddled subprime mortgages with exorbitant interest rates and no down payment requirement. Among the array of loans proffered, the interest-only mortgage emerged as a tempting option, luring borrowers with its initial low payments, sustained by covering only the interest. However, once the triumphant period elapsed, homeowners were blindsided by soaring mortgage payments.

This reckless practice echoed across borders, with governments and financial institutions turning a blind eye to the loans' distribution and failing to scrutinize the looming repercussions of these perilous practices. Banks, basking in the lucrative world of high-interest lending, scarcely fretted. Lenders, reaping commissions from these loans, were content. Builders gleefully watched their properties fly off the market. And borrowers, blissfully acquiring new homes without breaking a sweat, remained unfazed. The prevailing belief? Housing prices could only ascend. Lenders harbored the conviction that, should borrowers falter, they could simply repossess and flip the homes for a tidy profit. Borrowers, in turn, believed that if push came to shove, they could offload their homes at a handsome gain.

It seemed like an unending win-win game, devoid of losers—an irresistible gamble for all. No one could foresee the ominous conclusion lurking on the horizon, save for the innocent borrowers who would bear the brunt of this imprudent spree. In this high-stakes game, one party emerged as the ultimate casualty: the borrower.

As the repercussions of this economic tumult unfurled, millions found themselves stripped of their livelihoods. Concurrently, the housing market plummeted in the throes of a severe economic downturn. Pockets of homeowners grappled with the painful realization that their abodes had depreciated significantly from their initial estimates. Consequently, a deluge of homes descended into foreclosure, as families grappled with the insurmountable burden of sustaining their mortgage payments.

The ensuing foreclosure saga, catalyzed by the Financial Meltdown, inflicted profound damage beyond mere financial woes. Millions bore the brunt of this catastrophe, their credit scores plummeting alongside the unraveling of their lives …

The articles slide off Olivia's hands. Her head rests on the chair and with her eyes shut, she sees Naomi sitting between Ramona and Malcolm in their little apartment. They are speaking to a man, but Olivia can't see his face due to him having his back turned towards her, but she recognizes his voice.

(17) Plan

"Hi Miss Grace," greets Naomi as she visits Miss Grace. "You asked me to drop by. So… I am here."

"Yes! You were talking about a case," begins Miss Grace. "I wanted to know what you were talking about."

"It was about Mr. Anderson, I wanted Mr. Anderson to get back his regular classes, he taught us well, therefore I thought it was a good idea to speak to the principal ... so that he could teach us once again."

"Well, did you speak to the principal?"

"Yes, I did, but I could not convince her enough to change her decision."

"I see, in most negotiations, you need to have bargaining power in your favor. Something I learned in business studies."

"You went to business school, Miss Grace?"

"Not really, my expertise is in psychology and social work, but I did business studies as a minor area."

"Now that I am here and you have done business studies, I have an extra question for you."

"We can do both, answer your questions and discuss anything else that's bothering you."

"First the question, before the Financial Meltdown, did people know that they will have to pay a monthly amount, and what that amount was going to be."

"Yes, most of them did, but the great idea that was passed around was that prices of houses will never come down."

"So, did that really happen?"

"No, not at all! Also, some mortgage companies had hidden conditions like you pay a small amount for the first two to three years, and then suddenly your payment would increase so much that you won't be able to afford your mortgage anymore."

"The people in these banks that give out these loans are people who have a basic education, right Miss Grace?"

"Yes, unfortunately, nobody cared much. And by the time they took action to prevent this irresponsible lending, it was too late. Also, there were many unseen mortgage irregularities happening, which were not detected in time."

"So, this is the scam my parents got caught in. And it was set up by Utter's father."

"Sweety, I can't speak about other students or their parents. But the way I see it is, it was not a setup, it was irresponsibility, and gross negligence. And I am sorry to hear what happened to your parents … Now Imagine, what happened to your family happening throughout the country … Well, that's what happened, and the depression that came with it was later called the Financial Meltdown."

"Did everybody suffer the same way, Miss Grace?"

"On no, the people who owned these mortgage companies, the board of directors of the banks, the people in the construction business, did well and moved on. It is the regular people who work hard to earn their pay that suffered."

"Were the loans only to buy homes?"

"No, some people obtained huge loans to renovate their homes, huge loans with high interest and unreasonable conditions. Loans they may never be able to pay back."

"So then why didn't people just not take the loans?"

"Good question, that's because money is a great motivator, the world moves on economics. Nobody can resist the attraction of getting money."

"How did the country recover from this crisis?"

"The government bailed out many banks and many failing corporations."

"Miss Grace, I don't think anybody bailed out the people, because my parents lost their home and now, they're in a situation of not being able to get a new home."

"I am sorry sweety, you can research more on this, I just shared the information I know."

"Thank you, but there is something wrong in that whole story, it does not seem to add up. Where did all the money go, surely a lot of money can't just disappear like that."

"Well, it didn't pass your way, neither did it pass my way."

"Hmm …"

"Now to your other problems."

"Yes, it is about Utter's mom. He's devastated about his mom being in prison, also his mom and my mom were best friends once, now they are enemies. I want to solve that problem too."

"My girl, you have taken the whole world upon yourself. I don't know what to say."

"Miss Grace, when I see a problem, I need to solve it, so I find a way to do it. That's who I am."

"Naomi let's learn from our experience. The last time you tried to solve a problem, you got hurt. I don't want something else to hurt you again."

"Miss Grace, what I did, saved a child. Yes, I know that I got hurt, but I am healed now, and I am happy that I saved somebody."

Miss Grace contemplates for a moment and seeing Naomi's determination and good intentions, wants to find a solution for her.

"I think there is a way around this," Miss Grace speaks, "Now, this is only a plan, let's hope this plan doesn't go south."

"I am all ears, Miss Grace. Did it just get dark inside?"

Miss Grace observes the gray hue through her cubicle window, the sky is filling up with dark clouds stopping the flow of sunlight into her room.

"Let me switch on the other light, it's getting dark early today."

Naomi and Miss Grace have an extensive discussion about a solution to Naomi's problem. Rain splatters onto the windowpane and smog rises, cooling the setting. Naomi is impatient to put her plan into action.

It is still raining that afternoon as Naomi and Utter try to leave the school building. The school entrance is swarming with students trying to make their own rainy afternoon choices.

"Utter, what shall we do now, this is not stopping any soon! Can you run?"

Utter nods.

Several students push their hands outside into the rain to gauge the intensity of the downpour, others just wanting to have fun, chatter at the entrance. Sara, a student in Naomi's class, walks in the rain opening her mouth towards the sky trying to catch falling rain.

"Sara! Come inside, you'll catch a cold," cries Naomi.

"Can you hear me; I am singing with the rain," explains Sara.

"Are you trying to get sick, my girl," asks the traffic warden who assists three students huddled under a single umbrella.

At a distance, Miss Shepherd, holding a pink umbrella to shield her from the rain, watches the commotion with interest.

"Hi Miss Shepard," Sara waves with both hands, "I am singing with the rain."

Mrs. Shepard smiles.

"Miss Shepard, we need a real music teacher in our school," pleads Sara.

The rain loses its strength, and Naomi runs towards the bus stop with Utter following close behind. Once again, a haze of rain puffs down; finding it too late to turn back, they keep running.

Soaking and breathless, they sit next to each other, on a bench at the bus stop. Naomi gains her breath fast and watches Utter taking time to recover. A gust of wind sweeps off leaves from a nearby maple tree, and the smaller trees bow in the direction of the wind. The chilly wind causes goosebumps on Naomi.

"Utter, listen, I got a plan to save your mom. But we gotta play it really smart," says Naomi.

Utter's instant attention is not surprising to Naomi, as she continues. "I need you to be strong, much stronger than you are, not physically but mentally."

Naomi waiting for a response, "Nod your head Utter or give me a thumbs up, … if you can be that." Utter nods his head.

Naomi continues, "First, you have to put down your anger and hatred towards your father; and if you can't be nice to him, at least pretend to be nice to him."

Utter stands up, but Naomi pulls him back onto the seat.

"Look Utter, whatever past memory that's going on in your head, it's holding you back. You have to let go the bitterness … Like I did."

Naomi gains Utter's attention, he looks into her eyes.

"My parents hated your parents for what happened. They still do!"

"Utter keeps his fixation towards Naomi's eyes."

"Each time I overheard my parent's conversations about your parents, and thinking of what I lost, I hated your parents too … But after I got to know who you were, I decided to forgive everybody and move forward … that's why we are speaking here, sitting by each other, in this pouring rain at this moment."

Utter closes his eyes and keeps them shut.

"I know my mom cursed your family for what happened to her, I am sorry that she did. I wish your family only blessings, blessings powerful enough to break every curse against your family!"

Utter still keeps his eyes shut.

"Listen … I want you to do as I did! … stop blaming your father for what happened to you. Use that energy to free your mom!"

Utter opens his eyes, and Naomi notices the serenity in his eyes. It is as if she relieved him of a great burden.

"Because ... what would you do if you went down the 'rabbit hole?'"

Utter looks confused.

Naomi responds, "I like that look on your face Utter, at least now you can show feeling during a conversation. That shows progress, and that's good for our plan."

Utter looks more confused, with wrinkles on his forehead.

"What I mean is, if you go down the rabbit hole you will be wondering like Alice, meeting the Mad Hatter, the Crazy Rabbit, and the Wicked Queen. No, you don't want that! So, what if you turn back and come out of that same opening without going any further, then you are saved."

Utter's eyes are wide open, but his wrinkles remain.

"Oh, now stop looking so confused. Utter, let me put this to you in simple English."

A bus makes a stop on a puddle, and they hop into the bus, escaping the downpour and not stepping on the puddle. They find warmth on the bus, irrespective of their rain-soaked clothing. Naomi further reveals her plan.

"This is the way I see it. Your mom is definitely innocent, she couldn't have done it. Everybody thinks so, and I think so too."

Utter nods.

"The only other person who could be linked to this crime ... is your father. Because we need to ask ourselves, who would benefit from this crime … It's him."

Utter nods.

"This is why you should get your father's help to save your mom … and stop nodding like that… you might hurt your neck."

Utter's cheeks become red, and she sees his face bulge.

"When you're free, try to meditate. You may remember what made you dislike him; surely, he would have done something that makes you despise him that much. But listen, I am repeating this. Utter, you can't show him that you hate him … could you do that? … Tell me, could you do that?"

Utter nods his head again.

"Then, we'll find a way to save your mom."

Utter nods and smiles again.

"I just don't want you nodding your head and smiling, come-on, show me confidence, confidence like you believe it."

Utter offers Naomi a gesture of pointing both thumbs up. Naomi sees his smile grow.

She hugs him in delight.

(18) Conflict

The city council approves the principal's request for the renovation of the Science Laboratory at Admirable Academics High School, except its construction budget. The principal is not worried since a parent has pledged to cover that expense: Morgan Jr. The principal wants to offer Morgan a grand appreciation for his generosity, thus she is planning to host an event that welcomes him to the school to publicize his contribution. Morgan Jr., loving publicity, is eager to meet the staff and students of Admirable Academics, and more importantly to be able to speak to the press.

Being on the organizing committee, Miss Grace has recommended three addresses to be done at this event: the opening address by the principal, Morgan Jr.'s address, and an inspirational address by a student. Then for a press briefing at the existing science laboratory which is about to be renovated and brunch with a few staff members and students.

The principal sees Miss Grace hurrying into her office, "There you are Miss Grace, I was about to call you."

"I am sorry, I got held up at the guidance office," Miss Grace explains.

"How did the committee meeting go last afternoon?"

"Fine," continues Miss Grace. "I need to run a few things with you, just to check if you like it."

"Yes, sure, go ahead."

"First, let me talk about the program. You welcome Mr. Morgan at the front door and walk him up to the stage at the auditorium. We do not have enough room for the whole school to be seated at the auditorium, so I will let you pick the classes that need to be there."

"Nothing to worry about that, I will discuss it at our staff meeting on Friday."

"The sensitive issue here is Morgan's son, Lex. According to the psychologist's report, the recommendation was to keep the child away from the father, for the comfort of the child. And, when the father tried to force his point of view, the grandmother obtained a court order restricting the influence of the father."

"I see Miss Grace! Let me speak to the grandmother and Lex to see how we could proceed in that situation. What's next?"

"I am introducing an inspirational speech to be done by a student, and I have chosen Naomi Martínez to deliver that speech."

"Why Naomi Martínez? Shouldn't the speech be done by a senior; besides, we have good speakers among that group."

"I was thinking that way at first, but I don't want to hassle the seniors too much since most of them are studying for multiple AP classes. The others are so busy with their senior activities, and we need to give an opportunity to somebody new."

"Then, will you coach her, because I want her to rehearse the speech well."

"Then, I want teachers to nominate students who would take part in the Brunch. Ideally a mix of students - a student performing well in sports, a top-of-the-class student, a student with extreme disadvantage, a cognitively immature student, etc. We also need to have a balance of ethnicity, a balance between girls and boys, among other aspects that represent this school.

"Good, Miss Grace! I will put that out during Friday's staff meeting. What else?"

"I am concerned about Morgan's character; how will he influence these students."

"Miss Grace, we can't find a millionaire or billionaire without a flaw, that's the world we live in today. Morgan for whatever reason pledged this large donation."

"I heard that Jaylen Williams made the outreach."

"Yes, what I mean is, from what I have heard about Morgan, this is out of character for him."

"Well, I guess, people have different characters, but this has benefited our students."

"If he is not a good person, I hope when visiting this school, students in this school will influence him, to be that good person."

(19) Turning Point

Although her Sugarcane can't speak yet, he is able to display facial expressions, and Grandma is excited about it. Seated in the waiting room in the psychiatrist's office, Grandma and he are awaiting their turn. Grandma wants to discuss with the doctor a note her Sugarcane wrote to her. It was just two simple sentences; however, for Grandma, Olivia, it was a colossal leap of emotional progress for her grandson, or a possible psychological disaster lurking around. Olivia held the note as if a child were holding a precious toy, she had taken the note out of her handbag as soon as they had sat in the waiting room. She keeps reading the note as if there lies a deep message secretly encoded between the words:

Grandma, I think I am strong enough to visit Mom again. Also, Grandma, I am ready to meet my father.

When Utter had given her the note initially, she had been overcome with joy. Then, pondering on the note for, creates a mix of happiness, sadness, and confusion within her. Happiness to know that her sugarcane is emotionally recovering, sadness to feel that her sugarcane can't be with his precious mother, and confusion to think if a relationship with his father will help or hurt. Sugarcane, on the other hand, seems happy, as if relieved from a mammoth weight that was suppressing him; he calmly reads off his tablet and looks up to relax his eyes.

The school principal had spoken to Grandma the previous evening about the school event Morgan Jr. is to partake towards the end of that month.

"It's good to see you once again, and I am amazed at your progress. I did not expect you to progress this far so fast," says the doctor. "When Grandma spoke to me, she felt very happy for you, it's good to see smiles on both your faces."

"Thank you, doctor!" Grandma speaks as she pats Sugarcane's shoulder.

"Grandma informed me of your new thinking, and we need new thinking for progress."

"I just don't want him to push his limits too much, doctor."

The doctor continues, "The human brain is the most astounding entity, and sometimes we dare to test its limitations. Right now, we are moving through uncharted territories, and I am confident that he will make it through. Likewise, we will never know the answer if we do not attempt to find out, and I am pleased that you are attempting to find out whatever you're searching for."

"There is a new development," explains Grandma to the doctor. She informs the doctor about the school principal's communication with regards to Morgan Jr. being at Sugarcane's school and if Sugarcane should be involved in any part of the function.

The doctor, laughing, "Now we are pushing our limits."

Then leaving Sugarcane to have his psychotherapy session with the doctor, Grandma returns to the waiting room.

It is a long wait for Grandma, eager to hear her next piece of advice from the therapist, and eager to plan her next course of action. The digital clock on the wall informs the progression of time through its red illustrations; the seconds pulsate, reminding of a time when Sophia was little. Olivia remembers a walk through the park, Sophia running ahead, dressed in her favorite light blue checked dress embroidered with blue and white flowers, while wearing her favorite blue Alice-band.

Olivia remembers bringing Sophia to the park to reveal the most emotional wrecking information a mother can convey to a child. She remembers how she was finding the courage to tell her happy daughter that her father may never come back home. That walk through the park seemed eternal, and she remembers finding courage to speak up, when Sophia said to her.

"Do you know why I chose this pair of shoes, mommy?"

It was an old pair of shoes, a little tight on her feet, but the buckle had broken off and Daddy had fixed it for her when it had come out.

"Take me to the studio and get a picture of me. I want to send that picture to Daddy."

Thereafter, Olivia never found the courage to speak the truth. Sophia hoped that her father would come back, and Olivia never wanted her to think otherwise - afraid of breaking her little heart. Then Sophia found out the truth herself at a memorial service.

"Mommy, why is Daddy's name on the list, I thought only Ramona's daddy should be on the list."

Olivia remembers how she tried to hug Sophia and Sophia pushing her back. She tried again and again to hold Sophia, and again and again was pushed away. She loved Sophia too much to break her heart, but she broke her heart anyway.

Then years later, when Sophia was married to Morgan, Olivia witnessed the socially irresponsible path Morgan Jr. had taken. Olivia was silent, believing that it would hurt Sophia if Morgan's mistakes were pointed out.

Now she is in prison due to circumstantial evidence working against her without a true witness, and Morgan is enjoying life as if nothing is wrong. Could she have done something to protect the mother and child? The guilt of failure is overwhelming, but her strength to carry this affliction is her drive for rectification.

Now a great responsibility has befallen her, to protect her Sugarcane from any errors that he could make. At first, he is psychologically motivated to distance himself from his father, now he wants to do just the opposite. But how is she to know the difference between the correct and incorrect decisions he may make; then, how is she going to help?

She doesn't keep track of the red numerals on the digital clock, but the seconds still pulsate when Sugarcane walks out of the therapy session with his doctor following him.

"Hi Mrs. Tosco, he is good to go with his decision, I have to file paperwork with your attorney to modify the court order, give me a day or two."

"Are you certain that this will work out, doctor?"

"As I said, he has the situation under control. Don't worry, we will monitor him."

"Thank you again!"

(20) Error of the Past

A glass pane prevents a mother from touching her son, yet the glass pane is not resilient enough to hold off the tremors of her son's feelings towards her. As the hands of mother and son meet from either side of the cubicle, among feelings of sadness his hand conveys a fervent feeling of hope, and his eyes sparkle with a sentiment of courage.

The last meeting between the two only created a wail of tears, but today there are no tears, only reason between the two. Mother speaks, Son listens, and sometimes, he holds a note to her. Grandma sits opposite him and sometimes adds to the conversation. Grandma remains strong, Sophia transcends with sadness and joy as she uses the last of her allocated time to wish them well; her son is so attentive, so strong, and so calm. As Sophia walks away, she turns back to see her sweet boy holding his fist above, with his thumb pointing up. She sees the rejuvenating of hope.

Sophia walks through the extended corridor, face down, trying to keep a count of the waned floor tiles, and trying to recollect the count of days she has been in this misery. She recollects the past joys shared with her son, Lex, she recollects the nail that pierced her life, the card played against her by her man, Morgan.

As she sits in her cell, Sophia recollects her encounter with the extortionist, Sonny Segarra, a former employee of her husband's mortgage lending company. She remembers visiting that mortgage company at the request of her husband to sign off on any urgent documents, during the two weeks Morgan Sr. was in hospital due to having a minor stroke. She remembers how Segarra arrived at work habitually after 10:00 AM, dressed in a tuxedo and reddish glasses, while carrying a leather briefcase cuffed to his hand. He was well groomed, and he never drove a car. His excuse was having driver's anxiety, so he prefers a cab. His phrase "sweetheart," after each sentence he spoke, was the first thing she disliked about him. Next, the profane language he used in conversations as if he can't form a sentence in English, without adding profanity.

She remembers how Morgan Sr. wanted to fire Segarra when Morgan Sr. came out of the hospital, but how her husband found excuses to keep Segarra. She recalls how her husband liquidated that company after Morgan Sr. got his second stroke. She recalls how her husband and Segarra shredded off documents accumulated during that business, giving the excuse that customer personal information should not be compromised. She did not see Segarra after the liquidation of the company.

Then, she remembers how one morning, a couple of years ago, when about to leave her Staten Island mansion with her son Lex, Sonny Segarra was standing at her door. She was surprised to see Segarra, an employee she despised, being an uninvited guest.

He was in the same attire, the same way she remembered him: tuxedo and reddish glasses with a leather briefcase chained to his hand.

"Hello, Sophia! Do you remember me," he asked? "I worked for your company … I am Sonny … Sonny Segarra."

"Yes, I remember you, what brings you this way?"

"Sweetheart, won't you ask me to come in."

"In fact, I am in a hurry, my son has his graduation rehearsals, I don't want to delay him. You can try calling my husband."

"That cheapskate doesn't want to pick up my calls, and you will let me in when you know what I have to give to the feds. See … I am not worried about going down, because I have been there … nothing to lose. You and him on the other hand, will lose a lot."

"What are you trying to say, Segarra?"

"You remember all those documents we were shredding … just before you people closed shop?"

"What are you talking about?"

"You people suffer from memory loss … only when it benefits you."

"Say what you have to say, Segarra … I need to go."

"Lex Morgan Jr., your husband, was thinking that he was covering his tracks, when he shredded all documents, deleted all the computer files, and closed business in that mortgage company. He did a good job; I give that to him." Segarra says with a sly grin. "But he can't outrun me, sweetheart …. I am smarter than him."

"I need to go now."

Raising his briefcase closer to her face, and rapidly tapping the briefcase with his finger, he continues, "In here … these documents he wanted me to shred … I hid them: all original copies signed in ink, by you."

"Segarra, just tell me what you came here for," then she remembers shutting the front door behind her and walking towards the car with her son Lex following her. "I need to drop my son in school, so whatever you came for, deal with my husband. You worked for him, not for me."

"No, no, no, sweetheart, wait …I worked for you." Segarra pulls out multiple documents off his briefcase and shows her signature on each document.

"Can we talk now?"

Sophia remembers how confused she was and remembers how she, with contemplation, let him inside her home.

Segarra walked inside her home and made himself comfortable on the sofa. Segarra informed how her husband and Segarra forged documents to misrepresent people's financial information to banks, during the financial meltdown. According to Segarra, as the real-estate business slowed down due to the economic recession caused by irresponsible lending practices, her husband's investments became stagnant due to the unsold homes. During the housing boom, Morgan Jr. and his investors were in a rapid cycle of construction. The lending company Morgan Jr.

opened under his father's name, was rapidly processing loans to sell off the new constructions.

Sophia remembers Segarra explaining to her, "Morgan's investors were jumping down his throat, and he had to get rid of those houses. Those unsold houses were worth millions … So, he came to me … and I helped him."

"How?"

In the wake of the recession, financial institutions had become more vigilant about people's borrowing credentials.

Segarra continued, "To outrun the financial companies … we made-up documents for unqualified buyers … by forging … by forging."

"Gosh, what did you get my husband into?"

"I haven't got him into anything, I made him rich that's all. Every loan he made, he got a cut for the company, and the bigger cut was when he sold a house. I helped him to run that business, and what did I get, nothing much."

"So, what do you want me to do about that now," she remembers asking him.

"For a small lump sum payment within your means, I will make this information disappear. You know … I will not ask for an arm or a leg sweetheart!"

"You know this is extortion," she remembers telling him. "I know my husband is a good businessman, he has his faults, but I know whatever he did should be legal. So, just leave us, and don't bother us anymore."

"You and the old man signed these documents, so that makes you at fault sweetheart. The old man is dead … so that leaves only you."

"So how much are you looking for?" inquired Sophia.

"Good question … finally! Call Morgan … tell him I am here, and meet me now," And sweetheart, can you make me coffee without poisoning it."

Sophia remembers how alarmed she was when Segarra mentioned her signature being on those documents. Knowing Segarra at that time she should have verified what she was signing; an innocent assumption, a careless mistake of the past had come that day to sting her. Then, she remembers how angry she felt with her husband for his illegal undertakings, how angry she felt for mixing her with a fraud like Segarra.

She also remembers asking him, "Is that what you did to my friend Ramona, do you remember Ramona Martínez?"

"Their story was different. Boss Morgan wanted to get them the best deal possible, All I had to do was insert a few papers here and a few papers there, and voila, the loan passed."

"Did they know you inserted additional documents while processing their loan? Did they sign the documents, did you tell them?"

"Sweetheart, nobody cared back then, nobody cared reading a thousand pages. All they cared about was the house and a good monthly payment. What happens three years down the road …. who cared back then?"

"There's no hell made, to dump people like you."

"Sweetheart, you got that right also, there are too many of us, hell will be overcrowded. Everybody like me was doing it, and if I didn't, somebody else would have."

With all that anxiety, with all that tension, Sophia also remembers how she overlooked her son, Lex, listening to the conversation. She remembers how her husband dashed into the house and got into an argument with Segarra. She remembers how Morgan and she argued that day, how Segarra had wanted the payment in cash, how Morgan wanted time to raise the cash, and how her son Lex had followed the whole sequence of events.

She remembers thereafter, how her husband and she would get into lengthy arguments even over something insignificant. She remembers how much her son was worried. His mood had changed; so, had hers, and she did not know whom to talk to.

She thought her son would feel better after the graduation party and vacation she had organized for her close family friends at her holiday home in Port Aransas.

The vacation didn't seem to soothe him, yet she had hoped that her son would feel at ease after her husband paid off Sonny Segarra. She felt that she would feel relieved too.

(21) Day of Fate

Sophia is in jail for manslaughter in the second degree. Olivia has appealed for a retrial in her case, trying to prove that the circumstantial evidence used was not substantial enough. There was too much bad publicity in the case, there was too much speculation connecting the crime to corrupt mortgage practices; Sophia feels that due to the bad publicity, somebody had to go down, and she was the pawn. She is hopeful that the justice system will prove her innocence.

Sophia knows the effort her mother dedicates to proving her innocence, and Sophia is also aware of how her husband is afraid to interfere with the justice system due to being afraid his misconducts would be known.

She remembers the events of the ill-fated morning. She remembers how her husband had written a check and had a bag of cash ready for Sonny Segarra. Sonny Segarra had finally accepted the offer by Morgan Jr. to get a large sum by check and a smaller sum in cash. She remembers how Segarra had not shown up yet when she left home with her son Lex. That morning was chaotic. Stepping outside, she found paper burning on the barbecue grill; thus, entering the house through the rear entrance to yell at her husband for doing so; and not finding him, she went down to the basement looking for him. Then she observed misdirected cameras on the video surveillance system. Fixing the surveillance system and not finding him, she stepped out of the house, slamming the door. Then she drove off annoyed.

She was driving and her son Lex was in the rear seat; her attention was distorted due to Segarra's extortion and her husband's coldness. She was further vexed by her son Lex's apprehension to the circumstances: A child who was living a calm life, pushed into confusing circumstances. She too was living a cozy life, until her husband's faults began sequentially tumbling on her sanity.

Her distraction while driving that day may have stimulated her to disregard speed limits. She was aghast when the rear-view mirrors showed her car trunk opening and a resemblance of a human hand protruding. In her shock, she may have crossed an intersection with the lights against her and was T-boned by a truck, resulting in her son being thrown out of the car. Airbags inflated from all sides and trapped her in the driver's seat.

She remembers being dazed, yet heard the sirens of arriving ambulances, then her car door forced open. She tried to stand up but collapsed back onto the seat. She looked around, and saw a body bag zipped up, she screamed, "Lex!"

A paramedic said, "A kid is on that stretcher."

She stood up brushing the paramedics who were helping her, saw her son on the stretcher, unconscious, with an oxygen mask, and he was being pushed towards the ambulance. She forced herself on the same ambulance that carried her son Lex to the hospital.

At the hospital, they found brain injuries on Lex and severe external bruises. Lex had gone into a coma. He may not have had his seat belt on, if he had his belt on, he would have been trapped inside the car, and protected by airbags. Instead, he was thrown out of the car.

Detectives asked her if she knew the man who tried to get off her car trunk. When she said no, they showed a photograph of Segarra and asked her if she knew him. She said, yes. Segarra was pronounced dead at the scene of the accident. They asked her how Segarra got into her car trunk. She did not know. She was there beside Lex when her husband came in followed by her mother. She spent days waiting for Lex to recover, he did not. She was arrested for the murder of Sonny Segarra, was bailed out, tried, and a sentence was handed down. Her son never recovered.

During the investigation, detectives found Segarra's briefcase forced open next to the barbecue grill at the Morgan Premises and the grill had been used to burn documents. In addition, a tranquilizer dart, the reddish pair of glasses belonging to Segarra, and one of Segarra's shoes were also found on the Morgan premises. The most incriminating evidence was that the tranquilizer dart found on the Morgan premises had her fingerprints on it. Forensics revealed that Segarra had been struck by that same tranquilizer dart two hours before the accident. The angles of the surveillance cameras monitoring the premises had been remotely changed to face upwards three hours before Segarra's accident and turned back into regular view half an hour before the accident. Sophia's fingerprints on the surveillance device controls indicated that she was the last to operate the surveillance mechanism. Segarra also had one shoe on him which indicated to investigators that Segarra had been put into the trunk at the Morgan premises. Detectives believed that the large sum of money and check written in favor of Segarra, found at the Morgan residence, may have been a payoff for Segarra. Segarra's prior records indicated that his driver's license had been revoked due to multiple DUI's.

Detectives found out that Segarra had used a cab service to arrive at the Morgan residence and the surveillance could not record his arrival due to cameras being faced upwards by a member of the household, perhaps by Sophia. Then Segarra was attacked with the tranquilizer dart before he entered the house, and his lifeless body put in Sophia's car trunk. The fact that only Sophia's fingerprints were on the tranquilizer dart, created the assumption that the act may have been committed by Sophia. Then burning the documents using the grill, and turning back the cameras to the original position, she leaves the premises planning to get rid of Segarra. Since Segarra was not physically large, Sophia may have managed to carry out the act on her own. She never thought that Segarra would wake up on the way and attempt to get off the trunk. The detectives also believed that, given the fact that the money was ready, it may have been Morgan Jr.'s idea to pay off Segarra but Sophia's idea to get rid of Segarra due to her believing that Segarra had incriminating documents against her, which were burnt using the barbecue machine.

Another testimony was taken in court from a former employee of the mortgage company run by Morgan Jr. The employee revealed under oath that Morgan Sr. ran the company and Sophia took care of the company whenever Morgan Sr. was not able to. The employee also revealed how Segarra had hated Sophia at that time, and how she had tried multiple times to have Segarra fired. The employee also testified in court how Segarra once mentioned, “I have dirt on them.”

Morgan Jr. “Pleaded the fifth amendment,” therefore the prosecution did not find enough evidence to obtain Morgan Jr.’s testimony. Finally, due to finding evidence that Sophia had the means, the motive, and the opportunity to commit this crime, Sophia was convicted for manslaughter in the second degree.

Sophia believes that Morgan Jr. adjusted the surveillance cameras intending to confront Segarra outside of the house, then used the dart to subdue Segarra and lock Segarra in her car trunk. She believes that he then burnt the documents on the grill, to get rid of the evidence Segarra was using in his extortion scheme. She believes that Morgan Jr. did it to protect her from falsely being implicated for fraud; somehow, the plan was not perfect, and she had to pay in a different way. She feels guilty for causing the death of Segarra, even though she despised Segarra and even though Segarra was blackmailing the family.

(22) Old Friends

After Asher's and Antonio's meeting at the pizzeria, Antonio decides to invite Asher and his family to his new home on a Sunday evening. Asher and his wife Audre, Antonio, Veronica, and Veronica's sister Sally are outside on the deck, enjoying the cool fall weather. The children are inside watching a movie. At the corner of the deck, a loaded barbecue grill dissipates heat. Two candles burn at the center of their round table, one tall red candle flickering with a bright flame, the other, which is a pink candle dispelling a dull flame. Dim lamps lit at the four corners create tranquility, and above are the stars that twinkle at them.

"Why is everybody quiet," Sally asks, wanting small talk.

"This is a nice deck you got," Asher facing Antonio, "how do you power those lanterns?"

"Solar power, not that expensive," replies Antonio. "So, when is your daughter coming home?"

"She'll be with us for Thanksgiving," Audre informs. "Hey, why not you come to our place for Thanksgiving, our daughter would love it. I was telling Asher that I would like to ask Olivia and Sophia's kid to join us too."

Veronica being enthusiastic, "That's wonderful," they enjoyed themselves so much the other day.

Juliet, Jaylen, and Jaylen's little brother walk up to the barbecue grill. Juliet gives Jaylen's little brother a plate, napkins and helps him at the grill.

Sally sees the children and goes up to help them. "Let me help you guys. … they are all well done, we nearly forgot this ... Vero can you bring me those trays."

Sally, flexing towards Jaylen's brother, "Hi, what's your name?"

"Ashton Williams"

"What a lovely, lovely name. Let me give you a big hug."

The kids join the adults, and everybody enjoys their grub, sitting around the table. Ashton sits on Audre's lap, and she helps him to eat the kebab served. The flickering of the red and pink candles adds to the delight of everybody present. Still, they all feel unfulfilled.

Veronica says to Juliet, "Didn't Lex and his grandma have a nice time with us the other day?"

"Juliet chewing her stake answers," hmm!"

"So, we have been invited to celebrate Thanksgiving at Mr. Asher's place."

"Hmm!"

"Little problem here, how will young Lex react to the big man if he crashes in," Asher questions.

"Dad, that's under control," Jaylen confirms.

"What do you mean, under control? That boy hates the sight of Morgan for an unknown reason, although I could guess what. Anyway, I don't want that boy to get an anxiety attack on such a nice event."

"Dad, last Friday, we were planning out Morgan's visit to our school, you remember I told you about the donation."

"Yea, yea, keep going."

"Miss Shepherd was worried about that too, she had called Grandma Olivia to ask if Lex," Jaylen pauses, "Lex or … Utter … whatever we call him now."

"These children are so rude to each other," Audre interrupts.

"Mom let me continue, he likes that name."

"That's not his name though," Audre corrects.

"OK mom, may I continue! Grandma Olivia had informed the principal and Miss Grace, that everything is under control. He is looking forward to meeting his father. He also met his mom last week, and he was fine about that too."

Juliet acknowledging, "Hmm!"

Asher says, "I haven't spoken to Olivia for a while, let me find out about this miraculous recovery."

Antonio interrupts, "Do what I did. The day we had the party here, I told Boss Morgan to come late … when his son had gone, I mean, he understood, the guy may be crazy, but he wants his son to recover. That's what we all want right?"

"Hmm!"

"But we can't do that for Thanksgiving," Audre points out.

"Does anybody know how this girl Sophia's appeal for a retrial, proceeding?" Asher, checking from everybody.

Veronica says, "It is a difficult process, but Olivia is not giving up hope."

"I always said that it is that big guy who did the crime and pinned it on this girl Sophia. Antonio, don't we know about him, isn't he capable of anything? Otherwise, how did Segarra magically appear in that car trunk?"

"Yes, first the detectives thought that he put Segarra in, but there was no evidence to pin Boss Morgan."

"He would have cooked up the evidence. Tell me, why hasn't he visited her? It is because he can't face her, or he is afraid of going down. Do you think a man who did not care for his father, would care that much for his wife? Don't you agree Antonio?"

"Let me think!"

"Now without his wife to check on him, his son being taken care by the grandmother, and without Morgan Sr. to watch over him, who knows what that guy is plotting in that mansion."

"Asher, honey, you're getting a bit emotional here. I told you years ago that we should pull out our investments from there, take care of your tool factory in Michigan, and do something else here. I am telling you once again today, let's leave him and his business for good. If Morgan goes down, I don't want you to be involved with anything."

Nobody comments and Audre continues, "Knowing him, and with Olivia pushing for a retrial, we don't know what they'll find on him."

"We all got involved like this because of old Morgan, he was a nice man. He took care of our Antonio," exclaims Sally.

Antonio supporting Sally, "Old Morgan found me when I got thrown out of the pub by that John guy."

Veronica Laughing, "Why did you get thrown out now?"

"See Asher, those days were not good for me, I did not have the pizzeria, I was doing construction full time. when I got hurt at my old job, they just got rid of me."

Veronica continuing, "So he had to go looking for a job at the bar."

Everybody laughs and Antonio continues, "I was in pain, and I did not know what to do, I had Juliet to care for. I just went for one drink ... and hey, you have to do something to numb the pain."

"Like come crawling to my pizzeria," adds Sally, with a smile.

Veronica continues, "Sally called me ... Juliet was small, I couldn't leave her alone, so I took her and went to the pizzeria."

"He, he, he," laughs Asher.

"I was drunk, but I remember Juliet crying ... then old Morgan arrived after hearing the commotion at Sally's pizzeria."

"The first thing old Morgan said was, I will help them out."

"That's him!" reminds Asher. "Not like the other guy we know."

"I remember old Morgan driving us home in that old pickup truck, then he carried me and dumped me on our sofa," Antonio continues.

"Then I gave Antonio a job at the pizzeria, Sophia's Cafe was doing well, and our business was also growing, then Vero had to help us too."

"Old Morgan was a good man with a good heart, but it was Morgan Jr., who got me involved in construction once again, when he started building, I had to only supervise," Antonio adds.

"Then one day when Morgan Jr. and Sophia bought the building from John, our Antonio got the pizzeria part as a gift. how we own it now," Sally says.

"That was a nice story about your family, Juliet! So, your family is cool with Morgan Jr., right?" asks Jaylen.

"I've heard that story so many times Jaylen, let's go back inside and continue the movie ... come Ashton."

"Antonio, did you notice our daughter, did you get the feeling that she is not telling us something?"

"No, my dear."

The two partially burnt candles are vibrant, the flame on the red candle flickers while the flame on the pink candle dissipates a peculiar glow.

(23) Another Confession

While the adults enjoy themselves outside, the two teens are inside, seated on the sofa, continuing the movie they were watching earlier. Ashton enjoys the movie, sitting between Jaylen and Juliet. Juliet is not enjoying the movie; the conversation between the adults has made her uneasy.

Juliet moving to the edge of the sofa and turning toward Jaylen, "Utter knew that there was something terrible about to happen to them, I just did not get good help for him even when I saw the signs. I think I'm to blame too," Juliet explains to Jaylen.

Jaylen, turning his face towards Juliet, "How could you say that, Juliet?"

"When we were at Port Aransas," Juliet continues, "Utter was always in deep thought, something was bothering him."

"To think of it, I noticed that too."

"One evening his speech was slurring and he was shaking. I had never seen him that way before."

"Did you get help for him?"

"I asked him what was wrong, and I was trying to get help, but he begged me not to. He said nobody can help."

"Yes, I remember, he was like that just before the accident, so forgetful also. Do you remember how he blanked out during his awards night speech? People thought he was nervous, but I felt that something else was wrong."

"Yes, that also. He finally spoke to me during the vacation about what was happening at home. He made me promise that I talk to nobody about his problem. I agreed."

"What was his problem."

"So, that Segarra guy who our parents were speaking about, worked for Utter's father a while ago. Segarra knew something, and Segarra was blackmailing Utter's father, but somehow his mother was connected."

"I see, it makes sense now."

"I promised to find a solution for him as soon as we got back. I asked him to calm down and not worry. I asked him to trust me in this situation. Yes, my promise worked, and he felt better. Much better!"

"Did you find a solution then, Juliet?"

"That's the problem, I didn't have a solution. I said it to buy time."

"Damn."

"Then something worse happened, I slammed the door on Segarra, at Utter's house."

"I am lost, how did that happen."

"When we returned to New York after that vacation, I was at Utter's home, his mom had gone to the store, and the housekeeper was upstairs."

"So that guy showed up?" inquires Jaylen.

"Yes, he tried to force himself into the house, he was trying to pull out the door chain."

"I would have beaten him up," Explains Jaylen.

"That's when I slammed the door on his hand."

"That's good. Did he try anything after?"

"He left, but he called Utter over the landline phone and said something that scared Utter even more."

"What was it."

"Utter never told me, but he said we need to solve this problem Immediately."

"Damn that guy."

"Now, I was getting worried that he would feel worse than before."

"Why didn't you come to me, Girl?"

"I couldn't go to my parents because I had made a promise not to speak to anyone about this situation. This was giving me a headache," Juliet holds her head.

Ashton kneels on the sofa and rubs Juliet's head.

"Not now sweetie, back then," Juliet hugs Ashton.

Jaylen continues, "Why didn't you come to me, we could have planned something together."

"What would you have done Jaylen, what would you have done? This was a serious situation."

"So?"

"So, I set up a meeting with Utter and Valentine the Bully, at our pizzeria. Because Valentine's father is a Russian spy, and I thought he might be able to help."

"You told Valentine and not me, why?"

"I don't know, I am sorry Jaylen! I was confused. Because Valentine's dad was a spy, I thought he could help."

"Valentine is a liar, he imagines stuff. Why didn't you check with me first, Valentine's dad is an electrician, he's not even Russian."

"How do you know so much about Valentine?"

"His dad does work for my dad. Back then, Valentine and his dad used to show up at my place on Friday nights to get paid. When Valentine shows up, I can't get rid of him, he just walks into my room and pulls all my stuff. Damn!"

"I did not know all that, so for $25, Valentine promised to give Utter a plan. But he wanted to know the whole story."

"Girl, what advice can Valentine give anybody, he copies from others during tests, and still fails. He came to you for the free pizza, that's all. Do you know that he was left behind in class, three times?"

"Valentine said, if somebody is blackmailing you, they should know about something you've done wrong. So, all we got to do is get rid of that something, it is as easy as that."

"OK, that's correct."

"Then Utter said that his dad planned to pay the man off."

"So, Mr. Morgan had a plan."

"But Valentine said, if you give them money, they will keep coming back for more, over and over. 'You got to nip it in the bud,' he said."

"Sounds true, although it's coming from a guy like Valentine. Do you know how many fights he got involved in, and how many times that guy got suspended from school?"

"But I got to know him better after his first fight in school," exclaims Juliet.

"That guy!" responds Jaylen.

"After the discussion, Valentine said that he has this ultra-package to get rid of problems for a fee of $125/-, but because Utter gave him $25, he will only charge him $100/-"

Jaylen gets up from the sofa and bangs his right fist on his left palm. He walks around the hall in an aimless manner. "Damn … that Valentine! Did your mom know about this?"

"No, she would have thrown Valentine out immediately."

Jaylen lets himself fall back onto the sofa. "Did Utter pay him the money?"

"Yes, and Utter met Valentine at our pizzeria, before that accident."

"Damn! Are you telling me that Valentine set this thing up? Do you think he put that Segarra guy in the car trunk? … and framed Aunt Sophia? This is too far-fetched."

"I thought so too, but I never met Valentine after that. Anyway, he goes to a different high school now."

"Thinking about this, Valentine never showed up at my house for a while. But it also could be that my dad didn't give them any work."

"You see, I have to take the blame for this, Jaylen, I am to be blamed."

"Don't worry, I am going to meet that Valentine outside school tomorrow afternoon. I will take two of my football dudes too."

"No, please don't start a fight, I don't want any more trouble."

"No, I will only rough him up a little, he may say what happened. Who knows, we may get Aunt Sophia home for Thanksgiving."

"Please tell me you'd take care of this without getting hurt."

"I got this girl! You worry too much."

"Your last game is coming up, then at least go after Thanksgiving."

"I got this, Girl."

(24) Valentine the Bully

He is the center of attention because he has exciting tales to tell to his interested listeners; the stories he reveals are humorous and suspenseful, and in all those tales, he is the hero. His dimpled cheeks, his constantly animated deportment, and bushy hair are his traits the girls comment on: he loves it. He could act innocent, act facetious, act villainous, or act ignorant - all acts to suit his own needs. The naive fall for his schemes; and although not well crafted, those schemes most often end by jeopardizing his innocent participants' appeal. At school, he is not the most academically disciplined, but on the streets, he knows his way too well, and they call him, "The Trader." His name is Valentine, and during his middle school years, students called him, Valentine the Bully.

Using the full potential offered by the sublime weather on Monday afternoon, Valentine sits on the stairs at the side exit in his school building, displaying his antics to two attentive female listeners. Another student stops to listen to Valentine, and Valentine teases the student asking, "What are you looking at?" The student walks away, and Valentine rolls his eyes.

The rolling eyes of Valentine capture a distant image of a familiar person approaching in his direction, and besides this familiar person, are two other people of similar physique. The three well-built physiques are looking straight at him, prompting his heartbeat to spontaneously accelerate, and providing extra energy to his legs.

"Got to go," he reluctantly says to the girls, scampering down the stairs, and onto the sidewalk. Hurriedly crossing the street, he walks fast, going down the road trying to shield himself by the parked vehicles.

"Yo, Valentine, wait!" cries this person, freezing Valentine's feet. Now Valentine's brain must work at hyper speed.

Valentine acting surprised and waving at Jaylen, "Yo Jaylen, my brother, what's up, it's been a long time," and walks away hurriedly.

In the rush, Valentine bounces on a utility post; when he regains his alertness, Jaylen and the other two surround him.

"Why were you running from me, son; are you trying to hide something from me?"

"I wasn't running my brother, just in a hurry to get home."

"Answer this question, why did you trap Segarra in the trunk?"

"Segarra? What trunk?"

"I know you charged Lex $125, to put that guy in the trunk. Tell me everything, because you have committed murder, and you're going down now."

"What are you talking about, I know nothing?"

"Valentine, you can't lie to me, Lex told me everything, how he paid you money and how you put that guy in the trunk of the car."

"Lex is awake. From when?"

"From recently, and he's planning to go to the cops. He is going to pin you for the murder. He has footage of paying you money, do you remember you took money from him at Sally's pizzeria? I saw that footage, and I saw that you got Juliet involved in this too."

"It was she that came to me for help. But it is not the way you think it happened."

"You want to explain!"

"Did Juliet say anything to you, my brother?"

"Not a word, should she Valentine?"

"My brother, there are too many people listening. I don't feel comfortable, and it's not good for you either. Can you please send your friends away?"

Jaylen agrees. Jaylen and his two friends fist bump each other and leave. Valentine feels much relieved.

"Hey Jaylen," Valentine speaks, "are you hungry, I am starving. can you buy me a burger with all the stuff, from that burger joint, I can't talk much when I am starving."

Jaylen agrees, and the two dine at the burger restaurant to continue their discussion.

Valentine resumes his conversation with Jaylen, Valentine does not know what exactly to say to Jaylen, but his goal is to get Jaylen off his back.

"You know, Juliet did not trust you, that's why she came to me. I asked her to go to you first, but she still came to me. You know, she liked me more than Lex or you. Now she may lie to you, do not listen to her. You are my friend, brother Jaylen, she is not a true friend. She lies."

"Valentine, get to the point, you remind me of that character in my ELA lesson."

"Which character, I know many characters."

"My mistake for thinking that you read Shakespeare! Get to the story without bad-mouthing my friend. I am sure she'll find out that she trusted a liar and a cheat."

"I know Shakespeare, I know Romeo and Juliet."

Valentine sees Jaylen staring at him, Jaylen holding his fist tight and losing patience. "Valentine, it's nice talking to you son, now I got to go to the cops. Don't skip town."

"Wait, wait, don't be in such a hurry because you're involved in this too. You supplied the murder weapon."

"Say it to the cops when they get you. I'll finish my burger and I am out of here."

"Do you remember the tranquilizer dart you had, the one you brought from Australia or Kenya? You said that you found it on the safari grounds. Do you remember me asking you if I could have it?

"Yes, I did not give it to you because it was mine."

"Do you remember that it was loaded?"

"Yes, there was liquid in it."

"What if I tell you that, your tranquilizer dart was the murder weapon. The scammer was shot using your tranquilizer dart."

"The scammer died in the car crash you…"

"Yes, by being in the car trunk. Who put the scammer in the trunk? Can you please answer that, brother?"

"So, you are confessing to this crime, right, Valentine?"

"No, suppose you gave Lex the tranquilizer dart because he was your friend, supposing Lex shot the scammer with the tranquilizer dart, and supposing Lex put the scammer in the car trunk, then you have helped him to commit murder. So, you go down, not me."

"You loser! Now I know that you stole my tranquilizer dart, shot Segarra, and then put him in the car trunk."

"Can you prove your theory; I don't think so. Who was closer to Lex - you and Juliet- not me! I can tell the cops that it was a plot between you, Lex, and Juliet. Then, after committing the crime, you were trying to pin the act on me. Whom will the cops believe, you or me?"

Jaylen sits in astonishment thinking of how Valentine has spun a new diversion. Jaylen takes the final byte off his burger, not knowing how to react to Valentine. Valentine seems smarter than he thinks, and Valentine has spun a tale that may implicate him for murder.

"Hey, Jaylen, my brother, do you think you could buy me a fruit punch."

"The only punch I may give you now is a fist punch."

"Treat me nice brother, your secret is safe with me."

Jaylen is not in a mood for football practice, he throws a few dollar bills at Valentine to let Valentine get the fruit punch, and as Valentine heads to order the fruit punch, Jaylen leaves the restaurant.

Jaylen walks slowly towards the football field, not that he is in a mood for practice, it is because his father picks him up after practice. Jaylen does not want his father to know about the skipped practices because his father may ask too many questions.

As he walks to the football field, Jaylen feels that somebody is following him, he turns back and sees nobody.

(25) Lost Focus

After the conversation with Valentine the previous week, Jaylen's thoughts are in disarray.

What if Valentine gave Utter the tranquilizer dart, and what if Utter used the dart to subdue Segarra. What if Utter really put Segarra in the trunk of the car, and the fateful accident was due to Utter putting Segarra in the car. Now, what if Aunt Sophia is in prison due to Utter's fault, and sadly Utter doesn't even know who caused Aunt Sophia to be in prison.

Jaylen feels that he has just solved the case and his information may result in a new twist to the case or even exonerate Aunt Sophia, yet that same information may incriminate his friend, Utter.

Days go by, tormenting Jaylen's soul. His practice sessions have become a disaster, the coach had spoken to him multiple times about carelessness on the field.

Another day of practice is over, and the coach's final words were, "Get your act together, otherwise you're not making it to your fifty."

The coach dismisses the other players, to speaks to Jaylen, "I am counting on you, your school is counting on you, touchdowns forty-nine and fifty are happening on Thanksgiving Eve."

After the practice session, Jaylen sits on the bleachers gathering his thoughts; he sees his teammates leaving at a distance, Coach following them, and Dad parked at the gate.

From behind a tree emerges Valentine.

"Hey Jaylen, my brother! What's going on with you?"

"What brings you this way, Valentine?"

"I wanted to see you practice, my brother."

"Why do you want to see me practice, are you getting sick or what."

"You know, I am a big fan of yours. My school doesn't have a good football team like yours. So, I come to watch your games. I mean, I have watched every game of yours. Sorry I didn't tell you before."

"Valentine, what's your point?"

"After I spoke to you the other day, I followed you. I thought I may have rattled you."

"Valentine … you can't rattle me."

"Then why didn't you practice that day."

"Yo! Mind your business!"

"I didn't mean it that way, brother. I was worried that I may have said the wrong thing to you, especially when there is a big game around the corner."

"Get lost Valentine, don't bother me."

"I … I was watching you, my brother ... today … yesterday … the other day … and we have one more game left …I saw coach speak to you … I know you're not doing great."

"Valentine you are really sick, or did you come here to commit suicide."

"No! My brother, listen! The way you are going now with your practices … you're not going to make it."

Ignoring Valentine, Jaylen picks up his bag and begins walking towards the gate.

"I will tell you everything about Lex, I have nothing to hide. Please listen to me."

Valentine gets Jaylen's attention; Jaylen stops walking and turns towards Valentine, making Valentine hurry towards him."

"What about Lex?"

"I admit, I stole the dart from you but that was a while ago. I kept it as a souvenir from you. You have everything … I don't. When you said you can't give it to me, I took it from you, because I felt sad."

"You need a lot of help son, now get to the point where you gave the dart to Lex."

"Did you speak to the cops about it? Was my name mentioned anywhere?"

"No!"

"To Juliet?"

"No, Valentine, get to the point. How did you give Lex the dart?"

"I washed it and cleaned it. Then I wrapped it in a napkin and gave it to him."

"Why did you do it."

"Hundred bucks was a lot to me, besides I wanted to help. I wanted to be in your group."

"What group."

"You were the popular guy, Juliet was the pretty girl, and Lex was the rich kid. You guys got everything going right, the teachers loved you, you guys got awards while I got only detention. I wanted to be with you guys, be like you. So, when I got the chance, I took it."

"You waited all this while to tell me?"

"When the accident hit the news, I was afraid. I couldn't even sleep …I was tossing and turning in bed all night … I was afraid that they would arrest us ... I mean only me."

"Too bad!"

"Yes, days went by … I couldn't even think … I couldn't get over this … what happened."

"You look fine to me … I am not buying you anything."

"I got over it … I got over it when I took a potion … the one that my dad takes when he gets stressed."

"You mean you stole your father's medication."

"No, it is like an energy drink … I can give you that if you want."

"Thank you, but you could keep it."

"I am giving it to you for free, drink it only if you want. This will help you focus like an eagle. You need it more than ever now."

Valentine pulls out two small bottles the size of miniature perfume samples. Both bottles are affixed with rubber lids, "This is excellent stuff ... a syrup from Russia … that's what my dad said. Use this narrow straw on the side to puncture the rubber and draw the syrup."

"Another scam by you!"

"I promise my brother, this is not a scam. You owe me nothing. I am helping you when you need me the most. Like I helped Lex when he needed me the most. Because … I am your fourth member in the group."

"What?"

"Yes, you are the strong one, Juliet is the pretty one, Lex is the rich one, and I am the smart one. Together we make a great team. We know each other's secrets because we trust each other."

Jaylen once again begins walking towards the gate, and Valentine follows him.

"Be honest with yourself, if you're not feeling great, take this. It's your only chance."

Jaylen walks faster.

"Here take it, Brother, it is free. I am giving you two."

Jaylen does not want to attract his father's attention, and to get rid of Valentine, Jaylen accepts the two bottles, and Valentine stops following him.

"Take one before practice, you will feel nothing, and you will fear nothing. You will be unstoppable, and you will thank me!"

Planning to get rid of the bottles later, Jaylen puts the bottles in his bag before dad notices. He is relieved that Valentine admits to giving the dart to Lex, but what's he to do with the information? It's worthless! He cannot betray his friend, Lex!

Nevertheless, he cannot bear the idea that Aunt Sophia is innocent and serving sentence. And, he has to prepare for his final game.

"Damn!"

"We are going home straight; Mom has made dinner," explains Dad during the ride home.

"I am not hungry, Dad; I just want to sleep."

The next day before practice, Jaylen feels the same, and he feels tired. He had been tossing and turning during the night rather than getting enough sleep. He sees his teammates gathering for practice, and he knows that the practice session will be another disaster for him.

He thinks of Valentine's potion which he forgot to get rid of. Would it work? He takes a bottle out of his bag, it's colorless. He pulls the straw out and inserts the straw through the rubber lid, drops squirt out onto his hand. He rubs it on his lips but can't feel anything. He draws more drops, it reminds him of an energy drink that he used to take a while ago, he draws more, and they seem harmless, he draws it all.

Jaylen joins the others in the warmup sessions, he feels better. The coach yells out, "Jay," makes a wayward throw and runs towards the finish line; the ball spins through the air and Jaylen catches the ball with ease, then instantly taking a few steps back while holding the ball with his middle finger and thumb oriented in a straight line, he gets on top of the ball twisting his upper body and releases the ball giving it a perfect spin using his index finger. The ball, penetrating the wind, flies across the field towards the finish line, into the coach's hands.

"Welcome back, Jay! Forty-nine and fifty are calling you."

(26) Narrow Hope

It is Tuesday morning; Utter has left for school. Olivia waits impatiently for a visitor, a new investigator assigned to Sophia's case. Olivia is in confusion due to the conversations she had over the phone that morning: first with an investigator and then with Sophia's attorney. Olivia tries to process this sudden information she received that morning and has manifold questions of her own. Had her appeals about Sophia's case to multiple departments around the country worked out? Does she finally have an answer to her cries and prayers? What will she find out, her anxiety of waiting, torments her!

Sophia's attorney had insisted that she would be present with Olivia when the investigator arrives, but Olivia's reply to the attorney was, "Just get my daughter exonerated, it is long overdue. I will speak to any investigator myself because the truth can't be changed."

She looks out of the window, down towards the street, impatiently looking for any sign of her visitors.

"The truth is my daughter is innocent, why can't anybody understand that," Olivia murmurs to herself.

Now, sitting at the table, Olivia opens a binder stacked with documents relating to Sophia's case. Documents she had collected and arranged in a three-ring binder. First are the newspaper clippings of the case. One article had the title, "Husband and Wife are Murder Suspects." That was when both Sophia and Morgan were suspects of trying to get rid of Segarra. Another headline was, "Lender's Wife Murders Extortionist?" That was a time when Sophia was the focus of the media, and investigators could not find any evidence to link Morgan to the crime. The third article carried the title, "Dart and Grill Reveal Grisly Tale." The article revealed how Sophia's fingerprints were on a tranquilizer dart they found on the premises, and her signature being on the partially burnt documents. The most damaging headline was,

"Payback for Illicit Lender," and the article explained how Segarra worked for Sophia providing unreasonable loans to unsuspecting borrowers, and how these loans eventually sent those borrowers into foreclosure. These newspaper reports only victimized Sophia and not Morgan, and these reports took away any social sympathy towards Sophia.

Olivia peeks out of the window again, awaiting the arrival of the investigator. She remembers moments from long ago when she looked out of the window, waiting for Sophia and Ramona to return home from school, and when they appeared, she could almost hear their chortles. She remembers at a later time, waiting for Morgan and Sophia, the bliss she felt to see them walking hand in hand; having dinner at the same circular table, then going outside to sit on the bench below to talk for hours.

Sitting at the table once again, she flips more pages of the binder. She finds case transcripts; she begins reading when the doorbell rings. closing the binder, Olivia promptly opens the door. There are two investigators present, one male officer and a female officer.

"Mrs. Tosco?" asks the female investigators.

"Yes, that's me. Good morning?"

"Good morning, I am detective Madison, and this is detective Raj. We are the new investigators for your daughter, Sophia's case."

"Just being curious, what happened to the other two gentlemen?"

"One retired, and the other moved to another state."

"I see!"

"Mrs. Tosco, as we spoke earlier, it seems that your appeal and petitions to multiple places and the persistence of your attorney, have been heard."

"Does that mean they caught the real murderer? Can my daughter go free?"

"Mrs. Tosco, can we use that table so that we could go over a few things with you."

"Yes, please sit."

Detective Madison begins, "Over the past year, multiple appeals made by Sophia's attorney were rejected, but the new appeal has been reconsidered. Your attorney will go over the technicalities with you, but the news is that the DA and Trial Judge have ordered a new trial, which also means that there is going to be a reinvestigation. That's why we are here."

Olivia presses her hands against her chest and closes her eyes. Her closed eyelids can't hold her outburst of tears. She knows that her tears are not a show of sadness, but an announcement of light at the far end of darkness. A symbol of hope!

"My daughter is a good woman, and I know that she would have never done this. It is a miscarriage of justice that she is in prison today. I bless those judges who are willing to give her another chance to prove her innocence. I thank you for coming into my home and giving me this good news. My daughter and I have nothing to hide, because the truth will always remain as the truth, and nobody can change that."

"Yes, Mrs. Tosco, the truth is the truth, and we are planning to find that truth. We have a few questions. These questions and answers will be recorded, do you have any objection to that."

"No, just ask."

The discussion drags on for over an hour, and the two detectives prepare to leave, informing Olivia of the next meeting in their day's agenda. The meeting is at the prison with Sophia and her attorney.

"Just one question, answer this if you can, why is the retrial happening, what's the new situation. I am asking this as a mother, not as a witness."

Detective Madison hesitantly, "Your attorney got the attention of the DA and the trial judge when she informed them that three jurors knowingly or unknowingly may have been biased in the verdict."

"What do you mean?"

"See, Mrs. Toscano, your daughter was tried for manslaughter in the second degree, but three jurors had their family members going into foreclosure due to unethical lending practices, and one of them had obtained their loan through Sophia's father in law's lending company. Nobody considered that link at the time of jury selection, it is later that investigators found out how much this mortgage crisis had affected people's lives and those who are connected to the victims of unethical mortgage practices that happened at that time. So, your attorney used that situation to make a case for a retrial, claiming that those jurors may have been biased in their decision."

"Will my daughter come home then?"

"Your daughter has not been exonerated, and we don't have all the answers. But we know that there is going to be a retrial."

"Could she be bailed out?"

"It is for the judge to decide, I am sure your attorney will work something out. Thank you so much for your corroboration."

"My daughter is innocent."

Detective Raj adds, "That's what we are trying to find out. Have confidence in our justice system, it may not be perfect, but through my experience living in other countries before settling here, you can't find anything better outside. Now, it is our duty to perfect this system in a civilized manner."

"What a philosophical man you are, detective Raj," Olivia complements. "Will you be taking statements from my daughter's husband, Morgan too?"

Detective Madison continues, "The last time he pleaded the fifth. I am sorry, you know what that means right?"

"Of course, I know, my girl."

"We don't know his stance on the retrial. We are waiting for his attorney's response!"

"Thank you for coming, both of you."

(27) Inspirations

The hustle and bustle at Admirable Academics High School are exciting. Later that morning, Morgan is to commemorate the opening of the new Science laboratory at this High School. Students report to class as usual, but student organizers walk back and forth, hurrying along the hallways dressed in black pants and school blazers. Staff are more animated than usual, increasing their pitch to grab the attention of distracted students.

Miss Grace enters the principal's office and finds Mrs. Shepherd trying to force a file into the filing cabinet. Wearing the school blazer over a black outfit she looks taller with her heels on.

Seeing Miss Grace approach, she says cynically "I hope somebody donates us with filing cabinets."

"That would be nice too!"

The secretary interrupts with a melody, "I made that suggestion!"

"Mrs. Shepherd," continues Miss Grace, "It's time to meet your guest at the entrance."

"So soon? How time flies. Let's go, have the students taken their places?"

"Everything is ready, all you do is walk Mr. Morgan to the auditorium, and the students will take care of the rest. They are well-rehearsed."

Miss Grace walks with the principal towards the entrance, "Mrs. Shepherd, you got your speech ready, right?"

"In my pocket ... if I need it. It's not going to be a long and boring welcome address. Let Morgan speak and let the student's address happen."

"Good, then after all the speeches, you, the student council president, one of the science lab teachers, and the custodian will put on hard hats, and walk Mr. Morgan to the restricted area where the lab is about to be constructed - Just showing him what we are going to do with his money."

"Good! Miss Grace, you know that the money has already come to the school, right? I hope Morgan will like the show today."

"No doubt he will, Mrs. Shepherd."

Arriving at the school auditorium, Morgan waves at his audience and acknowledges their applause as he climbs up the stairs on his way to the stage. There is a row of seats laid out on the stage, and the principal ushers him to the middle seat, while she sits next to him. There are two assistant principals, the custodian, the student council president, and the PTA president, seated with them. After the brief jolt of welcome by the power vocals of Mrs. Shepherd, Morgan Jr. begins his speech:

My friends, it is a pleasure to be here, helping this great school to build its state-of-the-art science laboratory. I am doing this to honor my father's memory, remembering his fondness for society. It is also as a tribute to my son, Lex, who is a student in this school and who sits among you now.

Morgan point's his hand towards Utter, the audience tracks the direction of Morgan's hand, Utter looks down.

The audience applauds, Naomi squeezes Utter's hand saying, "Stay calm now, you're doing so well." Naomi gently releases her grip, only for Utter to grip her hand back.

"Breath in Utter, exhale, and calm yourself, only you can do it for yourself. Breathe in, ...exhale, ...relax."

Morgan continues. When I graduated from high school, my father was in prison and my mother was dying. Fact of life: most people who are around you when you're doing well, are not there when you're down under. Now, what would you do if you're alone and have no one to turn to? Ponder on that thought for a moment…

When my father got out of prison, he thought that life would be the same, it was not. He wanted to hold onto something that was not there, he was still trying to hold onto something that he had lost. We came here by accident. My father had this old pickup truck, the only thing that had survived. I must add, and all his old tools. We were living in a friend's garage, and one day after dinner, having nowhere to go, we just drove South, then we decided to turn East. We drove and we drove, we took breaks, but we drove until I saw the sunrise in New York City. We were looking for a place to get food when the pickup truck broke down, and we found ourselves stuck in New York. He fixed it, but it was not good enough to make our trip back. Then I asked him, "What do we have… to go back to."

The first few days after arriving in New York, my father and I lived in his old pickup truck, we celebrated my nineteenth birthday in that pickup truck. He gave me a birthday gift, an engraving on a piece of metal, a piece of metal like a dog tag but much bigger. The engraving was a quote by Hillel the Elder, it read, "If I am not for me, who will be for me." My friends, I am asking you that question, if you are not for you, who will be there for you. Just ponder on that thought for a moment…

When my father gave that engraving to me, it hurt me more. I was angry, but that saying captured me so deeply, I asked myself, what had I done for myself? I felt guilty that I had done nothing for myself. I graduated from high school because my parents wanted me to do so. I had planned to go to college because my parents had wanted me to do so. But what did I want for myself? I had no answer. In anger and frustration, with the help of my limited skill, I reverted the metal plaque to the back of my father's pickup truck. As I was trying to affix this plaque, I was thinking, what if my father had adapted a new skill, would he have been laid off, would he have gone to prison! He did not want to change, but I decided to be different, I decided that I wanted to change. That metal plaque that I affixed to the back of the truck, stayed there for a long time. As I moved ahead in life, I bought and sold off a countless number of vehicles, but I kept that pickup truck to remind me of the day I decided to do for me… and not wait for others to do for me.

You reap the reward of what you do for yourself! Now, I am not saying it is easy, because most often the odds are against you rather than for you. But continue with the odds against you, navigate those odds to the best of your ability, and when you succeed, those odds wouldn't matter anymore. One way to do it is by educating yourself, nobody is going to do that for you; you have to plan your career, you have to plan your enterprise, nobody is going to do that for you either, you have to learn new skills, and dare to improve on those skills. Although my father could not deal with change, although he could not seize the opportunity, I feel that I did, I learned new skills, I made use of opportunity, and we are having a conversation about it today. So, use this little window of time to plan your life's journey, enhance your skill, nurture your education, and never stop growing. This is my advice to you, pick a skill and career that can't be a victim of outsourcing, pick a skill and career where you could compete in a global market, and when you have chosen skill or career, do not be afraid to constantly update that skill, or you will be in danger of being redundant. Be for you, because if you are not for you, who will be there for you?

Thank you!

The principal briskly walks to the microphone, amidst the applause of the audience. "Thank you, Mr. Morgan, for that inspiring speech."

She looks at Morgan, "There is quite a lesson there."

Then turning her attention towards her audience, "The next speech is the continuation of Mr. Morgan's story and there is a twist to that saga."

"Ironic twist," comments Morgan Jr.

Using her extravagantly and excessively used vocals, the principal announces, "Let's welcome Naomi Martínez, who will deliver the student inspirational speech."

Raving applause glides Naomi towards the microphone; within those cheerful faces that decorate her visuals, she randomly identifies those closest to her – many! Juliet, Maya, and Sara compete with each other, in the applause, Utter with a standing ovation, and Miss Grace looking so anxious while granting applause.

"Thank you," Announces Naomi, and inferring that the applause may take time to drop steam, she announces again, "Thank you …you can stop now!"

Thank you for inviting me here!

When Mrs. Shepherd asked me to make an inspirational speech, there were so many things I wanted to share with you. But it all changed last Friday afternoon when I met Mr. Morgan by accident. Mr. Morgan was looking for Mrs. Shepherd, but not finding her, he accidentally walked into Miss Grace's office, where I was rehearsing. In his hand, he had a glass case, and in that case, was the engraving which he spoke of. He had removed it off his father's old pickup truck, and he wanted to leave it somewhere in the new laboratory, to pass on the lesson that had inspired him, to be what he is today.

Well now… me being me… I wanted that engraving at least cleaned up before finding its new home. So, we took the engraving down to the custodian's office, and with help, cleaned it up. To our surprise, we discovered that there was another engraving on the other side. An engraving Mr. Morgan had never uncovered since his nineteenth birthday. A message hidden to him, a message concealed between his father's old pickup truck and the outside world. It was another saying by Hillel the Elder. Now, before I say it, do you remember the previous quote, which Mr. Morgan mentioned?

Students call out, "If I am not for me, who will be for me."

All right, that's the quote; and while trying to restore this tablet, I commented to Mr. Morgan on how rusty and withered that that engraving had turned itself into. Now for the next quote, which was clear and new as the moment he received it, yet invisible to an observer without a keen eye - 'If I am only for me, who am I!'... I repeat, 'If I am only for me, who am I!' ... Reflect on that saying please!

Sometimes we are so egoistic that we think of only ourselves, our comfort, and our wealth. We will soon go out into the world and make great achievements - that's my wish for us. On that road to success, it will be nice to pick somebody who has fallen on the wayside, somebody who has lost hope, somebody who without your generosity may not make it. Generosity means not money, even though that helps. Generosity could take the form of a kind word, an action, or a solution.

I once knew this good man, who was kind, generous, and understood what it means to be down, somebody who truly followed the idea, "If I am only for me, who am I!" Then something happened to him, he felt betrayed by his son; hence, he was lost, he was fallen, and he was dying. I was little, and I recollect that moment. All that people had to do was help him to get back to his son or help the son understand the father. Nobody did it, they were only focusing on their personal gain; yet, it would have cost them nothing to help. If ever you experience a situation where you could provide a helping hand, just think of the quote, 'If I am only for me, who am I?'

Mr. Morgan, you may have followed the philosophy behind the previous saying, the saying that was obvious to the world. And although you never saw that engraving on the opposite side, it had been calling for your attention all these years. That's why you thought of us, and is contributing towards this momentous goal of ours. On behalf of my fellow students, I thank you and we wish you success in all your endeavors.

Thank you again!

As the students disperse into their classrooms the principal and the custodian walk Morgan Jr. to inspect the science laboratory construction area. The student invitees head over to the banquet hall.

"Naomi, you were so outstanding up there, I wish I could be like that too," says Maya.

"Maya, that's easy, I will coach you when we get the time."

"Please Naomi."

"You look so pretty today, with that colorful hijab, it looks so comfortable too."

"Yes, the material is chiffon, it gives a comfortable feeling."

"Hey, what about me, nobody commented about my tuxedo," says Juliet.

"Of course, you too, Girl! And you too, Sara. The two of you look as if you're top executives of a big corporation."

"Thank you, Naomi, you were something else, wow!" says Sara.

"You think so!"

"But nobody asked me to sing today," Sara says with playful sniffles.

"They're saving you for tomorrow Sara … are you ready with a victory song too."

"About that, what time are we meeting at the stadium tomorrow, we need to be there early," reminds Sara.

"I didn't think of that," says Maya.

"No problem, we'll sit together at brunch, then let's plan it out. We have time though" suggests Sara.

"Girls, we've been planning all month for tomorrow."

As the students enter the banquet hall, Naomi sees Mr. Anderson and two other teachers helping with the arrangements. Mr. Anderson is happy and energetic, and

Naomi hears another teacher say to Mr. Anderson, "I heard that you are back in your department," and Mr. Anderson replies, "Yes, I am alive again!"

Naomi, Maya, and Sara look at each other; and noticing their excitement, Juliet says, "Did I miss something?"

Sara says, "We are happy that Mr. Anderson is teaching us again. Bye Miss Pet!"

"A whole lot of happiness!" Maya adds.

Deep inside, Naomi is happy that she got Morgan Jr. to speak to Miss Shepherd about reinstating Mr. Anderson. – the bargaining power Miss grace was speaking to her about!

She is pleased that fate created an encounter with her and Morgan Jr., the day she met him bringing in the plaque to school. When they were trying to clean both sides of the plaque, she had the opportunity of informing Morgan Jr. that Mr. Anderson was Utter's favorite teacher, and sadly, Utter lost his favorite teacher due to a lapse of judgment by the school.

"One case closed!" Naomi whispers to herself. "Now for the big case!"

(28) Encounter

That was not bad, right, Utter!" Naomi and Utter walk through the school corridor heading towards the exit. Naomi is carefree and Utter gaining self-assurance.

"Hey Utter, do you know that a butterfly is riding on your back."

Utter tries to randomly swat his back with his hands.

"Wait Utter, you will hurt the butterfly. Let's step outside first."

When they are outside the school building, Naomi gently gathers the butterfly to her fingers and notices the elegance and mysticism of this sublime animation. She holds the butterfly above her head, and the butterfly circles around them and rises high and departs into the glaring sun.

"Son! Lex! I was waiting to take you home."

They realize Morgan Jr. waiting outside the school building, he is in the driver's seat and Naomi notices Utter ignoring his father.

Naomi does not want an opportunity for a bonding moment between father and son to go waste; also, believing that she may convince Morgan to work harder in getting Utter's mother free, she decides to be a catalyst in the father and son relationship.

"Hi Mr. Morgan, we were walking to the bus stop."

"I was waiting to drop you home, get in."

"That's very nice of you Mr. Morgan."

Then nudging Utter towards the car, "Your dad wants to give us a ride, now we don't have to take the bus."

Utter hesitates to move towards his father's car, but Naomi insists. "Utter, I am your attorney, remember. And we have a case to win, so please get in."

Utter squinting his eyes at Naomi, opens the rear door, slightly bowing and ushers her towards the seat.

"Thank you, Utter, what a gentleman, holding the door for a lady."

Utter sits next to Naomi, and Morgan drives. Naomi wants to convince Morgan to help Sophia, she has got a small window of opportunity, and she wants to make the best use of it.

"This is a nice car, Mr. Morgan!" Naomi pausing, "it's very comfortable."

Morgan focusses more on his driving, but she notices him glancing at Utter through the rear mirror.

"So, Mr. Morgan, why are you driving today, don't you have someone to drive for you?"

"Yes sweety, I gave him the rest of the day off. I must make an important trip tomorrow morning; I want my driver to be well-rested."

"That's very nice of you Mr. Morgan. Everybody in school said that you're a genuinely nice person, and your son is lucky to have a dad like you."

Morgan smiles. Utter pushes Naomi's foot with his foot, and Naomi hits his foot back with hers.

"Naomi, I notice you call him Utter, is it supposed to mean anything."

Utter, once again pushes Naomi's foot with his, and this time Naomi holds down his foot with hers.

"Yes, 'U' stands for unique, the 'Ts' stands for talking is tortuous, and 'E' stands for exclusive."

"Then what does 'R' stand for?"

"'R' stands for reassurance, we may reinterpret it as hope."

"That's mighty!"

She says to Utter in a soft voice, "Names evolve too."

"Now that makes sense, you say it so fast I couldn't catch it at the luncheon, and that other kid who was with you said it means something special, I was confused."

Utter manages to pull his foot free; thereafter, he does not try to stop her.

"You know Mr. Morgan, when I first met him in school, he was so sad …You know how a son feels when he misses his mom, right! … right Mr. Morgan?"

The question struck Morgan into a surge of bygone emotions, emotions shuddering him into the depths of his own past, the past he had suppressed for years. No one had dared to broach the subject of his mother, the woman he had lost when he was just as old as his own son now. Naomi's words resonate with memories of those days spent in the sterile, antiseptic environment of the hospital, fully aware that the clock was ticking down to their inevitable separation.

His father was in prison, distant, and perhaps unable to bear the weight of his son's pain. Relatives showed little care or concern, and his friends remained conspicuously absent, too proud to visit the son of a disgraced man. His mother's passing had been less about her ailment and more about the heartache that consumed her. Thereafter, his father's lips remained sealed on the subject, an unspeakable and heart-rending topic that was a shadow over their lives. Sophia, in her wisdom, had chosen never to broach the delicate matter, preferring silence over painful conversations.

Now, years of pent-up memories and unspoken grief surged within Mr. Morgan, threatening to overflow in the presence of Naomi and his own son. He vowed in that moment never to let his son endure the same desolation and despair that had haunted his own youth.

He hears Naomi speak again, "Your son was feeling so sad, so to cheer him up, I called him Utter, that was so funny, and he liked that name. Now, everybody calls him that."

He feels that his son has a true friend, and he sees the strength Naomi dedicates towards his son's progress. He himself was in the same condition when his mother passed and when his father incarcerated, and how he longed for somebody's intervention when he was at the threshold of emotional collapse. He remembers his high school graduation, walking out during the ceremony; for everybody, it was the beginning of something new, but for him, it was the beginning of nothing to look forward to. He remembers a family following him outside, a man and a woman carrying a baby.

The man said, "Son, don't leave. The ceremony is not over yet."

Ignoring the man, he hurried off, when the man spoke again, "We know your father, he asked us to be with you today."

He was confused, but they caught his attention.

"I am Asher Williams; I am a friend of your father. This is my wife Audre, and this is my daughter Tamira, we came to celebrate your graduation."

He remembers not knowing what to do next.

"If you are not in a mood to go back inside, we will go get something to eat," his wife said.

He recalls how Asher's family took care of him when he felt broken and how they nurtured his emotions with their kindness and generosity.

"Thank you, Naomi, for doing what you do. What motivates you! … What drives you to do what you do!"

He hears no response.

Morgan, speaks again, "What gives you this much energy?"

Naomi says, "My greatest wish, Mr. Morgan, is that he'll get his mom back, and he will be happy once again."

Morgan grapples with the knowledge that both Naomi's request and his son's heartfelt wish are within reach, all because he is aware of Sophia's innocence in the alleged crime. The cruel irony of Naomi's wish is crippling him, it mirrors his own wish to secure Sophia's freedom—a desire that haunted him ever since the accident. However, the daunting question looms: How can he unveil the truth to anybody?

Sophia resents him for his absence, Olivia's anger simmers due to his failure to check on Sophia, and his son bears a grudge against him for not actively working to release his mother. Confronting Sophia during her time of suffering becomes a seemingly impossible challenge, especially when he must admit that he's been concealing the truth. How could he confess that he knows her innocence yet allows her to endure an undeserved sentence?

In his agonizing contemplation, Morgan ultimately concluded that perhaps the best course of action is to refrain from visiting Sophia, allowing her to hold onto her beliefs, no matter how painful that decision may be for everybody.

However, with the new developments in the case, Sophia may have a finite chance of becoming free. He thinks of sharing the latest legal developments on Sophia's case with his son and Naomi.

"Actually, Naomi, we have a little hope of getting his mom out, I didn't even tell him because his grandmother and I didn't want to get him too excited, because we still don't know the outcome."

"Wow! That's so nice."

From the rear-view mirror, Morgan sees Naomi and his son hi-five each other, Morgan sees a smile on his son's face, a rare moment ... If only his son knew the truth!

"Now don't get too excited," he continues, "it all depends how things work."

"When is this supposed to happen, Mr. Morgan?"

He does not want to tell them that it may take place the following day, because he's not sure what the judge may decide.

"Sometime next week," he replies.

What would have Father done in this situation, how many times have Father taken the blame for errors Father did not cause. Father tried only to correct those errors just to give a lesson. How could he be like Father! Who was Naomi referring to in her speech, the analogy seems familiar!

"Naomi in your lovely speech, you said you once knew a man who was lost and was looking for his son, was it somebody you knew."

Naomi remains silent, which prompts his curiosity. He feels that Naomi was referring to his father and does not want to reveal it to him; but how could she have known about the last days of his father, the man he avoided during his last days.

"Is it a big secret, Naomi?" he probes.

"Mr. Morgan, this may not be the best of time to speak about it, but if you insist, I will tell you."

"Please, go ahead."

"The man was your father, Mr. Morgan."

He turns back for a moment to see Naomi's closed eyes and his son pressing her hand. He wonders how the memory of his father could disturb Naomi so much.

"I am sorry, I didn't mean to upset you, I was only curious."

"I am all right, Mr. Morgan, it is just that I knew your father when I was little, I called him grandpa Hope. He was a good man."

"Then you remember him well."

"Mom used to get a pain in her back pushing my stroller down Hope Avenue when the buses were not running. When the bus started running down Hope Avenue, she didn't get that pain anymore, and she felt happy."

"I remember that."

"When we moved to that new house, the one we lost, it was Grandpa Hope that organized the party. You were there too, can't you remember?"

"I remember."

"Then one day I met Grandpa Hope on a train, I think he recognized me, but he seemed delusional, and he spoke to me about you. I know well that he was sad as if something had hurt him too much, and I regret not knowing how to help him out."

They arrive at their destination; Naomi and his son get out of the car. He has one more question for Naomi.

"Naomi, when was it that you met him on a train."

"The day he died!"

"Gosh! What exactly did he tell you?"

"He wondered how you'd be remembered."

Naomi tries to tell him something else, but his son pulls her away towards his grandmother's apartment building.

He leaves them and drives off home. In the morning, he walked into that school as a hero; and in the evening, he is returning home in fragments.

The encounter with Naomi drives him towards self-reflection.

Father's last moments in life should have been spent with him. Instead, Father dies alone feeling abandoned. Yet how amazing, a moment before Father dies, he passes a message to a little girl, a message that he may have never understood if received at that time. Receiving that message today provides him with a better self-reflection of himself, about what he has done in the past and about what he will do in the future.

How would he want people to remember him, does he want people to remember him as the self-made rich man who abandoned his father, wife, and child; or would he want to be remembered as how people remember his father?

It is not easy, for he is not his father. Father never faced the conflict like the one faced now.

His conflict is knowing the truth but being unable to reveal that truth, his conflict is choosing between two people he holds dear – his Sophia and his Lex.

(29) The Game

Naomi gets out of the car carrying a stack of t-shirts.

"Dads, meet me at this gate when the game ends, please come five minutes early, and after the game, if you see Utter wandering around this gate, hold him until I come."

"Yes, captain!"

"Bye, Dads, love you."

"Good luck on the game, Baby Girl."

"We will win, Dads!"

"Love you, Baby Girl … what time do I come here?"

"I don't know, figure it out, Dads," Naomi hurries off into the stadium.

"Yes, captain!"

The Thanksgiving Eve football game is about to hurl; Admirable Academics High school's football team, the Cat-O-Pults, meet the visiting team. The visiting team remains undefeated thus far, and so are the Cat-O-Pults; it is a showdown for both teams because, at the end of the game, one team will remain undefeated. Fans arrive, and the teams are warming up on the field. The stadium has more A. A. High School fans than visitors. The stadium is ornate in green, magenta, and gold sails fluttering in the wind.

Utter sits among the spectators hoping Jaylen would add to his touchdown passes and Naomi would join him soon. Juliet is lost among the raves of cheerleaders.

"Utter, come on, join our group," is Naomi's voice, as he feels a tap on his shoulder.

Naomi, in a Cat-O-Pults t-shirt, hands him one too. "Put it on if you want, but join us, we are over there."

Utter joins Naomi's group, and they welcome him with fist-bumps and hi-fives. He finds them all happy and ecstatic, and they welcome him as if they have known him for a long time. This is his first sporting event after leaving the hospital, it is overwhelming, but Naomi's support and the students' friendly gestures towards him, are pacifying. The group wears Magenta t-shirts with the Cat-O-Pults' logo highlighted on their chests. The logo is a side view illustration of a single-horned Smilodon leaping over a horizontal football; in the bottom elliptical half sphere of the football are the characters that spell out, Cat-O-Pults. Utter gets a huge letter 'O' made from XPS-foam and painted in gold. spectators are rapturous, and he wishes to own at least a single scream.

The marching bands, the school chorus, and cheerleaders do their opening performances. Sara leads the National Anthem: her vibrant voice raves through the field and everybody stands at attention, everybody facing the Flag, and with their right hands over their beating hearts. After the virtue of that solemn moment, it is rapture at the stadium when the clock sets to zero.

The visiting team wins the toss and plans the kickoff. The visitors, the green shirts, are in a collinear formation and the Cat-O-Pults wearing their magenta shirts, are in defense. The spectators' chant, "A A, A A," exhilarates the kick-off. The commotion raves as the ball catapults towards the receiver, the receiver snakes forward and brushes through players until Jaylen tackles him. The crowd roars.

"That guy is so perfect," says a spectator.

The visitor's mascot and the Cat-O-Pults' mascot dance a few feet away from the gridiron, and the Cat-O-Pults' mascot somersaults.

Spectators chant, "go A A, go A A, go A. A. go Cat-O-Pullllts!"

Nine groups of cheering squads are in position around the stadium, each holding a gold alphabetical character carved off XPS-foam. They chant in sequential order.

The First group chants 'C' and the stadium hears them. In similar poise, the next group chants 'A', and the following group yells, 'T.'

"It is us now," cries Naomi, and the group yells 'O,' trying to outdo the other groups.

The chanting continues, until the word Cat-O-Pults circles around the arena. The chanting continues and continues. No team gets the advantage over the other, and the game stays that way until halftime.

During halftime Utter walks down the steps heading to the rest area, on arrival at the rest area, he needs to wait for his turn among the crowd. Inside the rest area, he hears the rumble occurring outside, and the rise of action signals the end of halftime. He puts on the t-shirt Naomi gave him, and hurries out of the rest area, hoping to get to the game fast. But he accidentally elbows an oncoming spectator while taking the turn out of the rest area. The elbow collision sends a painful pulse up his hand, startling him.

"Yo! Watch yourself," yells out the spectator.

The other person who accompanies the spectator adds, "Who does he think he is!"

Utter raises his hands in apology, although his hand still electrifies with pain.

"Hey, aren't you that Morgan guy's son who woke up." says the other person, pushing Utter. Utter feels the coldness of the wall on his back.

"He has that same arrogance as his father, and a scammer like his father too."

"Gabriel let's go. We got a game to watch," says the person who got jabbed by Utter's elbow, and turning to Utter, says, "just watch where you are going … OK!"

But the other person, holding onto Utter's t-shirt, explains to his friend, "Jose, you don't know what it's like to be scammed. His father took everything we had, we got thrown out like animals when our house went into foreclosure, and who buys it again when we are on the streets. His father! And for a cheaper price."

Jose releases Gabriel's grip on Utter's shirt, saying "Gabriel, it's not his fault, people are watching, let him go."

As Utter walks away, he hears Gabriel screaming, "His father then paints our house and sells it to make more money. He put us into misery and sold our misery for a profit."

Utter goes up the stairs, with his emotions in distress; It is not the physical assault that distorts him, it is by what he hears about his father. He notices that he has dropped his shirt on his way back to his seat but is too perplexed to go looking for his lost shirt. He sits trying to watch the game, but the game is a blur to him. He looks for Jaylen but finds him lost on the field, He looks for Juliet, but she too is lost among the cheerleaders. He sees Naomi waving the 'O' and cheering with her group.

"Don't give up A A Cat-O-Pults," she calls. "Please don't give up!"

The game and its ecstasy become an animation to him: noisy moving shapes of green with tones of magenta and gold. He tries to focus but fails, and the football moves from magenta to green and back to magenta. Within the distortion, he still hears Naomi's voice close by.

The magenta shapes on the gridiron, clutter and expand with the green shapes not giving up. Players crouch forward, he spots Jaylen, and the display begins the countdown. The points still stand at zero for each side. twelve seconds left, Jaylen receives the snap from center, a magenta shirt runs towards the end zone, and the crowd roars in excitement; alas, Jaylen fumbles, and the crowd make a horrible moan as if the sun sank instantly below the horizon; Jaylen recovers though, silencing the crowd, then stepping back, attempts to make the throw, but that three-second fumble delay makes the magentas and the greens collide, the crowd row and moan again, and Jaylen is lost between the players, but the ball is instantly picked up by a green shirt who snakes all the way towards the end zone and leaps for a touchdown.

The visitors spike in ecstasy; Cat-O-Pults are stunned into silence in disbelief. The green shirts dance, the magenta shirts fall, the Cat-O-Pults agonize, and Naomi cuddles the 'O.'

The Greens celebrate around the gridiron; yet, carrying disappointment, the magenta and gold sails decay and evaporate into the evening.

(30) Surprise

Naomi sits embracing the 'O' which is ripped; her head bent down, her eyes closed, and is desperately trying to hold onto her tears.

Utter stands next to her wanting to say, "It's not the end of the world."

He wants to say something to comfort her, yet what could he say to the tough girl, to the tough girl who gave strength to him, to the noble friend who has brought him so far. Her friends wait for her on the main aisle, and he gestures to them that he will take care of her.

Maya shakes her head refusing to leave, and Sara gestures to him indicating that she is waiting too.

Reluctantly and gradually, the other students head towards the gates in slow steps, turning back from time to time to check on Naomi.

He lays his hand on her shoulder and says, "Don't worry Naomi, let's go."

Naomi looks at him spontaneously, and asks, "Did you speak to me?" Her eyes still smothered in tears, she gets up and looks around.

"Did you say my name," she asks, pulling the 'O' which now splits in two, and the bottom part falls in-between the seats.

Did words come out of his mouth, or did she hear somebody else call her; then, if somebody did call, why didn't that person call her again? Clearly, she heard a voice that called her name, and he heard it too; was that voice from his vocals? He picks the fallen part of the 'O' still thinking of the mysterious voice they both heard. He walks towards the center aisle where Maya and Sara are waiting. Naomi follows him.

"Did the others leave?" She asks the two girls. They point to the others moving further ahead.

Naomi tries to keep up the pace with the others, and seeing her walking in their direction, they wait for her. Then, it is a long and silent walk to the gate, their chatter, their excitement, and their aspiration, laid to rest within the lamenting gridiron.

Naomi does not speak to Utter or her father on their way back home, by the end of the journey, she is asleep in the car, exhaling the day's exhaustion. Utter fist-bums Malcom and walks towards the apartment, feeling miserable that Naomi is sad, but also blissful that her parents are there to pamper her sadness. When would he experience such bliss, or when was the last time he experienced that bliss! He sees Grandma looking down from the apartment window, he knows she is waiting for him - waiting patiently until he comes home.

Getting off the elevator, he finds his apartment door open and hears a loud conversation and laughter between his father and Grandma. Are the day's surprises not over yet, he wonders, and hurries in. He finds Grandma seated at her favorite place at the dining table, his father on the opposite side, both grinning at him.

He can't remember the last time his father visited Grandma's apartment, he can't even remember the last time his father had a friendly conversation with Grandma, neither can he remember the last time he had a conversation with his father. He stands in front of them in doubt and in amazement.

"Hello Lex, my son!"

He hears a name that he hates but feels no emotion. He hears his father speaking to him and still, he feels no sentiment. Even Grandma's grin doesn't mean a sentiment because it is mixed with his father's grin; there is no anger, no remorse, no love, only the stillness and the darkness of the night outside.

"Sugarcane, I have a surprise for you, a Thanksgiving gift. Close your eyes!"

Utter closes his eyes and feels a soft pair of hands covering his eyes from behind. The breath of that familiar fragrance diffusing through the surroundings can belong to only one person he knows.

He says, "Mom!"

"Yes, my big son, I came home to you!"

Crying or laughing is not a response for him, sorrow or joy is neither a response for him, the stillness of the night just becomes packed with a band of animating musicians, the darkness of the night just becomes charmed with a cluster of gleaming costars, and he holds his most precious mother, never to let her go.

"Tell me everything my big son, oh! how much I missed you."

Sophia and Utter do not notice Morgan stepping out and Olivia following him close behind. Olivia sees two officers standing towards the end of the passageway.

"I will be good, thank you for taking care of my son …please take care of my wife too … You are a good person … I am lucky to have you as a mother-in-law … I love you!"

Olivia never imagined that it may come to a day when she would say again, "I love you too, Morgan!"

She is sad as he departs, "I appreciate you finally taking responsibility for your actions and freeing my daughter, my prayers are with you, may God give you strength!"

Morgan walks towards the end of the corridor, one officer handcuffs Morgan, and the two officers escort Morgan towards the elevator.

Olivia steps inside and closes her apartment door.

(31) Journey

The transport vehicle exits from Olivia's apartment complex, entering Narrow Hope Avenue, and Morgan sits behind. Olivia's apartment window reflects a yellow hue, he imagines mother and son in embrace, mother and daughter in embrace, and the smiles on their faces.

"If they only knew the truth!" he whispers to himself.

He passes 704 Narrow Hope Avenue and sees the younger him and a sweeter Sophia with baby Lex, walking under the moonlight, along the side of the house towards the basement entrance, the basement that was warm, loving, and friendly. The basement he first shared with Father until Sophia moved in, and the basement where they planned their future.

"Sophia, could you have foreshadowed this day!"

The traffic light pauses him at a cross street branching off Hope Avenue. He sees homes that he built and sold, standing close to each other on either side of the street and their windows illuminating alongside the rows of streetlights. Homes smirking at him and frowning at him. Most buyers got their mortgages from his lending company that he dissolved, those frowning homes went into foreclosure, and families evicted. How did those people feel when they became homeowners holding subprime mortgages, how did they feel when the real-estate market was crashing, how did they feel when they could not pay the banks and were thrown out onto the streets – did he ever find out?

"How will those poor unfortunates remember me?"

Mothers, wives, and children, brutally thrown against the wayside. No, he did not feel their pain, he overcame that pain when he was thrown out of his own childhood home when his mother was dying. A long time ago he was that helpless teen – not anymore. He repurchased those failing homes for a cheaper price and resold those homes for a profit.

"Mother, would you recognize me if you saw me now!"

The old brick house at the next stop sign is for sale; that's the third time within the last five years somebody is selling that house. It belonged to that old couple, whom he offered that huge high-interest loan. The couple had lived all their lives, the old man was a friend of his father, so the old man signed the paperwork without hesitation. The maple tree in the backyard overshadows the house and the old man guise as the branches contrasting in the shimmer of moonlight, but how could that be, that old man is dead. That old couple who was leaving that home for their daughter, that old couple who were living on their social security but needed to do renovations before handing that house to their daughter; how he made father offer them a loan to do their overpriced renovations, how he used Segarra to do his underhand paperwork, and how he secretly used his construction company to do those renovations and to take back all that money.

"Father, if you only knew!"

When that old couple's mortgage payment readjusted, they could not pay back their loan, they called him countless times, but he did not take their call; if they called Father how could Father have picked that call, Father was in the hospital. They say that the old man died of a heart attack the day the marshals showed up on their doorstep, they describe how that old woman wailed.

"Wonder what happened to the old woman, perhaps she still walks within the shadows of Narrow Hope Avenue. Will I ever know her name!"

The vehicle makes a right turn onto First Main Street, neon lights flashing, cheery crowds on the street, Antonio and Sally are busy at the pizzeria.

"Antonio, my greatest friend, I need a favor from you. Only you could do it for me."

At the end of the storefront, at the corner pub, he imagines father and John having a drink; he hears John relating to father, why the old storefront had to be sold off for cheap.

"But John, you accused me of living off my father. How could you think that way, John! Did you know that I was smarter than you, you'll never find out! If you only knew that it was Sally's husband whom you looked down on, the man I hired to pose off as a building department officer … he threatened you with building violations … Ha John, thank you for giving me that old storefront for cheap. John, thank you for throwing Antonio out of your pub that day, you did a favor when you threw him out. You saw a fallen man who was worthless, but I saw a fallen man who could rise!"

The transport vehicle gathers momentum, the cuffs on his hands put him in discomfort; how could Segarra have been carrying that cuffed briefcase!

"Segarra, you're dead, but you still haunt me."

He sees Lex coming between him and Sophia during arguments; like a sponge, absorbing the hindrance, absorbing the follies, and absorbing the rage. He remembers going through Lex's text messages after the accident and discovering all the conversations Lex had with Juliet about the Segarra incident, Lex's fear for the safety of Sophia, and Lex's feelings about his lost grandfather.

"My son, you hate me so much, you think everything happened because of me, and you took matters into your own hands."

The vehicle enters the expressway, heading towards his new home. For how long, he doesn't know.

"Son, I saw that tranquilizer dart lying in your backpack."

Morgan feels like a failure, the same way he felt just before coming to New York.

"I didn't do it, your mom wouldn't have ever done it, so the only person who did it is you, and I will cover for you my son because I failed you as your father!"

(32) Utter and Mom

There is happiness and surprise that Utter said, "Mom," and that delight is seen in Grandma when she exalts her hands, looks above, and chants, "thank you!"

He tries to speak again but fails, and annoyance sets in.

"That's your first word, soon we won't be able to stop you, my Sugarcane. So, relax now!" Grandma consoles.

Utter, crouched on the tabletop, his chin resting, and hands resting crossways. Mom and Grandma sit on either side, contemplating Morgan Jr.'s fate. Utter feels anxious that he can't continue speaking but feels happy, reunited with his mother. And the conversation between Grandma and Mom about his father is an exchange of words that have no depth to him. He gives ear to their conversation, although for him, the moon is bright outside, no clouds overshadowing, and no raindrops mocking him.

"I will never wish anything bad for either of you, but I was angry with Morgan, so angry about what he did to you," Grandma pausing and pointing, "and so angry for what he did to him."

"Mommy, did you know that I was coming home?"

"No, but Morgan called me on the way to see you there, 'It's long overdue,' I thought to myself.

He asked me what Lex would like for Thanksgiving, and I told him the only thing that Lex would like is to see his mother back home."

"Oh, Mommy!"

"Morgan said that the investigators and your attorney would also be meeting there, and the promise would be delivered."

"Did you ask him how?"

"No, I did not, because I knew you were innocent, and that truth can't be changed. I had faith that you would come home, so I began preparing dinner for everybody."

"Mommy!"

"Were you surprised to see him over there?"

"Yes, I was, because he never visited me before."

"Did Morgan tell you that he was going back, or you found out when you came here?"

"He asked me to go home; he said that he has things to take care of. I didn't know that he had to be escorted by the officers."

"While you were in the shower, we had a long conversation. It's funny, until this morning I was angry with him, now I feel sorry for him. He asked me to take care of the two of you, he thanked me for all that I did for Sugarcane. He spoke about his father, there was remorse in that tone, and he said a lot more, my Sophy. A lot more!"

"I don't know what to feel – sad – angry - hurt – dejected - I think confused is a better word. At least I am with my sweet son here," Mom rubs his back as he still lays crouched on that table.

"Now, look at him, he looks so exhausted. Sugarcane, go, get ready for bed, Mom is not going anywhere."

Mom and Grandma's chatter continues, he hears them while in the shower, he hears them in the room, and he hears their echo in his sleep.

It is morning, he is back with them on Grandma's table, seated outside Grandma's cottage watching the sunrise: a setting like the one from a fairytale read to him by Mom a long time ago, as a bedtime story. From the door of the cottage begins a gravel path that leads to the forest beyond. He follows the gravel path, Mom and Grandma are happy and laughing at each other's comments, and they do not see him walk into the forest. He walks until he cannot hear their laughter, the silence contributes an eerie feeling making him want to turn back, but the path behind him is gone, leaving only a path to move forward.

He hears a voice, "Lex you can't hide from me, I am back." The voice is familiar, but those words rebound from all directions.

He decides to run along that serpentine gravel path, where the trees loom tall on either flank, their branches reaching out to caress him. Strands of sunlight pierce the forest's embrace, casting blinding beams across his determined face and he maintains his frantic pace. Fatigue bites at his weary limbs, yet he has no choice but run to escape his relentless pursuer. Nature itself is against him, with branches and twigs maliciously slapping at him, as though aligning with his foe.

Amidst the frantic run, the sound of approaching footsteps echoes through the woods, closing the gap between him and his pursuer. Panic courses through him; In a moment of dread, he dares to glance behind, and spots the ominous rustling of branches, a sign of his adversary drawing near.

"You can't run from me Lex; you don't know what lies ahead."

Utter arrives at a three-way junction, and the path to the left has obstructions of jagged-edged rock. Seeing a clear path on the right, he bolts through, only to find himself sinking in a puddle of mud. Each step Utter takes, he sinks a little deeper. He looks for the pursuer, the pursuer's face is clear, he wears a tuxedo and reddish glasses, a briefcase is cuffed to his hand.

"You can't outrun me," says Segarra.

The words reecho while Utter goes deeper into the mud; he is now waist down in the mud, and in front of him lies a river, but there is no bridge to cross the river. Being stuck in the mud, he sees Juliet waving at him from the opposite bank of the river.

"Lex, you have to come out and swim across," she says.

"I can't! I am stuck in this mud."

"I can't swim well, Lex, I can't swim well! I can't come to you, pull yourself out."

"Now to wait until you go down … look how deep you got yourself into," smirks Segarra.

"Lex don't listen to him, he can't hurt you, you have to pull yourself out," Juliet screams from the other bank.

"She's lying to you. Lex, do you remember this?"

Segarra shows an object, it is not clear at first, but staring into the object, it takes the shape of a familiar tranquilizer dart. Now, Utter remembers Valentine giving it to him, and remembers why.

"Let me remind you. Lex, do you remember how I told you that you or your mommy haven't seen the last of me yet. I thought you would go crying back to Mommy, but no, you became the tough son. Look at what happened to you for acting tough, you got yourself stuck in this mud. Now, who is there to save you?"

Juliet screaming louder, "Lex, don't listen to him, pull yourself out, you can do it."

"I can't, I am trying."

Segarra laughs, "Don't even try to escape, accept who you are, you lost. I won once, and I will win again."

"Lex, if you don't pull yourself out, I am swimming to you."

"Do you hear that, I am keeping my promise to you," says Segarra.

"Juliet no!"

Juliet dives into the river and swims towards the other bank, the current is strong, and Juliet drifts away. Desperately trying to crawl out of the mud, Utter sees a bunch of weeds growing adjacent to the mud. He leaps to hold on to the weeds, he fails at first but holds on at the second try. Utter pulls himself out of the mud and finds Segarra standing Infront of him.

"You're not saving her; I have to keep my promise to you."

Utter pushes Segarra to the side, and Segarra's reddish glasses fall into the mud. Segarra glares at him, and utter glares back. Utter sees his reflection through Segarra's eyes, but Utter is not afraid anymore.

Utter dives into the water, "I will save you, Juliet!"

The current is strong and Juliet drifts further and further away. He can't keep up with her.

"Juliet ... Juliet!" In a louder voice, "Juliet!"

"Lex, wake up ... Lex, wake up!"

"Mom?"

"My poor child, did you have a nightmare?"

"Mom, where am I?"

"You're with me honey, you are with me here, at Grandmas … Does this happen to you often?"

His heartbeat rises and he holds on to his mother until he calms down. His mother wants to get him something to drink, but he refuses.

"It is three in the morning, get more sleep; I'll be next to you ... you don't worry."

"Thanks, Mom!"

Mom sits on the side of his bed, in a little while he feels that she is lying next to him, and the rest of the night is calm.

Olivia, waking up in the morning, finds mother and son peacefully asleep next to each other. Saying a prayer in her heart for her daughter and grandson, then saying another prayer for Morgan Jr., Olivia begins her day's errands.

(33) It is ok!

Jay! Why are you hiding your face from me, there's no shame in losing a game!" There is a moment of silence.

"I don't understand why you and your insane dad must make a whole big deal over a silly ball game," Audre calls out. "Jay, and everybody who is listening, I am repeating this; it was only some ball game!"

Asher hears Audre say as she leaves Jaylen's room, "It is Thanksgiving, and I need both of you to get your act together because we are having guests tonight."

Asher's home is in chaos on Thanksgiving Morning since his wife is not happy about his and Jaylen's conversation about the Thanksgiving Eve football game. In Audre's opinion, the football coach and all those who have negative comments about her son's performance, are out of their minds for picking on her sweet son. And Asher, being the father, seems to agree with everybody else except his son.

"You know Asher, if they know so much about that rough game, and they can do better than Jay, ask them to play for that team. Let my Jay do his studies and get involved in something else where he'll be appreciated, then he doesn't have to be stressed over this silly ball game," Audre roars as she moves briskly into the pantry.

Asher follows her into the pantry, "But honey, you don't understand."

The banging of drawers, the clanking of cutlery, and Audre's stomping footsteps, signals to Asher that a whole day may be destroyed if Audre does not calm down soon. He and his wife's battle began the previous night when he was speaking to Jaylen about his fumble that cost the Cat-O-Pult's the game. The conversation between him and his son had become rough, he can't remember how, but can remember that Audre had intervened.

Audre continues, "If I hear one more conversation about this between the two of you today, or you answer one more phone call from that bunch of people about my Jay, I am taking my children to Mom's and you can explain to your friends why we are not celebrating this year, and you can explain to Mom why she can't celebrate Thanksgiving with us, in our home."

"Agreed! ... Honey, what are we having for breakfast?"

Asher realizes that Audre is planning to use heavy artillery against him when she brings her mother into their little family dispute. Asher understands that the best way to bring about peace to such family disputes is through appeasement.

Asher noticed that his son was out of focus after halftime, and he wanted to find out why. He could not bear to hear what the spectators discussed about his son and all he wanted was for such an incident not to repeat. His son has his ego hurt, and it could be a reason why the conversation became rough. However, the error in the game had cost the team, and it was a game they were counting on Jaylen to be at his best. Now, Jaylen's teammates were blaming Jaylen for the loss. But Asher lost his cool when he saw Jaylen's face.

Audre is under stress because she must organize the family Thanksgiving celebration, and in addition to that, when everybody arrives home after the game, there is an explosion about something insignificant to her. What made the situation worse last night was his little Ash making fun of his big Jay for fumbling, and his big Jay, in a high-pitched rough voice asked little Ash to shut up, making little Ash run to his mother crying.

The final and undisputed conclusion made by family judge Audre about the previous night's rift is that it's Asher's fault for not being able to manage a situation with tact. And, when judge Audre gives a verdict, it's a difficult appeal.

"Asher, are you even listening?"

"What Honey!"

"Do you know you have a daughter!"

"Is that a question?"

"Good morning, Mom, good morning, Dad! What's going on here between the two of you?"

"My Baby Girl, I missed you!" Asher hugs his daughter Tamira." Ashton stands next to her clapping.

Father and daughter still hugging, "So, what's all this noise I hear," Tamira inquires.

"Your father is making a big issue about a football game Jay lost yesterday."

"Such a big commotion over a lost game?"

"Yes!" Audre conforms.

"Seriously Dad, was there a big bet involved?"

"No!" says Audre.

"Was it a choice between life and death?"

"That's what I asked."

"So, what's wrong in losing a game, somebody has to win, and somebody has to lose!"

"I said that too!"

Sometimes when the family gangs up against you, it is best not to stress your point of view. However, there is a situation that's bothering Jaylen, and he is determined to find out, even though the family may not agree.

"Asher, you didn't ask how your daughter just appeared at home."

"Hey dad, Mom picked me up from the airport last night, funny you were supposed to do that."

"With Jay's thing going on, I just got lost in it."

"Didn't I tell you!" Audre mentions.

"When I arrived, you were snoring. Dad, I saw empty bottles on the table, so I knew you were celebrating my arrival."

"Hee -hee-hee! I love you, my baby girl!"

"My poor Dad, everybody is hard on him." Tamira hugs him again.

His Baby Girl, the girl he loves so much and is so proud of; and to him, the prettiest, the smartest, the wisest, and the girl who grew up so fast.

"Who is coming tonight, Mom?"

"Veronica's family, Sally, and Sally's husband ... if he comes."

"Honey, I thought Olivia and Sophia's son were coming too."

"Utter," corrects Ashton, tittering.

"That's not his name, it's Lex!" recorrects Audre.

Ashton leans onto Tamira.

Audre continues, "There is a problem with that! Ramona invited them, and Olivia wanted to go there. See, Ramona's kid and Lex are quite close too, they study together also."

"I remember Naomi, she must be all big now. Did they call you today, Mom?"

"Yes, Olivia called me a couple times this morning, I was too busy to pick up."

Audre continues, "Besides this is the first time after a long time they have been invited by Ramona, Olivia doesn't want to miss it for anything. She thinks that this is a chance for the two families to put their past behind and move forward."

"It will be difficult though, for what Ramona went through, but somebody has to try," Asher acknowledges.

"Morgan can do something for them, Ash, you gotta remind him of that."

"Yes, I made that request a while ago, old Morgan made that same request as soon as they were facing problems. In his arrogance, junior said, if he did it for them, they may think that it was his fault and everybody who went into foreclosure would be knocking at his door."

"That guy! Everybody who gets mixed up with him loses. No offense Dad."

"None taken my girl, I agree with you. I have made plans to pull out, I am just waiting for pending deals to close to take my money out. I plan to get a little building for you to start your practice."

"Awe thanks dad, but I have to complete my residency which may take about three years."

"Good, but we can start early because time flies. Look at how fast your brothers are growing up."

"Talking about my brothers, let me check on Jay," and Tamira walks up the stairs to get to Jaylen's room.

Jaylen opens his eyes, the time 11:17, and since there is light in the room, he knows it is still morning. He remembers speaking to his mother earlier, he may have snoozed off after the conversation. There are multiple text messages on his phone and multiple unanswered phone calls, and he feels the phone vibrate again. It is Juliet, he's not in a mood to pick up. She too has called him multiple times, and he scrolls to find a text message from her.

Hi Jay, just to let you know that whatever happened at the game yesterday, does not change who you are. You are still that great football player on the way to stardom. Even the greatest of heroes make unforgivable mistakes, yours was not that severe. Therefore, show everybody that you have it in you to rise and do better. See you later, love, Juliet!!

Also, call Lex, you won't believe what has happened.

Jaylen hears a mix of footsteps on the stairs leading towards his room, they are not stomping, so he rules out Mom and Dad, the soft scamper should be his little brother, but wonders to whom the other footsteps belong to. The soft rattle on his door lock is definitely Ashton, and Jaylen opens the door.

"Hello, Jaylen Williams!"

"Sis?"

"Yes, your big sister arrived last night and found her star football player brother and her father snoring after an argument … now tell me what happened to your face."

"It was nothing!"

"So, did somebody from the other side punch you on your face?"

"No!"

"Then what happened?"

"Ok, it's those guys from school who were always bullying Lex … they didn't like me defending him."

"So, did they bully Lex at the game?"

"No, they made fun of me … they said that I became a loser because I was friends with a loser."

"So, is that true? … of course not!"

Jaylen nods his head.

"Then knowing the truth, you should have walked away. But no, you didn't have the courage to do that, you thought you must have the last word. They picked your weakest moment to taunt you, and you proved them right … now look at your face and cracked lip."

"It will heal!"

"Even the strongest have their weak moments, it's how you behave when you're weak that makes or breaks you."

"I am sorry, Sis!"

Alright, now shower up and meet us down ... and stop thinking about your lost game because you have more to win."

"Where's dad"

"He's in a good mood, he won't bother you. Not today. Anyway, Mom sent him out to get stuff for tonight. He wanted me to join him, but I must be with you guys to catch up. Now hurry up."

Jaylen picks up a towel and throws it around his shoulder and decides to read one more text.

It was good to be at the game, my first outdoor event in this life. Hey, you shouldn't win every game, you got to leave for the others too. As much as I would have liked to see you win, I am happy that you fought well. Brother, you played better than any player on either side. We need to do our best, we need to learn from our mistakes, and we need to learn how to move on. It is good to know that you can fall too, otherwise, you will never learn to rise. – Utter.

Also, a miracle happened, my mom came home!!!

"Mom, Sis," Jaylen screams, "Aunt Sophia is back home."

(34) Reunion

On Thanksgiving evening, a gentle tap at Ramona's door prompts her to open it, revealing Sophia on the other side. They both stand there, facing each other in silence, neither eager to be the first to speak. In the quiet of the moment, Sophia silently pleads for Ramona's forgiveness in her heart, while Ramona, also in her heart, offers her forgiveness. Physically, they remain unchanged, yet five years of guilt and anger have eroded their feelings toward each other. Sophia carries the weight of guilt, while Ramona bears the burden of anger. The fiery emotions within them could melt even the coldest glacier, yet no words are exchanged between them.

Malcolm decides to break the ice between the two former friends.

"Are the two of you standing in ceremony … no hugs and kisses … no hi or hello."

Both girls remain unmoved.

Malcolm attempts once again to take away the aloofness between the two, stands next to Ramona and greets Sophia.

"Happy Thanksgiving Sophia, nice to see you after a long time," then moving next to Sophia, playfully saying, "Happy Thanksgiving Ramona, nice to see you after a long time too."

The ice breaks, a little too much - Sophia breaks down, "Ramona I am sorry that I let you down."

In return, Ramona, brushing her own eyes with the middle and index finger, "I have moved on Sophia, we are doing fine. I hope you are fine too."

Ramona and Sophia sit next to each other on the couch, still not knowing what to say to each other. Malcolm understands that he will have to brighten the evening, so he decides to get help.

"Naomi! Baby Girl! Guess who's visiting. Naomi, do you hear me, where are you, Baby Girl?"

Malcolm hears Naomi's voice from her room, "Why are you screaming Dads, I am still getting dressed up."

"Guess who is here?"

"Have Utter and Grandma Olivia come already?"

"No, somebody else."

"Who is it then?"

"You got to see for yourself."

"Coming in a minute!"

Olivia and Utter walk in, and Olivia wishes the family, "Happy Thanksgiving Moni, happy Thanksgiving Malcolm. And where's my dear Naomi?"

"I am here," Naomi rushes out of her room saying, "happy thanksgiving Grandma Olivia," hugs Olivia.

Then and with a chirpy voice, "Happy Thanksgiving Utter!"

Naomi notices the other guest in their living room, for a moment she is speechless, and then overcoming her surprise, gasps, "Utter's Mom?"

Sophia walks up to her, "Hi Naomi, you have grown so big, how are you!"

Naomi, still in astonishment, gives into Sophia's hugs and compliments. Then Naomi sits next to Ramona on the sofa holding onto Ramona's arm and gazing at Sophia. Naomi feels she wants to cry, she feels that she wants to leap in delight, then she embraces her mother's arm and rests her chin on her mother's shoulder, still in shock. Ramona, moving her hand around Naomi, pulls her close. Naomi feels the serenity of her mother, so serene as if all other emotions in her mother is washed away.

"Turkey Time!" announces Malcolm.

"First, let's say a prayer in thanksgiving," advises Olivia.

"Good idea," responds Malcolm, "Olivia you lead."

The prayer is an intense and fervent moment for the families. Olivia is thankful that her daughter is exonerated and, she is thankful that her Sugarcane spoke his first word again when he said 'Mom' the previous night. Olivia is also thankful that Ramona and Malcolm can forgive Sophia's family for the heartaches caused in the past.

Malcolm is thankful for the great family he has and thankful that Ramona got her BSN, something she studied so hard for. Ramona and Sophia have much to say to each other but find it difficult to begin, and Utter being silent is obvious, but Naomi being silent is a rare occurrence.

Meanwhile, the Thanksgiving dinner at Asher's and Audre's home is merrier, with Tamira getting all the attention. The guests want to find out her future plans, Veronica wants career information so that she can guide Juliet, and Sally wants to find out if such a pretty and smart girl like Tamira has decided on somebody special yet.

After ample discussion, Tamira wanting everybody to take their attention off her, "Dad, you have good taste selecting furniture, I was admiring the details on this dining table."

"The wood is mahogany, it is Victorian style, and made in America. Little expensive, but sophisticated!"

The conversation at the dinner table takes a different turn when Asher receives a telephone call from the company attorney. He leaves the table for a moment and returns baffled. Asher reminds everybody how he was correct about Morgan being the catalyst in the murder of Segarra. Asher also informs the family that he must run the corporation during Morgan's absence.

"And you were planning to pull out on Monday," Audre reminds Asher.

"Now I can't do that, Sophia is just out, the kid is not ready, and I can't let down the old man. I am sure that old man is watching us from somewhere."

Antonio says, "Asher, fill us in about Boss Morgan's story."

"I don't know what got to him, but he confessed to putting Segarra in the trunk of Sophia's car. I think he wanted to do the right thing, he confessed ...Finally!"

Veronica being curious, "Olivia said that there is going to be a retrial because the prosecution felt that the jury may have been biased, and they were trying to get Sophia out on bail."

"Yes, but the judge had denied bail due to compelling evidence against Sophia and requested for the investigation to continue."

"Boss Morgan took the fault, to free Sophia!"

Asher continues with the information he has, "Yes, then Morgan confessed that he jabbed Segarra with the tranquilizer dart and put him in Sophia's car trunk only to check the documents that Segarra claimed he had. When he did not understand the documents, he set them on fire on the grill, and when Sophia came out of the house, noticing the grill on, she turned the grill off, leaving her fingerprints on the grill. He ran into the house when he noticed the surveillance cameras moving to readjust angles. Sophia was readjusting the surveillance cameras leaving her fingerprints on the controls."

"Did he say from where he found the tranquilizer dart?" asks Audre.

"I don't know, anyway, I plan to visit him next week, there's a lot to discuss."

Tamira sees Jaylen leaving the table. "Done already Jay?"

"Jay, now what's the matter? Come here!" Audre speaks to Jaylen.

"I am fine, Mom!"

Ashton tries to follow Jaylen, but Ashton is sent back to the table by Jaylen. "Go, finish your food!"

Asher and Juliet notice the sudden change in Jaylen after the Morgan family becomes the topic of discussion; Juliet believes that Jaylen's change in mood is due to his meeting with Valentine, but Asher can't make any connection. Asher wants to have a conversation with Jaylen; however, Asher is afraid that the conversation may erupt into another verbal mishap within the family. Juliet wants to subtly begin a conversation with Jaylen about the meeting with Valentine, and Asher thinks of obtaining help from Tamira. Juliet plans to speak to Jaylen at school, and Asher plans to speak to Tamira during the weekend.

(35) Discussion

Juliet is in school after the Thanksgiving break and is anxious to meet Jaylen to obtain answers. Not seeing him the previous day, and not seeing him in classes today, she texts him.

"Hey, are you not in school today?"

"No! why?"

"Are you at home?"

"No! why?"

"Where are you?"

"Why?"

Juliet feels that there is something wrong, she feels that she needs to speak to Jaylen personally.

"Jaylen, there is something important I got to tell you. Where are you?"

"At the doughnut place close to the bus stop, near our school."

"Wait for me there, I am coming."

"Are you going to skip class?"

"Haven't you skipped school?"

Juliet decides to skip class and meet Jaylen immediately. She has never skipped school before, but she feels the need to do so. However, she can't leave the school building without parental permission; therefore, she decides to take the stairs down to the boiler-room, since that door is a maintenance exit, no one may notice her leaving the building. She finds herself in luck when the maintenance crew are moving equipment through the boiler-room exit, and the safety agent assigned to the exit is having a conversation with another staff member. Unnoticed, she passes through the exit and shielded by a parked delivery truck, she finds herself on the street.

Arriving at the doughnut store, she finds Jaylen sipping a large latte while twitching with his phone. Juliet sits next to him to begin her interrogation.

"Why are you not in school Jaylen?"

"Why are you not in school Juliet?"

"I was in school, until I found out that you're not in school. So here I am. What's happening?"

Juliet wants to find out the cause of Jaylen's behavioral change, but Jaylen sees Juliet's arrival as an annoyance. He has just texted Valentine asking him for another bottle, and Valentine has promised delivery, this time for a price.

"I was not in a mood to do any work, Dad dropped me on top of the road, and instead of walking to school, I just walked here."

"Jaylen I can help, what's going on?"

"Nothing! … Can you get back to school now! I am fine."

"I am not leaving; I came here to help."

Jaylen irritated, "like you helped Utter, like how you fixed him up with Valentine?"

"Jaylen, I made a mistake, which was when we were in middle school, now I am sure we could find a better solution if we work together. Tell me, did Valentine threaten you?"

Observing Juliet's sincerity about her mistake and regretting being rude to her, Jaylen speaks in a soft voice.

"Valentine is not the issue here, he does not know the difference between adding and subtracting, it is that he helped me to solve Utter's case. I finally know the truth."

"What truth?"

He blurts out to Juliet, "Utter did it, Utter put that guy in the trunk!"

"Did Valentine say this, isn't it obvious that Valentine is lying."

"No, Valentine did not say it, I figured it out from what Valentine told me."

"But Mr. Morgan accepted the fault, right? He was my suspect all along."

"That's what's bothering me more, he took the fault for something Utter did. Added to the problem, I don't know what game Mr. Morgan is playing, and Dad is now the head of that company."

"Jaylen, can you slow down, let's go through this slowly. First, tell me what happened with Valentine."

"Valentine stole the tranquilizer dart from me and gave it to Utter. Utter did it, and that's what's bothering me."

"Did Valentine say that?"

"At first, he denied, later he admitted that he gave Utter the dart. If Valentine gave it to Utter, the only person who could have used it on that Segarra guy, is Utter."

"Then why did Mr. Morgan take the blame? So … you're telling Morgan is innocent and Utter did the crime. That's exaggerated."

"It is not, do you think Utter gave the tranquilizer dart to the father saying, 'Here Dad, use this on Segarra' and Mr. Morgan said, 'Thank you my son I will use this on Segarra'... could something like that happen Juliet?"

"No, that couldn't happen either. I see where we are going with this, but clearly, we are missing something."

"Utter is the suspect; I have no doubt about it. Sadly, he can't even remember what happened."

"Jaylen! Was that bothering you during that game? Is that why you were not at your best?"

Jaylen is not sure why he fumbled at the game, could it have been that he was out of focus due to knowing the truth. "Maybe! but I don't know."

Could it have been that Valentine's liquid that he took before the game, "No that can't be it."

He receives a text from Valentine. "I am here brother, what's Juliet doing with you?"

"Give me a minute Valentine, I will meet you outside."

"I got more deliveries to make my brother, can you hurry up and don't forget the money."

He pauses to reorganize his thoughts. "But when I heard Valentine's story my first suspect was Utter, I couldn't imagine Aunt Sophia innocently suffering in jail, and we can't do anything because we need to protect Utter. And I know, this bothered me a lot … did it cause me to fumble at the game, I don't know."

"Now, that Aunt Sophia is out … and we never liked Mr. Morgan … and we always suspected Mr. Morgan … and now that Mr. Morgan admits to the crime … why even bother."

"You got a point my girl, but I can't wrap my head around this. It's too much."

Valentine texts again, "Brother, are you coming out now?"

"Wait!"

"The case is closed Jaylen; the case is closed! Utter is free and Aunt Sophia is free! Can't you see - we won." Juliet's point of view takes off the pressure he feels, now what bothers him is his father's involvement in Morgan's problems.

"I know, but what if there is a catch in this. I think that there is a catch in this because Mr. Morgan never cared for Aunt Sophia, and now he suddenly cares. Dad wanted to move out of his company, but now Dad must run it. I am more worried for Dad that Mr. Morgan will get Dad into trouble."

"Jaylen, your dad is a smart man, nobody can dupe him. So, there is nothing you must worry about … Now, on the other hand … from what I see, the only person who is messed up is you! And we got to fix that! You have more to lose here, Not Morgan, not Utter, not even your dad, only you!"

Juliet's analysis may be correct, the change must happen within him, he should focus on himself rather than overwhelm himself with somebody else's problems.

Valentine again, "Are you coming out or not?"

Jaylen in surprise, "Hey! What's my sister doing here?"

"Yo Valentine, I will pick it up later, it is getting too crowded here."

"Brother, I came all the way for you. Don't let me down."

"I can't, there is a change in situation."

"Brother, I will leave because you're my friend, but you have to give me something extra for this hassle."

"Ok!"

(36) Sister Talk

Jaylen contemplates in surprise as Tamira walks up to them. "Hi, surprised to see me?" she inquires with a smile.

Jaylen is silent, not wanting to speak to his sister, but Juliet greets Tamira. "Hi!"

"You guys skipped school to secretly hang out here? If I were you guys, I would pick some other place far from school to hang out ... after skipping school," Tamira says.

Jaylen looking at Juliet, shakes his head.

"And … what were you two lovebirds whispering to each other about, hmm?"

"Sis, it's not what you think, but how did you know we were here?" he asks.

Tamira sits next to them, "Then what should I think?"

There is confusion in his mind on how Tamira got to the doughnut store, but Tamira seems as if she was expecting him to be at the store. He does not want to talk to Tamira hoping that she will leave, but Tamira sits facing them as if she has all the time to wait until he speaks. Juliet becomes anxious, her fingers sequentially tap on the table as the silence extends. He is anxious too; he has to overcome his emotional conflict between the truth and his loyalty to their friend whom they have been trying to help. The silence only extends his unease.

Unable to hold the silence much longer, he glares at Tamira, "What Sis, what are you looking at?"

Tamira moves her chair close to them and extends her hands, "Come to Sis, you can tell me anything. I can keep your secret."

"Sis, are you crazy, we are at a store, and I ain't little anymore."

"So shy to come to your Big Sis, but if I hadn't come here, the two of you would be smooching each other as if it's nobody's business."

"Stop! Sis, it's not what you're thinking."

Juliet blushingly tries to hide her laughter with her hands.

"Then convince me otherwise, my two love birds. Your Sis loves you both. Trust me, a lot more than you know."

Juliet explains to Tamira, "It is not what you think, we had something important to talk about."

"Tell me, Girl, what are you hiding?"

"Nothing!"

Tamira speaks, "Jay, Dad knows that you are going through something, I felt it too. I am sure Juliet has felt it also. … We want to know what you're going through, because we love you, and together we could help ... What do you say, Juliet?"

Juliet acknowledges, and Jaylen notices Juliet's response.

Tamira continues, "I won't tell Mom or Dad, your secret is safe with me."

Jaylen relaxes his defense against guarding his secret, he feels that letting Tamira know his findings may help him ease his conflict.

"Ok, here's the situation …"

"Go on."

On second thought, what if the truth terrifies Tamira, what if she decides to go to the authorities, what if Utter loses his freedom and Mr. Morgan is set free? Jaylen decides to hold on to his secret from Tamira. Now he needs an excuse to divert the conversation.

"I am waiting," Tamira reminds.

"Ok, my dear Sis, I confess! I came here to hang out with Juliet, we planned to come here to have a quiet and peaceful time together."

"See! was that difficult my sweet brother!"

Juliet holds her chin, slanting her face and staring at him, she tightens her lips.

"Sis, now tell me, how did you know that we were here?"

"After Dad dropped you, he drove here to get coffee. He saw you come in and you didn't even see him. He waited in his car for a while but seeing that you didn't want to go to school, he asked me to check on you since I am your big sister."

With a smile and a feeling of embarrassment, he looks at Tamira, not knowing what to say next.

"Another thing, I checked on you and found out that you had not reported to school yesterday either."

Jaylen sees Juliet acknowledging the same to Tamira.

"That's not all my little brother, what's that bottle I found in your bag. Are you trying to destroy yourself after coming so far?"

"You pulled my stuff, where is it, I was looking for it … I wanted to get rid of it."

"Like that would happen. I sent it for analysis to the lab that I work … I found what it is. From which enemy of yours did you get it? Who is trying to kill you, I want to know?"

"Jaylen, what's going on?" Juliet interrupts.

"My little brother, you don't have to explain to me, but listen."

Jaylen realizes that he can't outrun his sister. He remembers how she was always a step ahead of him before she went off to college. He remembers how she took care of him, prepared his food, and helped him with his schoolwork. He remembers the first football he had, it was a birthday gift from her, he remembers how she used to take him to watch games, and how much he enjoyed that.

"We go through difficult times in life, which is part of living, and sometimes those difficulties are so unbearable, we try to find a way out. The easy way is to numb yourself from the pain, which does not mean the problem went away, you just committed suicide. You brought pain to yourself and everybody who cares for you."

"I only took it twice, but I wanted to stop it. I understood my mistake."

Valentine texts again, “Let me know when you are ready brother, if it can’t be done today, I will see you tomorrow.”

“Ok!”

“Stop texting and listen, my Jay! A fish dies due to taking the bait, at one moment the fish is enjoying the most delicious snack, and sadly, that’s the last snack the fish will ever have. Don’t be that fish!”

“Are you going to tell this to Mom and Dad?”

“That’s not important, what’s important is, can my brother be man enough to deal with a situation and rise, or will my brother be a coward that hides by numbing himself. Jay, how would you like to be remembered?”

"What do you mean?"

"One day in the future, how would you like to be remembered by your family, how would you like to be remembered by your friends, how would you like to be remembered by the rest of the world?"

"Why me?"

"Because you are you. That’s why!"

"When you are doing well, there will be more obstacles for you to overcome. So, never swallow a bait in the process."

He remembers how he felt when he took the bait for the first time, he felt great. The next time he took it was at the game, he was not feeling that great. He has not been feeling great since then, as if he needs to take it again to feel better. Has he already taken the bait, is he that fish who is struggling for its last breath? He wonders if there could have been a better way.

“Sis, I ain’t taking that thing again … I don’t need it anyway.”

Tamira rests her hand on his hand, and he feels the comfort of her hand, the same comfort he felt when he used to walk with her before she left for college. “You are my brother, and I will take care of you always.”

Another text from Valentine, "Why the sudden change my brother, you and I could have done great things together."

"I will text you later," replies Jaylen.

"Is it Juliet who is discouraging you? Just don't listen to her brother, she's trouble, her feelings are fake."

Juliet keeps her hand on Jaylen too.

"I am with you on this," she says.

(37) Detective Madison

Good morning Detective Madison!"

"Good morning, Detective Raj," Detective Madison notices stacks of paper and files on Detective Raj's desk and is curious to find out new developments after the Thanksgiving break. She was there when the judge released Sophia and ordered Morgan to be taken into custody. Morgan's attorney requested to post bail for Morgan, but the judge refused.

"What a case! right?" She says, "The last time, the guy pleaded the fifth, this time he wants to answer every question."

"See Detective Madison, I am not convinced with Morgan's plea, there's something we aren't seeing here."

Detective Madison's instincts indicate to her that they may not be seeing the full story, but she is a detective, she must go by clues and evidence gathering, to build a case.

"I was thinking the same over the break, I thought Morgan wanted Sophia out, and he confessed to something he didn't commit. If that's correct, whom is he covering for."

"Let's begin with the tranquilizer dart, Sophia's fingerprints were on the dart and that incriminated her. She said that she saw the dart on the exterior window ledge and touched it out of curiosity and left it where she found it. The investigation did not buy the story, but now Morgan says that he left it on the ledge to subdue the victim, Segarra."

"Detective Raj, we never asked him where he got the dart from. Let me note that down."

"Also, according to forensics, the liquid in the dart was not the original compound put by the manufacturer, it was locally done."

"Did forensics do a full analysis on the content?"

"Yes, but it's too technical, we have to visit forensics to get an explanation."

"Let me put that into my list also."

"Then somebody turned the surveillance camera angles upwards and later turned them back to the correct angles. Sophia's fingerprints were on the controls, which was also something that incriminated her. She said that there was something wrong with the surveillance cameras and fixed it before she left. The investigation did not buy that story either, but now Morgan says that he did it."

"Detective Raj, there are only three people who could have done it: Morgan, Sophia, or the son. Because Sophia mentioned that the housekeeper and the cook left in the evening, and they didn't have any guests either. So ... go on!"

"The barbecue grill knob had Sophia's fingerprints on it, and it was last used to burn a stack of paper. That too worked against Sophia, and she said that she saw the grill on and switched it off. Morgan said that he used the grill to burn the documents that he took from the victim."

"Now Detective Raj, my question is, if Sophia planned this so well, wouldn't she have thought of at least wearing gloves. That's where this whole investigation swings away from Sophia. Whoever did this, wore gloves."

"I see your point, Detective Madison."

"That brings us to the next question, why did Morgan put the victim in Sophia's trunk. He knew that the victim would wake up soon, so why didn't he put the victim somewhere else."

"Morgan said that he did it in a hurry, it was not planned, and he didn't want Sophia to find out."

"Raj, do you see the irony in that story!"

"I know! But hold on, even if he put the victim in Sophia's car knowing well that he did something wrong, wouldn't he have at least followed her."

"That's what makes me think that we're missing something. Why would he have the money ready to pay the victim off, if he was planning not to pay the guy at all? Also, when the detectives arrived at Morgan's home, they found the extortion money and a check on Morgan's front table. Then, if he got rid of the victim, why didn't he put the money away? You don't keep a large amount of money just lying around for the cook or housekeeper to find."

"What if he was still expecting the victim, what if he didn't know that the victim was dead?"

"So, detective Madison, are you suggesting that there may be a third person involved here."

"I seriously think so, I think Sophia was a victim of circumstances, and Morgan took the blame to save Sophia. Known or unknown to both of them, there is a third person or another angle to this case."

"The known other person that connects with that day's events is the cabdriver who brought the victim to the Morgan residence. A statement was taken from the driver, it didn't say much."

"Yes, other than dropping the victim, what else could the driver say. It would be good to know where the victim came from, could someone have followed him?"

"Yes, we'll investigate that, hope the cabdriver remembers, or hope that the cab company keeps a record of their old transaction. Let me note that down."

Detective Madison goes over the evidence and note made by the previous investigators, "I see that they never found the tools that were used to open the victim's briefcase, neither the tool used to cut the chain that cuffed the victim's hand to the briefcase."

"Isn't that strange detective Madison, you secure the tools used, but leave behind the dart that was used as a weapon."

"Just being curious, why did the victim have a briefcase chained to his wrist, was he carrying something so valuable."

"Did somebody think that he was carrying something valuable in that briefcase and attack him with the intention of robbery."

"Then the cabdriver would be an initial suspect, and you find emergency toolsets in a cab."

"It's getting complicated now."

"I know, until we get a clear picture, let us keep digging. We'll start at the cab company. Then we'll ask Morgan where he got the dart from."

(38) Back Home

The house appears unchanged from the way he left it two years ago. The furniture remains in its original position, not a single piece altered or relocated. The walls still boast the same colors, untouched by any modification, and the art and ornamental fixtures maintain their pristine condition. As Utter descends the staircase, his hand instinctively finds the familiar banister. He allows his fingers to glide along the handrail as he makes his way to the basement.

The video surveillance system stands as a witness to the crime, with every component remaining in its original place. The controls are those which he last operated, retaining their familiarity. With each step, memories of his quiet descent down these very stairs at dawn two years ago come flooding back. He recalls ensuring his parents remained undisturbed in their sleep, adjusting the surveillance system from various angles, and the triumphant feeling that washed over him as phase one of his plans unfolded successfully.

The video surveillance system affixed on the wall covers the area surrounding the house. He sees the barbecue grill in its original place, zooming in, he notices the corrosion on the sides. He zooms in until the image pixelates, he sees a dull flame rising from the pixels into a fire that engulfs a stack of paper. He watches as the stack of paper wither under the ghostly flame, the white background transfiguring into the foreground inky script, and the paper scattering as dust within the same flames.

"Lex!"

"Mom!"

"Did I startle you?"

"No, Mom, No!"

"I remember how you zoomed in and out of those visuals when we first installed this system. It was a game for you."

He can't understand what Mom says and is too apprehensive to care after recalling the flame, yet he shows interest trying to fake a smile, and hoping that she may not see through his fake smile, he looks beyond her shoulder. He spots his guitar and recollects the first tunes he played.

"Grandma left, I am trying to tidy the house a bit, I am waiting on two others who will help me with the chores. How are you feeling?"

"Yes, I mean good, Mom!"

Mom leaves. Hoping to revive the memory of the grill flame, he zooms into the visual of the grill once again, but this time the pixelates are stubborn.

He creases his fingers along the wall until he reaches his guitar; he feels the guitar strings and plucks the first string letting it resonate.

"Not a speck of dust."

He takes the guitar off the wall; he has not played guitar since his accident, and he tries to remember. He lets the other chords resonate, then he strums a tune, "The guitar is perfectly tuned."

He plays another tune; he sings flat then gets back to pitch. Often words don't flow easy, but more often they do; then, on and off he sings flat but manages to come back to pitch, he fails but tries, he tries and succeeds. His voice is weary, but the pitch is soothing, and his spirit turns resilient.

He walks to the surveillance system trying to find the window ledge where he left the ill-fated dart.

The surveillance cameras do not point to the window ledge where he left that dart, the curvature of the wall obstructs the camera view of that ledge, which is why he left it there. Yes, his plan was to subdue Segarra and get the incriminating documents, and somehow the plan went into motion, he doesn't know how, and they all thought that Mom used that dart to subdue Segarra, of course, Mom would never have done it. Now Dad says that Dad used it to subdue Segarra, Dad can do that, but did Dad really do it.

"What if Dad too, didn't? Then that leaves me!"

He strums his guitar, "Yes, I had the dart, I left the dart on the outside window ledge, now why am I in denial of the truth?"

He plays another tune on his guitar hoping to suppress what he remembers, he thinks the tune is good, he thinks of how far he has journeyed from that hospital bed - the bed where he only saw shadows and only heard whispers.

In those whispers he heard people speak ill about his father, he heard people using the phrase, "The son of the mortgage scammer."

He wished never to wake up. But he heard Grandma's voice constantly asking him to wake up, and he heard her prayers.

He used to hear Juliet say, "Please don't leave us."

He used to hear Jaylen. "Yo, wake up Son!"

When those shadows gradually focused into images and those whispers gradually formed into phrases, the world conveyed a resemblance, he ached for his mother. She could not be heard.

One night as he lay on his hospital bed, there was an image of a woman who was wearing headphones. She was observing him and was singing a tune. Due to the silence of the night, he also heard the music that she was listening to through her headphones. The song was, "What a Beautiful Night," sung by the "Star Sisters."

Through the window drapes, there was moonlight pouring into the ward, and the woman was beside the window. She transformed into the image of his mother.

He sat up to touch the shape, his mother was gone, and it was somebody else.

The woman wearing the headphones spoke to him, "You are awake!"

Leaving the hospital, and resting at home, he wished that he never had to go out into the open world. He wished that nobody knew who he was; he never wanted to be linked to his father. He visited Mom once, but that was a failure. Yet, "What a beautiful night" kept playing in his mind, a tune that made him hold on to life and not let go. His grandma's favorite FM broadcast band played that song frequently, and she noticed his distinct liking for that song; therefore, when the "Star Sisters" were performing at the Hope and Main Amphitheater, Grandma bought tickets for Juliet, Jaylen, and him to go for the show. Arriving at the Amphitheater he found the crowd too overwhelming, and he did not want to go in. Therefore, they decided to leave the Amphitheater, and watch the performance on the giant LCD at the storefront. His desperate attempt to sing the song that day, Juliet and Jaylen helping him to express, and his silence, is a memory of the past, a suppression which he has overcome.

He's feeling of victory has come with a taint as he looks back at the video Surveillance system, it is his strategy that went into motion, but he can't remember if he carried it through, did Dad commit the act or was it him? He wants to know, and he wants to search deep into his memories.

Utter gains focus, he remembers. Utter remembers the tranquilizer dart wrapped in his left hand, and he sees Segarra standing Infront of him. He strikes Segarra with his right fist, Segarra's reddish glasses fall off revealing Segarra's eyes. Utter sees himself through Segarra's eyes and is aghast.

Utter can hear his own heartbeat, he needs to calm down, so he strums his guitar. He wants to forget his memory, he plays a tune, and he pacifies.

He takes a deep breath and plays another tune, his favorite: "What a beautiful night. He likes it, and being satisfied, now he sings with the tune. Mom walks down the stairs and listens to him sing, he continues singing. She is not an image anymore, she is not a fragment of his subconscious, she is real, she is in front of him watching him, he feels her applause, he feels that standing ovation.

(39) Thank You!

"Hi Sophia"

"Hi Moni, how are you!"

"Olivia mentioned that you went home yesterday, just wondering how things were," says Ramona.

"Yes, we came yesterday, finished tidying up the place, just relaxing now."

"Since I am not working today, I thought I could visit you if you needed anything."

"There is nothing much to do, the place is tidy but lonesome, therefore friendly company would definitely help."

"Ha!"

"So, please drop by."

"I am also bringing a guest with me, somebody who has turned so anxious that she hasn't seen another somebody for the past few days."

"Moni, that somebody is always welcome! In my home and in my heart."

Sophia goes down to the basement and finds Utter holding his guitar and in deep thought in front of the video surveillance system. From the time they arrived, he is fixated on the displays, playing his guitar, and singing.

"Are you going to stare at that thing today also?" she asks him.

Utter walks away and lounges himself on the couch. "Feeling bored? I think you should go back to school tomorrow."

"How could I, Mom."

"Tell me," She inquires.

"Because … because …"

She has not seen him move past the basement area, perhaps he needs company to get past his self-confined area, and soon he will have that company. She does not want to inform him that Naomi is visiting; she wants Naomi's visit to surprise him.

"Come on, let's go upstairs. We'll talk about it."

Leaving his guitar behind, he follows her to the living room and leaps onto the sofa. In a few minutes, he is asleep on the sofa, using a sofa cushion as his pillow.

Sophia plans to prepare food.

Her mother left to meet Morgan earlier; she calls her mother but there is no response. She was with Morgan yesterday too. Suddenly she has taken such a liking to him. When the food is ready, she calls her mother again, but still no response.

"Lex honey, wake up, we are having guests ... Lex!"

She opens the drapes to gather indoor light; outside is a flock of carefree geese gathering feed from underneath the shrubs. A goose pecks food off another goose's beak; soon, the geese are pecking off food from each other's beaks while their necks together curve to the shape of a heart, a silhouette so distinct against the wintergreen boxwood hedge.

She opens the front door and finds Ramona and Naomi walking towards the entrance, with Naomi trying to outdo the steps of her mother.

Receiving a smooch generously given and graciously accepting, Naomi walks inside to find the somebody she is looking for and finds him walking up the basement stairs.

"Utter, I missed you, your text messages hardly say anything, I was worried."

Utter waves at Naomi, making her follow him down to the basement.

"Can we come too," asks Ramona.

He does not hear Ramona, or he pretends not to hear her, nevertheless, Sophia takes Ramona down to the basement to join Naomi.

"Where is that surprise you were texting me about?" asks Naomi.

He gestures that Naomi sits on the couch first, she follows his gesture.

"Where am I to sit," asks Ramona.

He gestures to Ramona, asking her to sit next to Naomi.

"I'll sit on the stairs, I watched the performance earlier, now it's your turn," says Sophia.

He picks his guitar, and plays the tune Thank you girl, by the "Star Sisters." Naomi's jaw drops an inch as she turns towards Ramona, and they both look at Sophia.

"That's my son!"

Naomi holds her hand across her mouth, as the music continues, she gradually moves the hand towards her chest, Ramona stands to imitate a slow Merengue rave with an invisible partner. The music dies and Ramona is back on the couch.

"Utter, if this is your surprise, I am so happy, and the tune was so perfect."

He begins his next tune, this time he tries to sing, but words don't seem to flow. He begins the tune again and tries to sing but coughs and bends down. Ramona rushes to him saying, "Take it easy, junior, you need to rest now."

Ramona helps him up, he feels uneasy, but finds the energy to breathe and say, "I am sorry Naomi."

Naomi screams, "Mom he spoke, did you hear that, he spoke."

"Let's go upstairs and take a break, I cooked something nice for everybody."

Ramona helps him to walk, and Naomi is still yelling, "He spoke, can't anybody hear me, he spoke!"

Sophia having her arm around Naomi's shoulders, "I know honey, I know! He has been speaking on and off these few days."

Upstairs, having an early dinner, Naomi cannot get over her surprise, "Utter why didn't you say that you could talk,"

"He wanted to be perfect, I heard him practice that song earlier, I think he wanted to sing that song to you."

Naomi in a melodic voice, "Utter!"

Ramona mentions, "Don't worry, we'll hear you play…once you have rested yourself."

"Utter, are you going to talk in school now, or are you going to keep it a secret."

He nods his head, then shakes his head sideways, with a smile.

"Utter, is that yes, or no?"

"Moni, I like the way she says, Utter."

"You're telling me, Sophs!"

Sophia's phone rings, "Mommy, I was worried, what happened, are you on your way back?"

The voice on the other side, "Yes, just left."

"What happened?"

"I will speak to you when I meet you tomorrow, I am going home straight. Got to take care of something."

"Mommy, is everything okay?"

"Sophy, there is nothing to worry about, just relax. How is my Sugarcane? Did Moni drop by?"

"Yes, they're here! And, your Sugarcane, sang, became exhausted, now he is lighting the fire pit outside with Naomi."

(40) Twilight

Flames rise through the spherical net and bow into the fire pit. Enthralling every breath of the evening chill, burning applewood dissipates its flame of temperateness. The fragrance of apple scatters the atmosphere, adding to the ambient glow of the evening, and Utter plays another tunes harmonious enough to soothe the stillness of that twilight moment.

The guitar chords weaken into silence; Utter and Naomi smile at each other.

Within the bright interior, sheltered by the terrace glass, sits Naomi's mother and Utter's mother in conversation, in amusement, and in happiness.

"Three months ago, I never thought this moment would be possible," says Naomi.

"You made the impossible happen," replies Utter.

"Utter, was it you who called my name the other day, while at the game?"

"I don't know, but I tried calling your name when you were feeling sad that our team had lost."

It was his voice that she heard at the end of the game. The voice seemed to echo from every direction, and it was difficult to guess where that voice came from. But she is certain now, it was him.

"How do you feel when you talk?"

"Fine, I guess."

"I am happy that you are talking again, and I am happy that you got Mom back. …. Oh Utter, I am so happy for you!"

"Thank you, Naomi! Thank you so much! I wanted to sing that song for you earlier because I don't know any other way to thank you. It's like you picked pieces of me and put it back together.... how did you do it."

"I didn't do a thing Utter, you just refused to give up."

"But each day I looked forward to seeing you because you had something to do or tell that made me overcome how I felt."

"Good that you enjoyed my therapy. Tell me, what was my greatest advice to you?"

"You said a lot of things!"

"I told you that, it's only you who can change yourself, that the need to change has to come from deep within you. You can't wait for others to do it for you, you can get help, but you have to find the way on your own."

"Everything happened because you wanted it to happen that way, Naomi. Isn't it?"

"No, it is because you wanted it to happen that way. I pushed you a little bit, I mean here and there."

"Why did you become my friend, Naomi?"

"Why did you become my friend, Utter?"

Neither Naomi nor Utter can answer each other's questions; therefore, they turn their heads towards the bay to experience that cosmic view created by twilight. The geese fly away at a distance.

"So, are you going to talk in school, Utter?"

"I can't go to school, the school saw my dad as a hero before the break, and now they see him as a villain after the break."

"So that's why you didn't come to school."

"Yes, but I also wanted to be with Mom."

"You know, Utter, you don't have to answer anybody's questions. Your dad's issue is more in your mind than theirs, so just act as if you still can't talk."

"You mean, I just don't talk in school."

"Yes, does anybody else know that you can talk now? I mean Jay and Juliet."

"No, I didn't get time to tell them. Anyway, this is the first time I am really talking."

"Oh!"

"So, you think not talking is a better option for me in school?"

"I think so, but you should tell Jay and Juliet that you could talk. Because ... they'll be happy for you."

"I will do that!"

"When you are in conflict, it's best not to interact with those who may aggravate that conflict, do you get what I mean?"

"Yes, you want me to be like my father, act as nothing has happened ... I am just kidding."

Observing the flames becoming dim in the firepit, Utter adds more Applewood to revitalize the firepit; Naomi watches him and notices how much he resembles his father.

"Done!" he says. "Wonder if the wood was enough."

The flame's desperate attempt to brighten against the dark starless sky, is futile. Darkness wins, making it apparent that the added wood made no difference. Naomi wants to continue the conversation following the clemency of the night and the delight within her heart; yet a gentle feeling of dissatisfaction creeps into her, as she perceives that Utter's voice resembles that of his father's.

"Naomi."

Naomi's displeasure grows, and she tries desperately to fight that feeling.

"We ran out of wood, the flame will die soon," he says.

"I may be overreacting," Naomi thinks.

"Naomi!"

"What!"

"There's something I want to explain to you."

"What's it Utter?"

"Something that I see in our surveillance cameras and something that I remember."

Each time she hears him speak, she recalls that conversation she had with Morgan. Not only does Utter's voice resembles that of Morgan's, Utter's facial expressions and gestures too.

"Naomi!"

The Utter she knew before, was that listener who responded to her speech in a much different tendency; as much as she feels and adores his presence, conversely, she sees another person in him.

"Naomi, are you listening?"

She wants to be in his presence; nevertheless, she feels the need to clear her mind off these conflicting thoughts about him. Would he be like his father? What if he is like his father? After all, he is a Morgan.

"Naomi, what are you thinking?"

"Nothing … but what were you saying earlier … that you see something."

"Yes, I think I just discovered something about myself, something I didn't know before."

"What else can it be … I mean what did you find out about yourself … that you look exactly like your dad?"

"Something worse … I think I put Segarra in the trunk of my mom's car."

"You did what?" She thinks that she heard him wrong, "Can you please repeat what you said."

"I remember Valentine from my middle school giving me that tranquilizer dart, I remember leaving it on the outside window ledge, I remember fixing the cameras, and I remember burning documents."

Her feet become lifeless, she feels a chill running through her spine, and she feels her heartbeat rising. She sits down.

"Now tell me, did you really put that guy in your mom's car trunk?"

"I don't remember that, but who else could have done it."

"Utter, think carefully, you see nightmares of that guy, right, so could it be one of those nightmares that you're just speaking about."

"No, it feels all real to me. I know the difference between reality and a dream."

"Then why did your dad take the fault?"

"I guess, he did it to save Mom."

"Does your mom know this?"

"How could I tell her, I just found out this morning."

"Did you feel scared when you found out?'

"Segarra has scared me so many times in my nightmares, now nothing of him scares me … no, it didn't scare me."

"Wow!"

She is still in doubt if he's relating to fact or delusion. A pain rises from the back of her head, and she feels her head pulsating. Feelings of sadness with overlapping feelings of annoyance gather around her; she cannot look at him anymore.

"Utter, it's getting late, I should be going home."

"Did I scare you, Naomi? did I? … Please wait!"

"We got school tomorrow, don't we? Unless you want to stay away tomorrow too."

"No, I am returning to school tomorrow … as we discussed … right!"

"Yes, as we discussed."

Naomi, walking inside the house, "Mom, isn't it time to go?"

"Oh, My Baby, we thought you were having a good time outside."

"Yes, we were, but we have school tomorrow."

"I know, but since we were all having a nice time here, Sophs and I thought that we could stay over and leave from here tomorrow morning."

"Then what about Dads."

"He's bringing us a change of clothing and our nightwear."

"Oh!"

"Why My Baby, is everything good!"

"Yes Mom, it is just that I am too tired, and I have a terrible headache."

"Oh, my Poor Baby, come sit next to me!"

"Mom, when Dads comes, I will go home with him, you can stay here."

"Then what about your headache?"

"I will manage, Mom!"

"If you're so keen on getting back home, then we'll all go. Where's junior?"

"Lex went down to the basement to leave his guitar, there he comes."

"This is the first time I heard you call him, Lex."

"He's not Utter to me anymore! He's Lex. Lex Morgan!"

(41) Gratitude

Antonio Gill meets Morgan Jr. in Jail, "Boss Morgan, how are you doing!"

"Thanks for coming Antonio, I want to tell you something."

"I am listening, Boss."

"Your daughter, Juliet, knew that Segarra was threatening my family, Lex had told her what was happening."

"What are you saying?"

"What I am trying to say is, I am not the one who put Segarra in the trunk."

"But you confessed … right?"

"I did it to protect my son and get my wife out. But he did it."

"But … but how?"

Antonio thinks that Morgan is trying to show his innocence by portraying Lex as a criminal and Juliet as an accomplice. But he does not want to show his anger towards Morgan, he wants to listen to Morgan due to the financial benefits he has received from Morgan.

"Boss Morgan, this story you're trying to tell me is strange."

"I know, it was strange for me too, until I went through Lex's text messages to Juliet, before the accident."

Although skeptical of Morgan's story, Antonio calms down when Mogen reveals the conversations Lex had with Juliet, and Lex attempting to find a solution to the Segarra problem.

"Why are you telling me now. Boss, why didn't you tell me at that time."

"Antonio, with everything that happened, I was confused, and I didn't think that Sophia would get convicted."

"Boss, but everybody knew that she was in trouble due to bad publicity, I didn't want to tell you that, but I saw her conviction coming … anyway, she is free now."

"Antonio, I am happy too. Her innocence … her being in prison, was killing me, so I had to find a way to set her free and protect my son."

"Boss, just because Lex was finding a solution … and he was discussing this with my daughter, doesn't mean that Lex did it."

"Who else was in the house that day to fix the cameras? Who else was there to burn those documents?"

"Then Boss, who left that tranquilizer dart on your window ledge, to be used on Segarra ... on that exact day."

"Two days before the accident, I was doing accounts at home, and I had misplaced my calculator. Now, I know that Lex has one in his backpack, he was asleep, so I just opened his backpack to get the calculator. Then I saw something like that dart in his backpack wrapped in a paper towel."

"Why didn't you ask him what it was."

"I was sleepy, I thought it might be one of his science gadgets for school, and I forgot about it."

"I see the story, very clearly. Now…what do we do from here?"

"Try finding out where Lex got that tranquilizer dart from, Juliet may know something. Perhaps, Asher's boy may know something too."

Antonio being reluctant to hear his daughter's name mentioned, "Why now?"

"The investigators were here asking me where I got it from, I told them that I found it on the street."

Antonio is worried that his daughter is linked to this mishap and wants to leave. "Ok, I will check, if I find something, I will let you know."

"Antonio, wait, don't leave. I have one more favor to ask you. You know I seldom ask favors from my friends; I only help them."

Antonio once again thinks of how Morgan gave him the store and financed the cost of his new home. Morgan has supported him to move forward from that hurt construction worker to an entrepreneur.

"Antonio, thank you again, you are my true friend."

"Boss Morgan, you gave me my life back, you helped me to start a new business, you helped me to buy a house for my family. You have done a lot for me."

"Yes, a house without a mortgage… ha, ha, ha."

"Ha, ha, ha ... Boss, you are funny."

"Do you remember Antonio, how many basements we inspected, how many attics we crawled through, how many houses we put down. Yes, those were the days, Antonio."

"Not to worry. Boss, soon you'll be out of here. Now, your Sophia is free, your son is awake. And I have better news for you."

"Tell me, Antonio."

"Your son can talk; he spoke to my daughter yesterday."

"I knew he would be able to talk eventually, this is better news to me."

"I heard they moved back home too."

"Antonio, you always bring good news to me. Do you think life will be great again?"

"It will be, don't worry, it will be!"

"How is business for you?"

"Hey, people need to eat and drink, so my pizzeria, your café, and the pub are doing well. The other businesses are slow due to the meltdown. Asher and I don't have much construction work, but still, we're Ok!"

"Yes, I have a few houses still in the market, I am not worried about that, those will sell eventually. I get rent from all those stores …"

"The poor people around are suffering a bit."

"Antonio, in any problem, the poor and the weak are the first to suffer. Even in this meltdown, it is the average person that's suffering, they work hard, half of their earnings are gone paying taxes, then they must pay bills, and … do they have enough money to feed their families … "

"Do you really feel for people that way?"

"You feel for people when you realize that you're not on this Earth, to live forever ... In my case, much sooner."

"Nobody came here to live forever."

"Scraping off everything and leaving nothing much for the others will serve you no purpose because when you have to go, you have to leave it all behind ... Like I will do."

"Many people are hurting because a few people decided to take it all. But although the people who lost are hurting, they still live, by trying to do the right thing. I think we should all do the right thing."

"There was a house that went into foreclosure a few years ago, and I bought it from the bank. You know, I never felt guilty of buying the foreclosures I created, then remodeling and selling them off again."

"Boss, you did a lot of that, and made a lot of money."

"… but this house was something else … I never remodeled it; I just locked it and just left it there …"

"What was about it that stopped you?"

"It could be something that my father said about that house. What I want you to do is, renovate that house to look brand new. Can you do it?"

"No problem, where should I get the money from."

"I spoke to Asher about this, so the money is there."

"I'll start on it today. No problem then."

"One more thing, I want you to get Sophia involved in this, when you tell her the address, she'll know which house we're talking about."

"What if she says she can't get involved?"

"Tell her I plan to return the house to its rightful owner. Then she'll do anything to help you out."

"It shall be done, Boss!"

"I need you to do one more thing, Antonio."

"Go ahead."

"Just make sure Asher is fine, when he met me on Monday, he didn't look fine to me… like his mind was somewhere else."

"Did you ask him if he felt Ok?"

"I did, but although he said yes, I feel that something is going on with him."

"I will do that too. You're trying to be a good man now."

"The time when I was down, he took care of me. This is before I came to New York. I never said thank you to him."

"You should have!"

"I just did what I wanted if there was money in it. Sometimes he tried to talk to me, but I just did what I wanted anyway. He hates me for that."

"Yes, I know that. But Asher always cared for you; it was because he cared for your father."

"I know … I wish I could have said thank you to my father too!"

(42) Determination

Jaylen feels fatigued and anxious while at school, he can't focus and wants to ask Valentine for another bottle, at least for just one more time. He remembers his promise to his sister, and he knows that Juliet is keeping a watch on him. During break time, he takes a bite off his sandwich, but not wanting to eat anymore, he shoves the sandwich back into his schoolbag. He rubs his fingers against each other as they twitch, he gazes at his phone, tempted to text Valentine.

He types "Yo Val" then decides against it and wants to delete it, but accidentally touches the send arrow.

He hopes Valentine does not respond, but Valentine does a minute later.

"My brother, what's up. Can I bring you a few more?"

Juliet distracts Jaylen, "Hi Jaylen, did you eat?"

"No, I was not hungry."

"I just noticed you seated alone, usually you're with your football buddies. Is everything Ok?"

"Brother, you did not reply," texts Valentine.

"I will get back to you," replies Jaylen,

"Oh well!" responds Valentine.

"Jaylen, hello …" Juliet speaks.

"Sorry I got distracted."

Juliet sits next to Jaylen, "Did you hear the news about Lex."

"He called me a few times; I didn't pick up … he usually texts me; why, does he think that he can talk to me over the phone."

"Actually, it's more than that. Answer him the next time he calls."

"I'll try."

"I'll ask him to text you also."

"If you want."

"I got to go to class a bit early, but meet me outside after school, my dad will drive us home."

"Why, you think I can't find my way back home?"

"Your sister's orders. I thought she told you."

Jaylen sits at the school cafeteria scrolling through random websites on his phone.

"The l-o-o-o-ser sits alone!" He hears voices and laughs from those students whom he fought after the game.

"Everybody wants him out of the team," says a boy from the group.

Another goes down on his knees and begs from the others, "Please don't fire me, I am in the loser's club, that's all."

"Look at his face, he has exchanged faces with his brother."

Jaylen rises in anger, and his chair slides away and crashes to the ground. Then he remembers his sister's advice and walks away. He feels that he became the stronger person.

Jaylen hears a clap from the corner of the room, it is Mr. Anderson.

"You did the right thing my son, you're still our star player."

Soon other students in the cafeteria join Mr. Anderson's clapping, and a girl screams, "Jay, we love you!"

Later that afternoon, Antonio waits outside the school building to take Juliet home. Antonio, seated on the driver's seat of his pickup truck, having a panoramic view of the outside, observes the hustle, vigilantly. A person wearing a striped hoody watches the school building from the opposite side; two students from the school cross the street and approach the person in the striped hoody. In an instant, money and miniature bottles exchange between them. Jaylen comes out of the school building, too; the person in the striped hoody crosses the street and does the same exchange with Jaylen and briskly walks away. Juliet comes out of the school building, and both Jaylen and Juliet get into the pickup truck.

Antonio remembers his conversation with Morgan and wonders if what he just observed was related to the distraction Asher had displayed to Morgan. He wonders if he is to let Asher know about what he just saw, or if it would be better to first approach Audre to inform her that Jaylen may be taking an illegal substance.

"So, Jaylen, how is football doing?" Antonio asks.

"There's a break now, we'll start practice after Christmas."

"You're doing well my son, keep it up."

"Thank you, Mr. Antonio."

Juliet and Jaylen hardly speak during their ride home, although usually, they are vocal. Are they tired after school, or does their silence indicate that there is something else that's bothering them? Jaylen gets off at his house, and Antonio wonders if he could get any information from his daughter.

"Is Jaylen feeling ok or is something bothering him."

"Why, Papi?"

"Juliet's tone is an indication that she may know something about Jaylen but wants to keep it to herself.

"I asked you because he is a good friend of yours and the son of a good friend of mine. Jaylen is a good kid, and he's like a son to me too. Because he is your friend, you may not want to speak about anything that he's going through, but if he is in trouble, as a friend you have to help him."

"What are you saying, Papi?

Antonio decides not to reveal to Juliet what he has seen but thinks of a better way to deal with the situation.

"Just make sure he's ok, that's all."

The following afternoon, Antonio waits for Juliet outside the school building; he observes the same individual, the person wearing the striped hood and jacket, waiting across the street. Antonio wants to be absolutely certain of his discovery the previous day, he is ready with his high-resolution recorder. He captures the exchange between Jaylen and the individual with the striped hood and jacket.

"Got it, now to plan this out with Tamira," Antonio says to himself.

The previous day, Antonio had visited Asher and Audre's home; however, he did not want to discuss the situation with Asher, due to being afraid that Asher may unleash his temper against Jaylen. On second thought, neither did Antonio want to discuss the situation with Audre, due to being afraid that Audre may get too emotional; therefore, he had a discussion with Tamira about Jaylen's situation. Together, they have alternative plans to protect Jaylen.

The following day afternoon too, Antonio waits outside the school building for his daughter to come out; he sees the same person whom he saw the previous day, the person who wears the striped hood and jacket waiting across the street, facing the school building. Antonio sees a female student crossing the street towards the person with the striped hood and jacket, then an exchange takes place. Three individuals, a female and two males, approach the girl and the person with the striped hood and jacket. A dean comes out of the school building and escorts the girl and the female back into the school building, while the two males handcuff the person wearing the striped hood and jacket. The hood falls off revealing the face of the individual.

Juliet gets into the pickup truck, "Papi, what's happening?"

"They're making an arrest, that guy was selling something illegal to the students."

"Papi, I know that guy ... he was from my middle school, they used to call him Valentine the bully."

"Is he the guy who used to come to the pizzeria to get free food from you?"

"Yes Papi, that's him. I feel bad for him, what did he do?"

"He's the guy who sold stuff to Jaylen yesterday… where's Jaylen, isn't he getting a ride with us."

"No, he went to the doctor today … what? …yesterday? Why didn't you tell me? Papi, if you saw something, why didn't you tell me?"

"I didn't want to upset you."

"Papi, I was supposed to watch Jaylen … Papi?"

Juliet in an angry mood texts Jaylen, "Hey Jaylen, I know you got that stuff from Valentine, and why did you get it yesterday after I spoke to you so much?"

"Hi, my girl, sorry I disappointed you, please forgive me, but I didn't take it though. I was going through the withdrawal symptoms, I thought I should take it to feel better, but I didn't want to dig my hole deeper. Most of all, I didn't want to let you or my sister down. So, I asked my sister for help, that's why I am at the doctor's office today."

"I forgive you Jaylen!! You're my hero, I Love you!!!"

(43) Jaylen's Advice

Jaylen and Tamira are on their way home, after Jaylen's visit to the doctor regarding Jaylen's withdrawal symptoms. Jaylen cannot comprehend Lex's involvement in the legal twist that sent Aunt Sophia to prison, and Jaylen cannot comprehend that it was Lex that jostled Segarra in the trunk.

He recollects feeling miserable each time he remembered their circumstances. He remembers how during the days of the trial, people who had never known Aunt Sophia, making derogatory comments about her by reading a newspaper article. Certain people in the storefront would wish her bad judder and bad fate during the trial, without even knowing that wonderful woman he knew and called Aunt Sophia. He remembers how people were happy about Aunt Sophia's sentencing; how people had falsely judged her for Morgan Jr.'s actions.

Mom used to take him along when she visited Aunt Sophia in prison, and how much he hoped that they could bring Aunt Sophia with them on their way back home. Only he knew that she would never commit such an act, only he knew that she was innocent, and who would believe him if he said so. Therefore, he prayed for her every night, prayed for her to come back home.

Then, seeing his friend Lex motionless on life-support was heart-wrenching, because he believed that Lex's life was ending. Then the happiness he felt when Lex woke up, the time he spent with Lex helping him to remember, and the times he responded to Grandma Olivia's call when Lex was not having a good day.

"Lex, what have you done? You …"

"What are you saying under your breath, my Dear Brother?"

"Sis, nothing."

"But I heard you say, Lex."

Jaylen does not want to respond.

"I spoke to Sophia yesterday, and Mom spoke to her too. We wanted you to speak to her, but with your thing going on, I didn't want to bother you too much."

Jaylen still does not want to respond.

"Jay, you never told me what bothered you so much that you had to take alternative measures."

"Nothing … but do you think Lex will be at home now?"

"We could pass by and find out, why don't you text him."

"No, I want to see him in person. I have something to ask him."

"OK, I will drop you there, you can say hi to your other Mama."

"Where are you going Sis, won't you wait for me."

"I remembered something I had to do today, then I will pick your prescription before I come back."

"Do I have to really take that?"

"It's a mild medication for you to overcome your situation. The doctor wouldn't have prescribed it if you don't have to really take it."

"Sis!"

"Yes, Jay?"

"I am sorry that I put you through this, I think I had a moment of weakness."

"I don't know what you experienced. But remember that when situations go wrong, your weaknesses are what's compromised. Then, asking for help is not your weakness, it is your strength."

"Thanks, Sis!"

"Can I ask you something … the other day when I met you at the donut store, did you mean it when you implied that you loved Juliet?"

"No Sis I was trying to get you off my back ... but yes!"

Another surprise awaits Jaylen when he finds out that Lex can talk.

"Why didn't you text me! So that's why Juliet was insisting that I speak to you."

"I was planning to go back to school. But, because of my father's issue, and because I didn't want anybody asking me too many questions, I thought it is best to act as if I can't talk yet."

Jaylen in an irate mood, "So, you wanted to hide that from me too?"

"No! I wanted to speak to you, to surprise you, that's why I called you several times and texted you asking you to call me. But you just declined all my calls and didn't even respond to my text messages."

Jaylen abruptly, "Yes, I was going through a situation, but it's OK now."

"Something you want to talk about?"

"Yes, but you may not like it."

"Me? What's it?"

Jaylen sees Aunt Sophia approach, "Hi, my Jaylen, so nice to see you, how are you!"

"Aunt Sophia," Jaylen being happy to see Aunt Sophia, embraces her, "I missed you, Aunt Sophia."

"I did too, look how tall you've become, you've gone through a growth spurt during my absence."

Meeting Aunt Sophia makes Jaylen's annoyance leave him, but can he ignore the distress which his friend Lex is responsible for. After a brief conversation, Aunt Sophia departs, giving him the opportunity to sort out matters with Lex.

"Where were we now?"

"You arrived in a smiley mood as if you won something, then you were annoyed that I had not told you of my new ability, then Mom walked into our conversation."

"Yes, about your abilities, I know everything, Lex. I know you did it."

"Did what?"

"I know that you knocked out that guy Segarra and threw him inside the trunk of your mom's car."

Lex, in collective expression, "Jaylen, I don't have to lie to you, yes I did it."

"Your actions and what happened is what's bothering me … how to go about it has driven me insane."

"That night when I saw Mom at home, was my happiest moment. She felt happy too. I thought that life would turn out to be the way it was before."

"I felt happy too when I read your text the next morning."

"But moving back here and finding out the truth has made me so depressed. Now I feel the same way I felt when I woke up."

Since Jaylen's annoyance has cleared up after observing the calmness and happiness of Aunt Sophia, he feels that he should not be hard on Lex.

"That's not a good thing, I remember you during that time you woke up, you were living but we felt that you were still dead."

"Yes, thanks to you and Juliet I became better. Naomi carried me to this point; she gave me hope. Now, I can talk again. But am I going to lose it all"?

"You won't lose it all, Son; you got your mom back."

"Yes, but to think that I caused Mom to be in prison for all those months while she was innocent, the fact that she doesn't even know it, then Dad taking the blame for what I did, and how much I hated him."

"Jaylen! Lex! Come to the table, I made something for both of you," Sophia calls.

Seeing their delay, "So now I have to call you twice, Jaylen."

Utter and Jaylen, in hesitant movements, walk to the table and slump on the dining table chairs.

"So, Jaylen, what have you been doing lately. I heard of all the games you've won for your team."

"Aunt Sophia, please don't remind me of those games."

"Jaylen! Mom was saying how down you were feeling after losing that last game, but what defines you are the things that you do right, what you go wrong are the things you fix. So, congratulations on all your successes."

Jaylen does not want to respond to that advice, because to him, the situation is not an easy fix. He dips his fork into his food. "So, Aunt Sophia, how have you been."

"I am fine, but your visit will help Lex become motivated. He's been feeling so down since yesterday, I don't know what's going on."

Jaylen remembers his conversation with Juliet the previous week, she mentioned that however crazy the circumstance may seem, their end goal is achieved.

"He will be fine Aunt Sophia!"

"Thank you, Jaylen! I hope you are right, so I will leave the two of you here, got work to finish."

Jaylen waits for Aunt Sophia to leave and begins his discussion. "Listen, Son, can you change what happened … can you ... can you?"

"I guess not."

"Then be happy that she is back home, be the good son she wants you to be from this moment. Make it up to her some other way."

"Then what about my dad, he's innocent."

Jaylen raises his voice, "Then admit that you pushed that guy in the trunk, go to prison and hurt your mom. If you go to prison, it will break your mom so much, nobody will be there to help her. Do you think your dad could help? He'll do nothing."

Unable to speak, Lex can only stare at Jaylen.

Jaylen in a louder voice, "I am serious here ... dead serious. So, suck it up, and move on."

Lex is silent and unmoved.

"It was your dad's fault in the first place, you don't know all the things he has done. It is because of what he did, that you had to protect your family from that dude who went in the trunk."

Lex contemplates Jaylen's reasoning. He has never seen Jaylen having such a serious disposition.

Jaylen continues, "I heard a lot from my dad about Grandpa, your grandfather; towards his end days Grandpa's main job was cleaning up after your father. At one point, your father was so ruthless that he was doing whatever he pleases, your father didn't care what went wrong because he knew Grandpa was there to take the blame."

"Like what my father is doing for me now."

"Yes, something like that."

Lex looks down at the table.

Jaylen tasting the food, "This is good!"

As Jaylen eats, he looks at Lex and wonders if Lex is still processing the discussion.

"So, you don't have to feel guilty, your grandpa covered for your father, now it is your father's job to cover for you, not the other way around."

Lex looks at the food laid out on the table. "Your mom has not lost her touch in her cooking," says Jaylen.

Lex too, picks up food and begins munching. In a little while, the two continue eating as if they have been starving for days.

"Jaylen, one question."

"Yes."

"You didn't tell me how you figured it out, while I am still trying to figure it out, myself."

"Valentine told me."

"Wow, Valentine."

"Yes, he told me how he supplied you with that tranquilizer dart."

"Yes, I clearly remember that. I remember leaving the dart on the outside window ledge the previous afternoon. I remember fixing the cameras. I also remember setting the documents on fire. And ... I can remember seeing that guy that morning and looking into his eyes."

"Why did you leave that dart on the window ledge the previous afternoon?"

"I think it was Valentine's plan, but I remember him asking me to leave it on the other window ledge."

"Why did you deviate from the plan."

"I didn't want the camera spotting me."

"Then did he want you to be spotted by the cameras when you were leaving the dart on the window ledge ... I am just thinking … why would he want you to be spotted?"

(44) Valentine's Recollections

Valentine is at the police precinct awaiting interrogation; experiencing arrest for the first time, he feels dismal and anxious. The anxiety in the dimly lit room, which has no windows, is compelling him to break the cuff that holds him and search for one of his confiscated miniature bottles to clinch his yearning. The scurrying footsteps outside vibrate his restraints along with his bones up to his jawlines, he clenches his teeth and holds onto the cold chain that refuses to console him. The female voice outside that recites his name, vaguely resembles his mother's, but how could she be there, how could she even know that he still lives, breathes, and has a pounding heart.

If Mom didn't leave, if she stayed back, then he would not be here, cuffed to a table, waiting for judgement, and waiting for ridicule. Who is there for him now, Jaylen will never understand that he was only trying to help for a fee. That's how Dad explains to him the benefit of this product - people will never know that you are trying to help them, but when they understand, they will come to you over and over. That's what he was trying to do to Jaylen, but Jaylen was rejecting the benefit of this product.

Valentine thinks of Jaylen, and the admiration Jaylen receives from friends and peers. Valentine wonders why he can't be Jaylen; Valentine reflects on the setbacks in life that contrast him from Jaylen. As a little kid, he meets Jaylen when he accompanies Dad to Jaylen's home every Friday where Dad collects payment for the week's work done. Those were fun times, like Jaylen, he too had a family. Then Dad said business got slow and those visits rarely happened. Then, after Mom left, and after twice repeating the same grade in school, he met his friend Jaylen again in middle school, in grade seven.

Because Valentine's father had threatened to report the alleged subpar quality of education Valentine was receiving to the newspaper, the school decided to move Valentine to the accelerated class. In class, Jaylen knew every answer to every question, and every teacher longed for Jaylen’s response as if their day may not transpire unless they hear Jaylen’s reply. Valentine, equally thrilled to be in Jaylen's class, made sincere efforts to participate and provide answers to questions. However, when he did, his classmates often exchanged puzzled glances, unsure if he was making a playful comment. Or they would just burst into laughter. Unfortunately, this pattern of reactions frequently led to Valentine being assigned detention. Valentine vividly recalls being unfairly labeled as a teacher's nightmare through no fault of his own and causing some educators to question their career choices.

Valentine further reflects on his difficult period in school. Could it be the bag of chips he secretly munched due to being hungry after missing the school breakfast program, could it be because Dad dropped him off in school at the end of the first period, or because he had this urge of socializing with his peers during class time and students complained. Could it also be those curse words he used in school, but Dad uses them freely as if they were conventional English. Why was he that way, why was he different, if Mom would have stayed, he could have asked her. No, she had to run away from dad, didn’t she? She had to take his baby sister with her, didn’t she? She wanted to hurt dad, didn’t she?

“Mom, you hurt me too!”

His baby sister should be big now, surely, she is as pretty as Juliet. How he longed to speak to Juliet in grade seven, how he longed to be spoken to by Juliet in grade seven, but no, she was the front row kid seated next to the rich kid, Lex. She sat with Jaylen and Lex during lunch breaks, they brought nice food and shared with each other, they did not notice him munching on the rest of his bag of chips, sipping his cheap colored drink, and gazing at the inedible free school meal.

One day he was so hungry he had the courage to ask her if he too could have one of her sandwiches she was so generously passing on to Lex and Jaylen. She did give him one, and that was the most delicious food he ate since his mom left. Thereafter, Juliet was kind to him with their remaining food, she felt pity for him, they would have thrown away that left over food anyway. But it did not bother him, that left him not hungry until his dad returned from work, bringing him food from the corner deli.

When that rough bully kid Arnold pushed Juliet against the wall, it was he who punched Arnold to the ground that day, not Jaylen, and not Lex, either. He got a week's suspension from school for punching Arnold, and a beating from his dad because dad had to lose half a day's pay due to the meeting at the principal's office. But everything was worth it because he did it for Juliet. When he returned to school, Juliet smiled at him for the first time, and she asked him how he had learned to fight. He did not know what to tell her because he was imitating Dad; therefore, he made up the story saying that his dad was a Russian spy who escaped to America. He asked her to keep that secret, but to speak to him if she was ever in trouble. Because Juliet began speaking to him, kids began liking him too, then he kept maintaining a status of acting tough. Two more fights later, the kids began calling him Valentine the Bully.

Towards the end of his middle school days, Juliet did come to him asking for a favor because his father was that Russian spy. He did not want Juliet to find out that he had lied about who his father was, therefore, he promised to help Juliet. When he heard that he was going to help Lex to save his family from a criminal, he thought that Lex's rich parents would reward him. He always suspected that Juliet liked Lex more than anybody, but if he proves to Juliet that he is a hero, Juliet would like him more. He would be like the prince in that fairy story, who slew the dragon, won the princess's heart, and received half the kingdom. He remembers his mom telling him that one day, that he too would be like that prince, a hero.

He sometimes saw Lex's mom arriving to pick Lex after school, she used to drive a beautiful car, Lex takes the front seat, and Juliet, the back seat. After he helps Lex's family to slay the dragon, he believed that Lex's mom would adopt him as her son. Maybe he too would have all the nice things like Lex has, maybe he would not feel that hungry anymore, and maybe his own Dad would not be angry with him again.

But today, if he goes home, Dad will be truly angry with him because he lost his supply, he imagines his dad's rage, his dad will make that regular insult, "you idiot," then beat him up, and deprive him of dinner until the lost money is made-up. Dad says that this is the only job suitable for a possible high school dropout, and this job where there are no benefits, and this job where he gets only insults, and this job where he must give back all the money earned to Dad.

This is a job that is not worth having.

"I am firing myself, Dad!"

He thinks that in jail they would treat him better and provide him with three free meals per day, the food in jail is much better than that deli sandwich Dad gets from the corner store. It's a good thing that they arrested him, and this could be a turning point in his life.

"I am not going to cover for you, Dad. You should have treated your son better."

(45) Interrogation

"Hi Valentine, I am detective Madison, I have questions to ask you, and our conversation will be on record. I want all answers to the best of your knowledge. Do you understand?"

"Yes officer, and I too, have a question."

"First, state your full name for the record."

"Valentine V. Valentinus."

"Now for your question."

"If I tell the truth, will I be sent to prison or will I go free."

"If we can't bring charges against you, you will be set free today; if we do bring charges against you, then it is for the judge to decide."

"I am guilty, please dump me in prison."

Detective Madison wonders why Valentine would be making such a request. It could be that Valentine cannot face a situation in the outside world, and he is looking for an escape.

"Supposing I let you go now, where would you go?"

"I don't know, I will walk down the street until I find food, then …"

"Then what Valentine?"

"I don't know Miss, I don't know."

"Don't you have a home to go to?"

"Yes, but I don't want to face Dad, and I don't know where my mother is because she left me years ago."

"What will Dad do to you."

"He will kill me for losing his stuff or beat me and starve me as punishment."

"Did Dad give you those bottles that you were selling on the street?"

"Officer, I am the one that needs prison time, not my dad."

"Why do you need prison time?"

"Because I will have a place to stay and will get three meals per day."

"Other than Dad, is there anything else you're scared about."

"Life itself, no job, no education, no money, so what's the point."

"Valentine, don't you have anybody you love to be with?"

"Yes, but Mom left, and Juliet likes somebody else."

"Juliet?"

"Yes, she was with me in middle school, and now she is at Admirable Academics."

"I see! Don't you have other friends?"

"Not important friends, just the hi and bye type."

"So, from where did Dad got that stuff?"

"I think he steals it from the hospital where he works."

"What does he do in that hospital."

"Part-time … he does clean-up stuff… Janitor."

"Janitor ... right!"

"Officer… Miss … I am the one that needs prison time, not him."

"Valentine, in life we got to make our contributions to society, and that's the correct thing to do. Doing what's right, sometimes hurts you, but doing what's right achieves the greater purpose in society."

"What's this greater purpose you're talking about."

"By living a good life, you can achieve that greater purpose. Trying to destroy lives, trying to destroy yourself, and trying to hide like a coward, doesn't make anybody great."

"I am not a coward."

"Being a hero is not doing an impossible feat, being a hero is doing the correct thing at the correct moment. Even if people don't agree with you, if you did the correct thing, you have achieved that greater purpose."

"I want to do the correct thing, but each time I fail."

"That doesn't mean you are a failure; you have to get up and try again."

"How can you help me, Miss?"

"You don't have to go back to your father, social services could set you up with accommodation …"

"Miss, I don't want to go to a homeless shelter, I would rather go to prison."

"No Valentine, we could set you up with reasonable accommodation, job training, and provide you with food. So, you don't have to live in fear of doing the right thing."

"What should I do now?"

Two hours of questioning go by, which includes a half-hour break where Valentine gets food and drink.

There is a commotion outside the interrogation room, with a cry, "I need to see my son, where is he?"

"I am sorry, you can't see him," is a reply by an officer outside.

"Miss, I don't want to see him either," says Valentine.

"Don't worry, I will take care of this," says detective Madison, stepping out of the interrogation room and shutting the door.

"Mr. Valentinus, you're under arrest for theft and the manufacture of an illegal substance. You have the right to remain silent. Anything you say can and will be used against you in a court of law. You have the right to an attorney. If you cannot afford an attorney, one will be provided for you."

Valentine's father screams, "Valentine, you idiot, when I get my hands on you, …"

"Take him away!" orders, Detective Madison.

"Miss thank you for saving me, what's going to happen now?"

"Social services will see to your next steps, now I am not saying it's going to be easy, but change will happen. I will also make outreach to certain organizations that I know, that would help you."

"So, I am not going to prison now?"

"No, you won't, let me take these cuffs off your hands."

"Thank you, Miss."

"Follow me, you are going to stay in the office until I finish your paperwork and we get you set up. We will bring you in tomorrow to make a statement at the DA's office."

"I will come."

"Meanwhile, if you think of anything else, about those bottles, about your dad, doesn't matter how insignificant you may think it is, let me know."

Valentine thinks of his future in the outside world, it is about him being alone, with no family and no friends. The only family he had, Dad, just only thought about himself. If Dad didn't treat Mom badly, they would have still been a happy family, he would still have Mom and his sister. Then, Dad had to make this illegal syrup saying that it would rejuvenate people, and due to taking that, Jaylen lost the game, obviously, the syrup didn't work, and now Jaylen acts veered. If he had at least solved Juliet's and Lex's problem, he would have them as friends, and Jaylen too would be his friend. No, Dad had to interfere there too; Dad had to put that guy in the trunk, and due to that, Lex's mom had to go to prison.

Valentine thinks, "Dad asked me to keep that secret, Dad said that since I stole Jaylen's tranquilizer dart, that I would be in trouble. Dad lied again, Dad put that guy in the trunk and got that guy killed."

Valentine sees Detective Madison filling out information on the computer, and he wants to speak to her immediately.

"Hey, Miss … Miss … hello!"

"Yes, Valentine?"

"I have to tell you something else ..."

"Give me a moment, Valentine."

Then, Valentine has second thoughts, what if he is charged as an accomplice for supplying the tranquilizer dart to Lex. Then he will have to be in prison with Dad, and Dad will not treat him well.

"Valentine, you were trying to tell me something," reminds Detective Madison.

"No Miss, just a question, what time should I come tomorrow to the DA's office?"

(46) Stalemate

"Where's that kid," asks detective Raj.

"He's speaking with the social scrvices person, while enjoying the pizza you brought."

"That kid can eat well."

"You Noticed!" She continues, "I have made an outreach to an organization to take care of him until the system takes over."

"That's great, bless you!'

"Now detective Raj, how did the interview with the cabdriver in the Morgan case go today."

"The cabdriver said something extra that may be of interest to the case. See, the guy thought that the two previous detectives were accusing him of actions that he did not commit, so he gave them very short answers to get them off his back."

"What's the new information?"

"He described a tall individual, with tattoos on both forearms, coming out of the premises and getting into an old black pickup truck. He also mentioned seeing a kid in the truck."

"Did he give any further descriptions of the pickup truck?"

"No."

"If the cabdriver saw this individual leaving the premises while dropping Segarra, then that individual may not be a suspect. But it will be good to track this individual and get a statement."

"I thought that too. But I found out that the cabdriver was asked to come back in exactly fifteen minutes, to drive Segarra to JFK. So, the cabdriver decided to use that time to pump gas to his car, it is when he came back that he saw this individual leave the premises."

"Now that's one more twist in the case, could this individual have done the deed and pinned it on Sophia."

"Unless Morgan arranged this guy to be there to commit the crime."

"That's a possibility. Where could he have found someone to do it?"

"You know Raj, when you are free, just swing by Morgan's construction company, give the description to Mr. Williams, check if Mr. Williams could think of somebody that matches this description."

"I'll get on it right away."

"Ok! What else did you find out."

"Segarra had pulled out a hundred-dollar bill from his briefcase to pay the cabdriver, asking him to keep the change."

"Yes, Segarra had made two ATM withdrawals that morning."

"Hmm, then, after coming back, the cabdriver had tooted his horn many times but there was no response, so he decided to get a cup of coffee for himself. Even after coming back, he tooted the horn many times, and since there was no response from Segarra, the cabdriver had left."

"Your theory of a third party being at the scene is correct, but how is that third party connected."

"We'll see! Are you ready to make a trip to the DA, tomorrow?"

"So, Morgan's trial is on then."

"It is what it is, what will Morgan's fate be now, I am sure the prosecutors will have a lot of questions for him."

"Yes, it's late now. I gotta go home."

(47) Guilt

Valentine leaves the DA's office after the interview; he understands that he has got a second chance which he wants to put to his best use. He is happy to be free, yet he carries that guilt of not revealing the whole truth about his father's involvement in the Morgan case.

While at the DA's office, he wanted to divulge his father's actions in the death of a person but was afraid that he may lose this freedom that he enjoys. He is free to make his own choices now, he is free to think of his progress in this vast city.

"If guilt is the price I should pay in exchange for my freedom, then that's what I'll pay."

As he keeps walking, he notices a person following him, and at the turn to a side street, that man speaks to him. "Hey, Valentine!"

"Who are you, how do you know me."

"I was outside the DA's office, I overheard you speaking to that officer about an evening job."

"Yes, but why were you listening to our conversation."

"Because I heard your story, and I can offer you a job too."

"As what."

"Does it matter, we will pay you well. It's money that you want, right?"

"I have already been given a job at a store."

"A store where you'll work for minimum wage and be taxed too. Do the math, hours you put times the minimum wage, then minus about one-third of that - that's your weekly pay!"

Valentine does not want to show that he cannot make that calculation, "So?"

"So, we could pay you double that or even three times that."

"Is it a legal job?"

"Who cares as long as you're making money!"

"Mister, I don't mind earning less as long as I know that I am doing the right thing. I got a second chance, and I will make use of it."

"The world doesn't give you a second chance kid, if you think that way, you're not thinking right."

"I got a second chance, and I will use it. Please, mister, don't bother me."

Valentine walks fast and the man slows down.

"See you later kid."

The sun shines on Valentine's face, forcing him to raise a hand to shield his eyes from its persistent glare. In that searing moment, he can't help but feel the tender caress of impending winter, an emotional reminder of seasons past. As he paces onward, the majestic Stars and Stripes unfurl above a nearby firehouse, its colors swaying in the breeze.

With each step, Valentine's heart quickens, anticipation coursing through his veins. The world around him seems to come alive, vibrant and full of possibilities. As he approaches the convenience store, every heartbeat echoes with the promise of discovery and adventure, making his journey more than just a walk down the street—it becomes a passionate, vivid odyssey of the soul.

"Hi, my name is Valentine, may I speak to the manager," says Valentine, excitedly.

"Hi Valentine, I was expecting you."

Back at the Morgan residence, Lex struggles with a difficult decision about returning to school. Each time he discusses it with his mother, he can't help but feel frustrated with himself, and his mom has noticed his changing mood. The thought of going back to school is daunting, and he dreads facing his peers and teachers, even if he wants to act as still verbally challenged. Before his father gained notoriety at the school, very few people even knew that he was Morgan Jr.'s son. Now everybody knows that he is the son of that villain who acted as a hero. Lex believes that the unwarranted attention he receives will hinder his emotional recovery.

Lex also carries a heavy burden of guilt because his actions led to his mom's unjust imprisonment. Whether he reveals the truth or keeps it hidden, he knows the consequences will be equally challenging. Adding to his emotional burden is his father's ongoing trial, where that guilt is heavy too. Despite his father's potentially unscrupulous deeds, Lex can't help but feel that his father is paying for a crime he never committed. As his friend Jaylen pointed out, admitting to the truth could further hurt his mother, who, given the circumstances, values her son's freedom over her husband's.

After a discussion involving his mom, grandma, and himself, they are considering homeschooling as an option due to his emotional state. Lex's mom believes that a semester of homeschooling could provide him with the time needed to heal. However, Lex questions if healing is even possible, given the immense guilt he feels for his mother's wrongful imprisonment.

Lex hasn't been in touch with Naomi since her last visit to his home, and she hasn't reached out to him either. He wonders why she hasn't spoken to him, but he's also apprehensive because discussing the Segarra incident in detail might become necessary if she contacts him. Lex had shared his inner struggles with Naomi to be honest with her, as she had been a steadfast friend who stood by him throughout. Regardless of what unfolds and how Naomi feels about him, Lex understands that it's now beyond his control, and he can't change the past.

(48) Who are You?

Naomi's trembling fingers flicker through the digital pages of her tablet.. From recent, the minutes drag on as the class periods stretch out endlessly - each day a yawning chasm of emptiness. The past few days, Naomi fought desperately against the encroaching melancholy, hurling herself into random errands and tasks in a futile attempt to escape the grip of despair, but every effort only served to reroute her back to the same relentless sadness. Hoping to catch up on studies today, she was seated at the desolate corner of the school library for the past hour for what she felt like an eternity, yet all she had accomplished was an unproductive cycle of page-flipping. The content she'd attempted to absorb, slipped off her memory like sand through her fingers, leaving her with nothing but frustration. With a heavy sigh, she surrenders to the futility of her efforts, closing the tablet.

She attempts sanctuary through her notebook and pen. She weaves intricate patterns of ink as her mind swirls with conflicting emotions. Those emotions churn within her, as she sketches in her notebook. She found a flicker of relief that Lex could talk, but that was overshadowed by his actions. Yet, she misses his company, but dreads having him in her vicinity, being afraid that she may dislike him due to what he has done. What if she cannot forgive him; what if their friendship is irrevocably broken? Perhaps, it maybe for the best, she did what could be done, and now it's time to move on.

The bell finally rings, snapping her back to reality. She wraps her arms around herself, hugging her own form tightly as she walks along the corridor. The once-familiar halls of the school now felt alien, cloaked in an unending shroud of monotony. Each step echoes uncertainty, and her heart is an emotional battleground. She feels that she has to move on, she can't allow anything to hold her down.

Yet, she wonders why Lex has not texted her or called her, on second thought she is more relaxed due to not getting a call or text from him. She thinks she knows why he never came back to school after the Thanksgiving break.

"Hi, Naomi," Maya waves her hands Infront of Naomi, "hello, hi, hi."

"Oh! Sorry Maya, did you speak to me?"

"Yes, you overshot your class."

"Oh! Did I?"

"Yes, now do a U-turn … Ok, like that … now let's walk down … right turn coming up … and in you go."

"What's Miss Pet doing in this class."

"Naomi, I think she is substituting, yep, free time!"

"Good, I am not even ready for this class, I couldn't do a thing."

"That's not like you. Let me sit next to you today, that seat next to you has been empty for too many days."

Mrs. Pet speaks, "Your teacher is absent today…"

"We figured that out," interrupts Sara.

"No interruptions please, use this time to catch up on your missed work if you have any."

"Tell me, Naomi, what happened to Utter?"

"I guess he's going through something."

"I know you're not ok with it, in fact, Sara had the same opinion too."

"I am fine."

"You don't look so, that's why I sat next to you now, to check if we could help. If we were going through something, you'd be there for us."

"I am fine, serious!"

"If Utter returns to school, would he still sit next to you?"

Naomi faces an interesting question, how would she feel if he is seated next to her, or how would she feel if he does not sit next to her. Either way, it will be uncomfortable for her. She feels that she should ask Maya not to call him Utter, because in her mind Utter is gone, or morphed into something else, something that's not pleasing to her mind.

"His name is Lex, I just called him Utter for fun."

"We know that, but we caught the name Utter, from you."

"Yes, but he is more Lex now, than Utter."

"Why do you say that?"

"He looks like his father, everything about him resembles his father."

"Hello! biology, genes, chromosomes, DNA …"

"Stop, I didn't mean it in that sense."

"Tell me what happened between the two of you."

"When I saw him the first time, he was that kid who seemed lost and emotionally down. I felt bad for him, I wanted to give him a hand."

"When did you see him for the first time. In school?"

"No, during last summer in my neighborhood. That day people were congratulating me over something."

"Yes, we know that story."

"I may have been the attention of people for something I did, but nobody cared for a person who was confused, who was broken, and who really needed a hand. So, I did it my way."

"How many others would have done it! Others may have been sympathetic to him, but you were empathetic towards him."

"I didn't see it that way though."

"We all saw how you did it, in such a short time too. He was that kid who looked different, we were keeping our distance from him, and we were worried about you too."

"You were scared of him!"

"In a way, yes, but we saw how much he liked you, and you were like his guide. You were bossy too … to him I mean."

"Me? … Bossy? … I was?"

"Yes, you were, and he only seemed to respond to you. Then, he began to smile, he got his facial expressions back, and we were not worried about you anymore."

"Wow! I never knew this."

"Ok, let me ask you a question, what was the greatest thing you did in your life?"

"Me? … I think it was that speech that I made to the students, during that function."

"We were discussing about you the other day, and we agreed that, by taking care of Utter even after his father hurt your family, is the most righteous act anybody could have done."

Naomi wonders if that was a righteous act; well, it is that act that turned him into what he is now. Does she want him to be what he was, or does she want him to be what he is? Everybody's team effort has brought him to where he is so fast, and she feels that she drove that team. But drove it to a wrecking halt.

Maya continues, "We thought that the greatest deed you may have done was giving life to somebody who felt empty inside."

Naomi doodles on her notebook. "What if I found out something about him that I did not know before, what if he is not who he is."

"Was whatever you found out about him, something that happened before you met him."

"Yes!"

"So how could he have changed that, he did not let you down."

"I don't know."

"You accepted him the way he was, and you made him into somebody else. You molded his future, but how could you rewrite his past!"

Naomi continues doodling on her book, subconsciously she has sketched a pair of wings.

Maya continues, "You can't expect people to be perfect, but we know, your expectations are high."

"I did not expect anything in return, I only wanted him to recover."

"You mean recover to perfection like you."

"I am not perfect."

"Yes, you are. You inspired me when you were on stage the other day. I wanted to become like you."

"Anybody can do it; you have to try."

"True, but only after that day that I understood that you should dare to try."

Naomi adds depth to her drawing.

"Naomi, I know who you are. You're an angel walking among us in disguise!"

"Sorry to disappoint you."

"I think you are! We know how you helped Mr. Anderson too."

"What?"

"Don't pretend, somebody overheard the principal speaking over the phone about you. About how you used Utter's dad to influence her."

"He's Lex. And I can guess who was snooping on the principal's conversation."

"It had been a positive conversation about you, Miss Shepherd had referred to you as a fascinating personality."

"All right ...!"

"Sara is grateful for the way you helped her in Math. without you, she would have failed her midterm."

"You helped her too, Maya."

"But you made the outreach."

So whatever problem you're going through, I pray that you'll find a solution. Enjoy your Holiday Break, I guess we'll meet again next year."

"I forgot about that. Yes, meet you next year!"

Sara is right, she has set high expectations on Lex; nevertheless, the silent conflict about Lex is that he has committed an act that sent his mother to prison, and now his father has taken the blame for it.

"That's the past, the future needs a new foundation … a better foundation!"

(49) Holiday Season

Juliet and Antonio are changing the drapes around their home, Antonio on a stepladder asking Juliet to correct the alignment.

"That's perfect Papi."

Antonio jumping off the stepladder, "Let's move the Christmas Tree to this corner, it will look better."

"Ok Papi, we'll do it later, first we must go shopping."

"Shopping? I got important work to finish …me and Sophia."

"I got to buy gifts; can't you go after? I haven't bought a thing for anybody."

"Ok, I can ask Sophia to wait. let's buy the gifts quickly."

Antonio in a hurry, calls Sophia in a whispering tone and informs her that he will be late.

"Papi, where are you going after … with her?"

"Got to take care of something. Oh, is Lex and Jaylen getting gifts too?"

"Yes Papi, everybody."

Antonio with a fake wide smile, "We'll buy Jaylen a football and for Lex … we'll buy a dartboard for Christmas."

"Why is that Papi," Juliet gets nervous remembering the dart Lex allegedly used on Segarra.

"Because he has darts at home and has no board."

"Papi, what's that supposed to mean?"

She understands that her father knows more about Lex's involvement in the Segarra incident. She knows her father's fake smile too well, and he obviously is implying that he knows what she is hiding.

His fake smile becomes wider, "He's your friend, you should know that he has no dartboard. Why, didn't he tell you?"

"Papi!" Juliet sits on the edge of the center table.

Antonio sits next to her, "My sweetest …you come first for me, not anybody else."

"Why are you asking me all these questions, Papi?"

"I know about Lex; his father knows it too. Tell me, who gave him that dart?"

"It was that guy Valentine, the guy who got arrested Infront of our school."

"That same guy? Isn't that the guy who supplied Jaylen with drugs? ... Now, this is that same guy who gave a dart to lex?"

"Yes!"

"He comes to our pizzeria and gets free food from you, then this is what he does?"

"Papi, he's not that bad, his mom had left him when he was in grade six, and his dad doesn't take care of him."

"He told that to you to get your sympathy. Hope he's in jail for distributing those illegal stuff."

"No, they set him free."

"What? And how do you know that?"

"Jaylen told me."

"Jaylen still keeps contact with that guy?"

"I think so, but it was Valentine's father making him do all those bad things, so they arrested Valentine's father and let Valentine go."

"Where does this Valentine live?"

"I don't know, but Mr. Asher should know."

"How could Asher know where he lives?"

"Valentine's father is an electrician, he worked for Mr. Asher."

"Oh my gosh! I remember now, I think he's the guy who fixed the video surveillance system at Boss Morgan's. It makes sense now."

"What, how?"

"Remember, the cameras didn't capture the incident."

Antonio picks up his phone and dials Asher. Juliet tries to prevent him.

"Papi, leave him alone. Jaylen will get into trouble. Papi, why did I even tell you this!"

"Don't worry, I won't mention you or Jaylen."

Juliet waits to listen in to the conversation between her father and Asher, but her father's call goes into Asher's voicemail.

"Papi, what are you planning to do?"

"Boss Morgan is in prison because somebody framed him. We got to somehow get him out."

"Papi, Lex will get arrested. Lex is my friend, and I don't like Morgan."

"Do you think Lex could have done it?"

"No Papi, he's not capable of doing it. I knew him well at that time, he was desperate to solve the problem, but he is not capable of doing it."

"We're having the same thought then."

"What do you mean Papi?"

"When Boss Morgan told me about his theory of Lex committing the crime, I thought to myself that it's wrong ... because you and I know about his son, more."

"You think he's innocent too then."

"Since the time Boss Morgan told me his theory, I was thinking of all the possibilities on how this may have happened."

"Tell me one way."

"This is one way I saw it, whoever put the dart there had a bigger plan, like frame a family member. Now when I see where the dart came from, I know who may have done it."

"Papi!"

The phone rings, it is Asher.

"Hey Asher, I just wanted to check. Who was that electrician who worked for you, he had a kid called Valentine?"

"Valentinus, why?"

"Was he the guy who installed Boss Morgan's video surveillance equipment?"

"Yes, it's him … His work is good, but he gets annoyed too much. So funny, a detective in the Morgan case came this way asking questions about a guy, and the descriptions match with Valentinus."

"How funny. Can you text me his phone number and address when you get a chance?"

Juliet, who was listening, "What did he say, Papi?"

"The detectives are after Valentine's father, he's a suspect."

"But his father is in prison."

"But Valentine may know something, If Valentine speaks, maybe, just maybe, Lex and Boss Morgan would be free."

"But Papi, if Valentine carried the dart to Lex, Valentine will be too afraid to speak … unless."

"Unless what?"

"Papi, can you drive me to the mall, if I don't get the gifts today, I may not have the time to wrap them.

(50) Eve

The Hope and Main Plaza is swarming with merriment and cheery faces. The decorations of twinkling lights animate the storefront, and the pulsating jingles liven the temperament. People display extra courtesy to each other, people swiping credit cards as if no limit holds them back, and children wanting to have everything that's bright.

Except for Mom, Utter feels. She is so different, she depicts an impression of excitement, rush, and exhaustion; and she is in long conversations with Antonio, but she stops talking when she sees anybody else around. She arrives at Dad's office at Hope and Main Plaza daily, and spends time in the office, and arrives home late. He knows she had meetings with Dad's attorney, but those meetings were during the mornings. Accompanying Mom to Dad's office today, he walks around the plaza hoping to uncover Mom's secret.

"She is not exhausting her energy on Dad's upcoming trial," he thinks. "She's involved in something else."

On a display window, he spots an elegant ornate which Mom and he saw during the thanksgiving weekend. It is two silver bells tied together with silver bows rotating inside a glass dome. They both agreed at that time that it was a masterpiece of artistry, which also carried a hefty price tag. They both agreed that there was a specific attraction to it, which neither of them could explain. They wanted to buy it, but they didn't have the money to spend on it at that time.

The ornate is still emitting that peculiar elegance, and the glow captures him. Now he wants to buy the ornate for mom but does not know how to do it. He remembers draining all of his Christmas allowances to buy gifts for Grandma and friends.

"That ornate is so expensive, but I have to get it for Mom. I will borrow from her and pay her back later."

He rushes into the office to ask if mom may lend him money to buy the ornate, but as usual, she is on the phone with Antonio.

"... then what time did you finally get home, Antonio," he hears her ask.

He does not hear Antonio's reply, so he gets close to her on the pretext of wanting the can of soda next to her on the table.

Mom says, "It's Christmas Eve, so we'll not meet tonight or tomorrow, but I'll see you on the twenty-sixth."

He does not hear Antonio's reply, but Mom continues.

"Moni and I are planning to do something for our kids tomorrow, besides I don't want her suspecting anything. Haven't seen them for a while after we started this ..."

She ends the conversation as soon as she realizes that he is eavesdropping on her conversation. He wonders what she is hiding from him and also hiding from her best friend.

He forgets what he came for and steps outside the office to speak to Juliet to find out if she suspects anything. As he dials Juliet, he reasons that if he could hide something important from his mother, his mother too has the same right to hide something from him.

"But Juliet is my friend, and this is crazy," he says to himself as Juliet answers.

"Of course, you're my friend, after all we've been through! but what's crazy."

"Sorry I was speaking to myself, but I want to ask you a question."

"Go ahead"

"Do you notice something strange about your dad?"

"Like what?"

"Do you know where he is, and where he goes these days?"

"He has been awfully busy these days."

"About that, is he having long conversations with my mom?"

"Ha, ha … oh Lex, are you getting jealous that my dad is hanging out with your mom too much these days … ha, ha … my mom is though … ha, ha …"

Juliet continues to chuckle, but he does not see it as funny.

"What? you don't mind?"

"Why not … ha, ha …" She continues to chuckle. "Shouldn't you be happy for her?"

"Yes, I mean no. What about your mom then?"

Juliet chuckles and even louder, she says something to him, but he can't understand a word she says due to her chuckling. He allows her to keep laughing hoping she may stop soon.

He hears her say, "You and I are like brother and sister, in middle school everybody thought that, so why not make it official … ha… ha …ha."

A bus stops at the corner of Hope and Main, he sees a familiar person, "No, it can't be."

"It can't be what?" Juliet asks. "Of course, it can be."

"No! I see Naomi, It's Naomi. Yes, it is her … walking this way."

"Go, say hi to your sweetheart, dear brother, ha…ha … ha."

Naomi walks gently, glancing into stores, and abruptly stops to inspect that lavish ornate by the store window, the same ornate he wants to buy for Mom.

"She finds it charming too."

Naomi walks into the store, and he knows that she wants to buy the ornate. He is desperate to speak to her but is afraid to face her, afraid that she may have passed judgment on him. He walks to the store entrance and sees her in discussion with two store employees. She shows them a stack of gift cards, one store employee shakes his head, and she walks towards the door. The other employee asks her to wait, and once again she shows her stack of gift cards to them, this time they agree with her, she is getting what she wants. The employees begin gift wrapping the ornate for her.

"She's buying it for her mom, that's ok, but does she have enough money," he thinks. "I must speak to her somehow, what if she wants help."

He is afraid to speak to her and needs a plan fast.

Juliet calls him. "Listen, not a word to a soul, only listen and don't talk. My dad, your mom, Mr. Asher, and we all are planning a big surprise for Naomi and her mom on New Year's Eve. Oh, Mr. Malcom is in this too."

"Why didn't anybody tell me?"

"I just found out from mom; you know she can't keep a secret. They're all afraid that you might blurt it out to Naomi, that's why it's a secret from you."

"But I can keep a secret."

"I know that too well, but others don't know that."

"Wait, what's the surprise. I haven't met her yet."

"Ok then. Your father wants to honor a request made to him by his father, I think your father is looking for redemption."

"At least he can redeem himself, but how can I."

"Lex, you are innocent."

"According to Detective Juliet, I was a suspect a few months ago."

"Yes, a few months ago, Detective Juliet had you as a suspect, but Sister Juliet gave you the benefit of the doubt ... but now, Detective Juliet has dropped the charges against you."

"What changes Detective Juliet's mind now?"

"Evidence."

"You didn't have to prove my guilt, I proved it myself."

"No! Detective Juliet crossed your name out. You're free to go, Lex, and Sister Juliet loves you."

"Juliet, thank you for being my sister."

The night is clear. A distant star twinkles at him.

He runs to the café, gets two hot medium pumpkin spice lattes and a chocolate cake. Naomi's favorites! He buys one single red rose, clips off the stem, and inserts it on the cake. He is back at the store entrance where he saw Naomi before. And they meet.

"You!" says Naomi, with a smile.

Holding the latte and cake to her, "Yes, it's me!"

"Good that you are here, would you mind walking a few blocks with me down Hope Avenue."

"Yes, let's go."

They walk down Hope Avenue in silence and sipping hot lattes. Utter carries the giftwrapped Ornate for Naomi, and Naomi holds Utter's gift. The digital display above the storefront indicates minus two Celsius, for him it is warm summer weather. He remembers the first time he walked with her down this road, summer was ending, and although the weather was still warm, there was a coldness in the air.

"We're turning onto this street," Naomi informs. "What happened to the streetlight here!"

He remembers the exhaustion he felt on that summer day, but today he arrives at that same place in no time. He remembers that woman with the walker they met that day; she lives beyond. In quick steps, Naomi walks up to the woman's house and rings the doorbell. A much younger woman with a similar resemblance, opens the door.

A little boy and a little girl come out and stand beside the woman. The boy greets Naomi, "Hi!"

"Hey, I know them, the kids I saw getting ice cream," Lex remembers.

"Is your grandma at home," Naomi asks the children.

The little boy and girl look at the woman, and the woman seems to be in distress.

The woman, taking a breath and stammers, "Who ... who are you?"

"I am Naomi. I know your mother. May I speak to her, please."

The woman breaking into sobs, "Mom died two weeks ago."

Naomi steps back shaking, and Lex holds her.

Naomi recovering quickly, "I am so sorry, I didn't know."

"And you are here because …"

"I wanted to wish her for Christmas. I got this for her, for some reason this meant a lot to her."

Utter hands over the ornate Naomi bought at the store.

The little boy observing the exchange of gifts, and referring to the cake in Naomi's hand, inquires, "Is that for us too?"

"Yes, you and your sister can have it."

Naomi wants to leave, but the woman insists that they come inside. The woman opens the gift.

"Where did you find this," the woman asks.

"I met your mother at a store in the plaza during the thanksgiving weekend. She wanted to buy this, but she did not have the money. She asked the store to hold it saying that she would buy it soon."

"This was a gift from my father to my mother on their twenty-fifth wedding anniversary … look, it's engraved with their names on it."

"Wow! … that's why she wanted to buy this so desperately."

"And she's gone now!"

"I am sorry that I couldn't get this for her in time."

"I will keep this to remember them, thank you so much."

"No worries … it was just that, she asked the store guy to hold it for her and that she'll be back to get it. I remembered her when I saw it, so I thought that this would be a nice Christmas gift for her."

"Their heart broke when they had to sell it to a gift shop because they needed money to settle bills … My dad was alive then."

"It came back to you after all these years."

"I don't know how this came back to the store, and I don't know how to thank the two of you either. At least let me wish you a Merry Christmas and offer you something for Christmas."

"No, we got to go home now. Merry Christmas to you and your family too."

As they leave, they hear the little boy's scream of excitement, "Mom, there is a real red rose in our cake."

Hearing the little boy, Naomi punches Lex on his shoulder. "You!"

"Ouch," He runs playfully.

"Wait, I am not done with you," Naomi runs behind him.

He runs faster, towards Hope Avenue, with Naomi running behind him.

"Wait for me, I am your attorney," she cries.

Turning onto hope avenue, "I thought you sentenced me."

"I was never your judge," Naomi calls out.

He hears a rustle and a thud, turning back he sees Naomi on the ground with a knife-wielding man standing next to her.

"Keep running kid, this is not your fight," the attacker says to Lex. "I got out yesterday. I want to celebrate tomorrow after I am done with her. It took months for my foot to recover."

Lex looks around and sees an empty street, and a spotless sidewalk with cars parked by the curb. He remembers the can of soda in his jacket pocket, he runs around a car while pulling out the soda can and hurls it at the assailant.

The assailant jumps aside avoiding the flying can.

"You're next, kid." The attacker says, then turns towards Naomi.

Naomi is still on the ground but facing upwards and trying to raise herself. The attacker gets closer to her.

A round kick from the ground by Naomi, startles the attacker, giving time for Lex to make a leap towards the assailant. Both the attacker and Lex go down. Naomi gets back on her feet. The screeching sound of tires and slamming of doors make the attacker get on his feet and limp into the darkness. It is Antonio and Malcom, and Naomi wraps her hands around Malcom.

Antonio wants to run after the assailant but seeing Lex having a gash on his upper arm, tends to Lex.

(51) Outreach

Juliet has a plan to get Valentine to reveal what he may know about his father's involvement in Lex's sequence of disastrous events.

She agrees with her father that Lex couldn't have committed the act which Jaylen and Morgan think Lex may have committed. Also, she prefers to leave the situation as it is, since according to her reasoning, Lex is back to normal, and Sophia is free. However, her father is determined to find information that may be favorable to Morgan; thus, he wants to make a statement about her information on the tranquilizer dart, to detective Madison who oversees the Morgan investigation. Juliet agrees, only if her plan to get Valentine to speak, fails.

Antonio and Juliet drive towards the store where Valentine works. Antonio yawns.

"Papi, do you want to stop for more coffee, you came home at three in the morning."

"We were at Malcom's until the Police arrested that guy ... what were you doing at three in the morning without getting your rest."

"Talking to everybody ... Lex was at the emergency getting sutures ... how could I get any sleep with all that was going on."

"That's behind us for good I hope, now for the next arrest."

"Papi, as I said, I want to try out my plan first, Valentine will do what's right."

"The only reason I don't want you going to Valentine is because his involvement nearly wrecked Lex and Jaylen."

"He was misguided Papi, now let's give him a chance."

"The next thing that'll happen is, he will start coming to the pizzeria, this time not only looking for free food."

"Papi, have confidence in me, you sit in the truck and watch, I will go inside the store and talk to him."

"Now are you sure he will be in the store at this time, today is a holiday."

"Let's find out, Jay said we got to pass that firehouse."

"Look for the store."

"This is the place. Wow, the parking lot is empty."

Antonio grinning, "Yes, on a day like today, people are at home with their families, not chasing after criminals."

"Papi!"

"What? He gets a gift too?"

"Yes!"

Juliet gets off the truck and walks towards the store entrance; she thinks of how she would begin her conversation with Valentine. She does not want Lex or Valentine to be in any difficulty, and she prefers the situation to be as it is because she feels it's peaceful that way. Yet, her father's determination to free Morgan may jeopardize that peace; she hopes that she may get the correct words to convey her message to Valentine so that everybody would be free.

The store door swings open with a gentle chime to announce her entrance, and the welcoming aroma of freshly brewed hazelnut coffee greets her. She finds herself in perfect harmony with the store's music, "Drummer Boy," and nestled in a far corner of the shop, she sees Valentine, arranging a store aisle.

Rather than approaching him directly, she decides to linger at the end of the aisle, hoping that he will notice her presence and initiate a conversation. Her wish is soon granted when he accidentally drops a box from a shelf and bends down to retrieve it. Their eyes meet, and for a moment, he seems unable to place her. Then, a glimmer of recognition sparks a warm smile on his face, and he makes his way towards her.

"Is it you, Juliet?"

"Merry Christmas, Valentine," Juliet says, holding the gift bag to him.

Valentine accepting the gift bag, peeking into it, “You remembered me after so long. What brings you this way?”

“Jaylen told me how you had a rough time, and I felt bad for you. So, I thought that I would drop by and wish you for Christmas.”

“What else did he say about me, did he say about anything specific.”

“Not really. Well, only that you were going through a difficult time; still, you had the courage to do the right thing.”

“I made a few mistakes, and I hurt Jaylen, so I had to call him to apologize. I am happy that he’s fine and practicing once again.”

“I am sorry about your father, Valentine.”

“Yes, that’s a long story.”

“Other than that, how have you been, Valentine.”

“That’s my life, how is yours.”

“You remember, I asked you a favor on behalf of Lex, because your father was a …”

Valentine continues, “Russian spy, right. By now you should know that I lied, I don’t know what got into my head back then.”

“I seriously believed that till recently. Anyway, I was thinking of asking you for another favor.”

“What’s it, Juliet?”

“It is going to be difficult for you, but I know that you will understand.”

“Go on, what’s it?”

“Ok! Well, it’s Lex again, he remembers you giving him the dart and my dad somehow knows more of the story than anybody else.”

“What’s he planning to do?”

“He plans to give that information to the detectives.”

“So, you came to tell me that, not that you really cared.”

"No, I came because I cared, I am happy that you chose to do the right thing, I don't want you to lose it all again."

"You're lying, you just want to help Lex again. But when I helped Lex that time, I was really helping you."

"Why me?"

"Because you were the first kind person I met after my mom left."

"Valentine!"

"And do you remember giving me food in school? Then do you remember me coming to your pizzeria to get something to eat?"

"Yes, sometimes."

"For a kid who's thrown a bag of chips when he's hungry, that meant a lot."

"I am sorry, Valentine, I didn't know."

"Yes, Juliet! Here we are now."

"Lex is like a brother to me; I have to help him. That's why I came to you."

"But now, I am trying to put my second chance to work."

"I know that Valentine, and I know that you're a good person, and I want only the best for you. That's why I came to warn you on Christmas Day."

"What do you want me to do now?"

"What would you do when the truth is staring at you."

"What truth?"

"The truth that you are keeping and can't bear to hold onto anymore, the truth that can set somebody free, and the truth that can set you free too."

Valentine rests both his hands on a store shelf and looks away from Juliet. She waits for him to respond, but he does not. He keeps his face away from her, still holding on to the shelves. In slow steps, she walks away from Valentine, towards the exit.

Valentine yells out, "I will do it for you again … for you again, Juliet …because I love you!"

(52) Valentine Again

Valentine is once again making a statement to Detective Madison, this time in a more comfortable setting. His attorney, provided to him by the State, sits next to him. Valentine is assured that there will be no charges against him, in exchange for his full cooperation.

"Miss, I wanted to make this statement a long time ago. That's because I wanted a fresh start."

"I know Valentine, you don't have to repeat, we know."

"Lex only wanted to scare that guy off to never bother his parents again."

"Why a dart?"

"Well, I don't know, I thought it was something strange and unique."

"Thank you, Valentine. How did your father know about your friend Lex's problem?"

"When Dad saw me washing that tranquilizer dart to give it to Lex, he asked me what I was doing with that thing. Then I told him the story."

"What did he tell you."

"He asked me why I was helping Lex, at first he asked me not to help because Dad didn't like the Morgan family."

"I told Dad that I am doing it for the hundred dollars I took from Lex … but Miss, I was really doing it for Juliet."

"What exactly did Juliet tell you?"

"She said that there was a rude guy who frequently visits Lex's house when his dad was not at home and demands money. When Lex's dad comes home, Lex's mom and dad end up in terrible arguments, which gives Lex headaches … Another thing, one day Lex's mom wanted to run an errand … so she had left Lex and Juliet home … and this guy showed up. Juliet had slammed the door at him … this guy had said that when he sees Juliet again, he would throw her into the bay."

"Now get to the part where your father puts this man in the trunk."

"I told Dad how much money this guy had asked from Lex's family. When he heard this, he said how dare this guy … what's his name … Cigar …"

"Don't worry, go ahead."

"… Dad said that he wanted all that money for himself… and if I helped him to get that money, he'll buy me new clothes, we will have good food at home, and we would go somewhere far where living is cheaper."

"How did you help him."

"Dad asked me to find out from Lex, the exact day and time that Cigar would come to get the money."

"How did you do that."

"Our meeting place was Juliet's pizzeria. I felt that we were a team going after a bad guy … What's that TV show where there is this pretty girl and all the smart guys …"

"I can't remember Valentine; did you get your father the exact date and time?"

"Yes, I did."

"How did he carry out the plan?"

"Dad asked me to tell Lex to follow his exact instructions."

"What were the instructions?"

"Dad gave me the instructions; I passed it on to Lex … Lex had to leave the tranquilizer dart on an outside window ledge the previous day."

"Any window ledge?"

"No, he specified the ledge."

"Then?"

"He said that Lex should remotely turn the camera's up when his parents were asleep … and attack Segarra with the tranquilizer dart as soon as Segarra enters the premises, take the documents off the briefcase and burn them on the barbecue grill."

"How did Dad know what to do about the cameras."

"He installed it at Lex's home."

"So, your father knew his way around Lex's house."

"Yes, he was the electrical contractor for them."

"I see! Now about that tranquilizer dart, was it the same tranquilizer dart you were washing?"

"Yes, Dad said that he needs to refill it with something that will knockout the Cigar character."

"What did you do then?"

"Then I cleaned and wrapped it in a paper towel and gave it to Lex."

"Now Valentine, Let's go to the day when your father put this guy in the trunk."

"We drove in Dad's pickup truck and parked it near Lex's home. Then we saw Cigar outside the house."

"What was he doing."

"He was talking to Lex, then Lex swung a fist and knocked out Cigar's glasses."

"What happened then."

"Cigar stood looking at Lex, and Lex stood looking at Cigar, then Lex threw something away that was wrapped in a paper towel and walked towards the back of the house."

"Do you know what Lex threw away?"

"Yes, that was the tranquilizer dart I gave him."

"Keep going."

"Then Cigar walked up to Lex's mom's car."

"Do you know why?"

"He left his briefcase on the car trunk and opened the briefcase ... then he counted some money that was in the briefcase and put it in his pocket."

"Was it the money he had taken from Lex's parents?"

"My dad thought that way. Dad said, if Lex can't do it, that he will have to do it himself... to get the money."

"Do what?"

"Knock Cigar out. It was Dad's idea to get Lex to knockout Cigar so that Dad can get the money."

"What did Dad do then."

"He put on his work gloves and approached Cigar."

"Did the guy see your father approach him?"

"He did, only when Dad got closer. The Cigar guy quickly shut his briefcase, but Dad got him, and this Cigar went down. Then he picked the tranquilizer and jabbed Cigar; he popped the trunk and put the Cigar in the trunk."

"What about the briefcase?"

"Dad cut the briefcase off Cigar's hand, but the briefcase opened, and all the papers went flying out."

"Then?"

"Dad left the briefcase and picked an envelope that had fallen. Then he was searching for something else, but a cab guy started tooting the horn outside the home."

"Did Dad drive off then?"

"No Dad came back to the truck to count the money he got… he was cursing because there was only eighteen hundred in the envelope … he said 'you idiot … there were supposed to be more zeros here…' He was upset."

"Did you leave then?"

"No, we drove around the hills and came back, the cab was gone but we saw Lex outside, picking up the paper."

"Did you drive off?"

"No, Dad said he wants the rest of the money … it could be still inside the house he said … so we waited until Lex picked up the paper and went … I guess to the back of the house."

"Then."

"Lex came back and got into the back seat."

"Go on."

"A little while later Lex's mom came out and she … I guess she too went to the back of the house, then she came out again through the front door and got into the car and drove off like in a hurry."

"Was it the same car where …"

"Yes, the Cigar guy was in the trunk."

"How long did you wait?"

"A few minutes. Then Dad got off the truck, he said he knows how to sneak into the house."

"Then?"

"Then the cab guy came back and was tooting the horn … so we waited … then the landscapers came … then we left."

"Did you come back?"

"Yes, Dad said that if Cigar didn't have the money, it should be still inside the house, in cash … and he wanted that money … so we came back, but as Dad was about to get off the truck again, two police cars arrived … then we left and never went back."

"Did you want to talk about this with anybody?"

"Dad said that if I did … that's the last thing I'll ever do. He asked me never to speak to Lex or Juliet again."

"Did you follow Dad's instructions?"

"Yes, it broke my heart not to speak to Juliet, but I managed. Besides, after hearing of what happened to Lex's family, I was too afraid to speak to any of them."

Later that day Detective Raj is having a coffee break when Detective Madison walks up to him.

"I have set up the identification parade for tomorrow afternoon, the cabdriver is coming in to identify Valentinus."

"I see that tranquilizer dart was a naïve plan by kids wanting to solve a mess-up created by adults."

"And Valentinus manipulated this kid stuff to his advantage."

Detective Raj voices his opinion, "Kids suffer due to the erratic behavior of adults."

"Yes, the kids were pushed against the wall by adult actions, what else could these kids do - only try to survive."

"None of this would have happened if that Morgan didn't get involved in the mortgage business."

"In that measure, none would have happened if lenders, banks, and higher-ups did their jobs without trying to scam the system."

"They should make the system better," exclaims Detective Raj.

"No system is perfect, you can't plan out a law to deal with every situation, but people who are given responsibility should adhere to their ethics - unfortunately, a few, don't.

"I guess, nobody was there to teach them ethics."

"You're right, then they pass on their erratic behavior to the kids they influence."

"I have plenty of examples to support that."

"Watch this Raj, now that the truth is out, Morgan will find a way out of his misery, but who is going to wash away the trail of misery that he created for the others. … Similar story between this kid Valentine and his parents."

"Are you updating Morgan's attorney?"

"I will let it go through the system, on the other hand, about this kid Valentine, I will personally make sure that justice works in his favor."

"You're so empathetic, Detective Madison!"

"We need to be empathetic in this job, Detective Raj, and also need to be careful not to incriminate the victims of this big game, because there are sharks outside who know how to scam the system and get away."

"Are you calling Olivia Tosco?"

"I plan to do that. I feel bad for that woman too. She's another victim of people's imprudent behavior."

(53) New Year

"Antonio! is everything going according to plan?"

"Don't worry Sophia, everybody is here, everything is ready, all you have to do is pick our boys and girls,"

Antonio says with his humor. "Don't forget to bring our chief guest, Moni."

Sophia hears Malcolm and Asher laughing in the background.

"Thank you, again!"

"No problem, Boss Lady."

"Ha! … Somebody's at the door, got to go."

"Happy New Year, Sophs."

"Happy New Year Moni, aw, what's this?"

"A little something for the New Year."

"Thank you!"

"I don't know what's going on with Malcom. Malcolm's been spending his holiday break helping Antonio, I asked Malcom to at least be with us today."

"Right, I forgot. I am sure he's doing a great job."

"He said Antonio wants to finish off before the end of the year, which is now."

"I am sure they managed it."

"Hope so! ... Sophs, I am happy to know that your husband is not responsible for the crime."

"Yes, I met him yesterday. ... But what I can't get over is how my Lex had been feeling all along, I told Lex that he should have come to me."

"Do you think that he could have come to you? ... My Naomi didn't come to me; she was bottling up all her emotions and reacting, and I couldn't even read it."

"Sometimes we think of nurturing our children by giving them what we think is good, but deep inside, they may be calling for something else, things they can't ask by the use of words."

"And we unload our own baggage on them, without even knowing it."

"We shouldn't underestimate them too, just because they're young. They are quite resourceful than we think."

"Oh yes! ... How's Junior's feelings about Morgan?"

"Good ... they had a lot to talk about."

"Sophs!"

"Yes, Moni!"

"Thank you, for Junior! I mean, he was a great influence in Naomi's recovery."

"No, it is the other way around."

"Naomi was going through this strand of anger, I thought she will have a breakdown, I thought that I will have a breakdown too. But meeting Lex was therapeutic for her ... for both of us."

"Actually, Naomi was therapeutic to all of us, even Morgan."

"That's nice! ... Is Olivia joining us."

"She went off with Vero and Audre to get the food."

"Hope they come fast; I am getting hungry."

"They will. Until then let's have something to drink and wait for the fireworks."

"Good idea."

Observing the view through the wide glass window of the dining room, Ramona exclaims, "Let me say this slowly with feeling - Bee-u-ti-ful ll!"

"I missed this so much when I was away."

The Morgan mansion, perched on a hill, overlooks the bay, and their eyes capture the distant view of New York City. The long and short oblong structures puncture into the night sky with its glowing ambiance radiating into the New Year.

Sophia smiling and Ramona continuing, "I have come here many times, but I have never admired this view as much as I have today. Today is something!"

"It is something about the years to come, for us and for our children," Sophia wishes.

"You think so?"

"Yes, I do!"

"The fireworks should begin soon; I hope they make it to the boat on time."

"Wow, the bay looks so bright. Somewhere there, the Hudson River ends its three-hundred-mile journey, meeting the Atlantic Ocean."

Ramona cynically, "I am getting a geography lesson, now; how about a history lesson also!"

"Ellis Island is close by," comments Sophia, "Mommy used to tell me stories of her parents arriving on Ellis Island as children."

"Amazing!" exclaims Ramona. "The Statue of Liberty is so bright, how awesome!"

"The amount of history you could memorialize from this view is astounding."

"Smarty, how many bulbs are on that bridge ... answer that if you can."

Far towards the right, the Verrazano Narrows stands in majesty, propagating a swarm of glimmers onto either side.

"Our parents witnessed the Verrazano being built, and now we drive over it. That bridge will stand there, remembering us, centuries after we are gone."

"My turn now," adds Ramona. "Those beams of light mark where the new tower is rising. It will rise even higher than before."

Ramona and Sophia are silent for a moment, reflecting on the vast horizon across a calm bay.

"Moni, now that we have given so much tribute to our city, here's our plan for the rest of the night or I wonder if we should be calling it the rest of the morning."

"I know, watch the fireworks, pick our children from the Ferry Terminal, and finally feed ourselves … I am hungry."

"Correct! But we are not going to feed ourselves here in my home. We're going to a special home for a special feast that's being organized for a special person."

"Where ... and who?"

"Don't ask me questions, just follow me."

"You got to tell me … where?"

"Look! The fireworks!"

Bathed in the glorious radiance of sequential silver showers that shimmer in the sky, the Staten Island Ferry glides toward Staten Island. The graceful boat and the flames in the sky, glide along the tranquil but exciting waters; aboard this ferry are Naomi, Juliet, Lex, and Jaylen, homeward bound, to celebrate the dawning new year.

Coincidentally, not far from them, standing on the deck, is Valentine. He believes that there was no physical distance between him and the others, despite the many admirers of the dazzling fireworks who stood in between. Given his past actions, he is reluctant to face Jaylen or Lex. He prefers to keep it that way and be close only in memory.

Another burst of fireworks simultaneously paints the night with a medley of colorful arcs; Passengers applaud, contributing to the fervent spectacle in the heavens. Amidst this, Jaylen's eyes spots Valentine's gaze on them.

"Valentine, what's up, Son!"

"Jaylen, my brother, Happy New Year!"

"And to you, Man!"

Valentine gets the courage to walk close to Jaylen.

"My brother, I am sorry again, for what I did to you!"

"No fuss, Son! It takes more than that to kill me. We're past that now."

Jaylen returns his focus to the mesmerizing fireworks. The brilliant bursts once again capture every attention, except Valentine's.

"Thank you for setting us free, thank you for setting yourself free too!" Juliet's words are much louder to Valentine than the collective babble of all passengers.

"Juliet, I am making a surprise visit to my mom, she lives in Staten Island. I hope she remembers me!"

"I hope you find what you're looking for, Valentine; I wish you good luck with everything!"

Valentine wishes to linger in their presence, but they continue to move forward, and passengers close the gap in-between. He watches them revel in the fireworks, and a fervent anticipation of going home burns within him.

Naomi leaps with excitement at the next wave of oncoming spirals. The spirals hover high above them and splitter-splatter a rain of silver and gold dainty. The brightness irradiates her exhilaration, and Lex smoothly reorganizes the disarray in her coiffure.

Juliet leans on Jaylen and points towards three bright clusters of light racing each other in the sky; these clusters elevate high into the heavens before transmitting a rainbow of ripples that overlap; the ripples do a desperate dance as if to fight for their own space in the dark sky, nevertheless, other glimmers that come after, consume those early ripples - only to last a while longer.

The End

Author's Statement

The story narrated in this book was a work of fiction. Thus, any resemblance of these fictional events happening to individuals or any resemblance of a fictional character to an individual living or dead was coincidental. However, the Financial Meltdown was an actual economic event that occurred.

ISBN: 978-1-7370060-1-5

www.ingramcontent.com/pod-product-compliance
Lightning Source LLC
LaVergne TN
LVHW010605100826
845148LV00014B/2860

* 9 7 8 1 7 3 7 0 0 6 0 1 5 *